I0690929

THE
BEAST
KEEPERS

JULIE FUDGE SMITH

Boyle
&
Dalton

Book Design & Production:
Boyle & Dalton
www.BoyleandDalton.com

Copyright © 2023 by Julie Fudge Smith

All rights reserved.
This book, or parts thereof, may not be
reproduced in any form without permission.

SUMMER WIND
English Words by JOHNNY MERCER
Original German Lyrics By HANS BRADTKE
Music by HENRY MAYER© 1965 (Renewed)
THE JOHNNY MERCER FOUNDATION and
EDITION PRIMUS ROLF BUDDE KG
All Rights Administered by WC MUSIC CORP.
All Rights Reserved
Used by Permission of ALFRED MUSIC

Passage from *The Feejee Mermaid*
by Jan Bondeson, copyright © 1999
by Cornell University Press, used by permission of the publisher,
Cornell University Press.

Paperback ISBN: 978-1-63337-739-4
E-book ISBN: 978-1-63337-740-0
LCCN: 2023911600

Printed in the United States of America
1 3 5 7 9 10 8 6 4 2

PRAISE FOR
THE BEAST KEEPERS

INDUSTRY RECOGNITION:

Literary Titan Gold Book Award, 2025

American Writing Awards Finalist, 2025

Digital Book Today Award Honorable Mention, 2025

Eric Hoffer Award Nominee, 2024

Wishing Shelf Awards Finalist, 2024

Wishing Shelf Awards, Winner, Best Cover, 2024

SPR Awards Finalist, 2023

"I would recommend this book to anyone who loves gentle fantasy with real emotional stakes, especially readers who enjoy animal stories, cozy rural settings, and small-town friendships. It is also a great pick for people who want fantasy that feels new but still comforting."

—Literary Titan, 5-Star Review

"A wonderfully original novel with a memorable cast of characters. A FINALIST and highly recommended!"

—The Wishing Shelf Book Awards

"Julie Fudge Smith, weaves a magical story . . .Benjamin Fife, the narrator, delivers a captivating performance with his rich tones and inflections. This is a truly delightful story!"

-Audiobook Reviewer

"If you are an animal lover, if you loved stories like *Old Yeller*, and *Narnia*, if you are still a kid at heart, this is for you. Julie Fudge Smith could hold her own at a meeting of The Inklings. I hope this isn't the only adventure we get in Carroll County."

—Tales of the Book Dragon, reviewer

"I loved this novel—just a perfect escape into a lovely Midwestern town with a few extra special quirks :) The pacing of the story was almost fairytale-like in its prose . . . A great example of what fantasy in the modern-age should look like :)"

—EMK, Amazon Verified Purchase Review

Adult readers looking for a light, easy fantasy read will enjoy this twist on the more traditional veterinary memoir books and precocious younger readers will likely enjoy it too. I can tell you that while I liked this as an adult reader, I would have LOVED this as a middle-grader—animals, mythology and humour—all my childhood favourites in one story!

— Steph W., Goodreads Review

"My husband and I both read and really enjoyed Julie's first book. This in itself is pretty amazing, since we have widely different tastes in books and rarely read the same book. I loved the blend of mythical, romance, ethical ponderances, veterinary knowledge, and Ohio landscape facets that were woven together to make this unique book. I look forward to the sequel and the continuation of Jonathan F. St. Roche's interactions with the mythical beasts of Carrollton, Ohio. Well done Julie!"

—Emily, Amazon Review

"Beautifully written, this book is fun, charming, and uplifting, even while dealing with serious themes (the nature of evil; our duties to ourselves and the animals over whom we exercise dominion). It's an easy read, but not just empty literary calories."

—Gatsby100, Barnes & Noble

For Brad, for everything.

And for my grandchildren,
Henry, Sophia, Edward, Robert, Elizabeth,
Grace, Peter, Eva, and Gregory:
May your lives be filled with hope, faith,
and boundless imagination.

Not to hurt our humble brethren is our first duty to them,
but to stop there is not enough. We have a higher mission—
to be of service to them wherever they require it.

—St. Francis of Assisi

PART I

CHAPTER 1

In his second year at the Elkhorn Creek Veterinary Hospital in Carroll County, Ohio, three seemingly inconsequential things irrevocably changed the life of Dr. Jonathan F. St. Roche, DVM. The first was a dog with dry eye, the second was a goose who started seeing in black and white, and the third was a woman he'd known since the first day on the job. As fate would have it, at the end of this most unusual season, things between him and DeeDee Guzman, MD, would never be the same.

But first things first.

Jonathan's journey back to the Midwest began while he was studying at the Qi Institute for Chinese Veterinary Medicine in Wellington, Florida. Many of his classmates from Cornell vet school were ensconced in lucrative suburban small animal practices, and others were pursuing research or finishing specialties such as orthopedics, ophthalmology, or oncology. But Jonathan's horse work in Malaga, Spain, right after college, had convinced him of two things. He wanted to be a veterinarian, and he wanted to specialize in equines—despite the memories it might stir. He also believed that knowledge of integrative medicine would boost his marketability in the highly competitive East Coast horse show world.

But thanks to an encounter with a particularly narcissistic member of the horsey set, any reservations he'd quelled about the elite equine world bubbled to the surface, as well as an unexpected longing for a connection he thought was consigned to his youth. As he paced his small apartment, consciously breathing in through his nose and out through his mouth, his eyes landed on the classified section of the *Qi Institute News* he'd tossed aside. *Hmm . . . maybe there is another way!* He reached for the paper and his phone and called Nathan Jackson.

If Jonathan had a platonic soul mate, it was Nathan. They'd met during a tour of the horse facility at an open house for the Cornell University College of Veterinary Medicine. They found they shared a passion for all things equine, as well as one for playing squash. But, more significantly, Nathan had left the Kentucky horse world for a staff position at The Animal Care Center in Lexington.

"Yes, that's a two. Sorry about my handwriting—Jon! Hey, I'm between cats, so I can give you five minutes, or I can call you later," Nathan said.

"Five minutes should do it." Jonathan hesitated a moment. "I was just wondering if you missed the horse world at all?"

Silence.

"Did you fall and hit your head?" Nathan finally replied.

"Noooo."

"Are you sure? 'Cause I can't believe you just asked me that."

"Well, you've been out of the business for a bit, so I was just wondering if there were any second thoughts on your part?"

"No. *None.* My assistant nearly breaks his back, and the first thing out of the owner's mouth is, 'How's Warlord?' followed by, 'Was he even qualified to ride my thoroughbred?' Well, that was the last straw." Nathan took a deep breath. "Seriously, who needs that brand of craziness?"

"And you don't miss the horses?"

Nathan exhaled. "Funny you should ask. I was just telling the ophthalmologist—who, by the way, is my new squash partner—that I *really* enjoy small animal practice. As far as the horses themselves, I consult with the University on endocrine issues, but I don't have to interact with the owners, so that's cool. Why do you ask?"

Jonathan mentioned his irritation with the equine world and then read him an ad: "*Vet retiring and looking for clever, open-minded individual with diverse skills to join rural Ohio practice. Not much money, but a stimulating and varied clientele, with an opportunity for growth. For more information text or call Dr. Xavier Pratt.* So, I was thinking that maybe I'd take a closer look. I miss the Midwest, and I think this job might give me a chance to use my skills with people who, I don't know, have their priorities straight."

"Look, Jon, I don't need to tell you about the good, the bad, and the ugly of the horse world, so if you're feeling even half the frustration I did, then yeah, take a good look at this job. Maybe it will give you what you're looking for. But I gotta go. Mr. Mittens is waiting."

Jonathan stared at the now-silent phone and contemplated his future. Then, without further hesitation, he called Xavier Pratt.

The man who met Jonathan at the Pittsburgh Airport was not what he envisioned from the deep and raspy voice on the phone that invited him to visit. Instead of being medium height with a solid build, full beard, and arms like tree trunks, Xavier Doolittle Pratt was tall, exceptionally lean, quick to smile, with brilliant white hair frantically trying to escape the confines of a Steelers ball cap. Gone was the gruff voice on the phone (he had been getting over a cold), replaced by a honeyed voice that put Jonathan immediately at ease.

"Welcome to Ohio, Jonathan." Xavier smiled at the lanky young man with equally unruly hair, dressed in dark-wash jeans, a blue oxford button-down shirt, and a navy tweed blazer. He steered him toward the short-term parking. "Madge, my office manager, is eager to meet you, as is my wife, Janice, who also works in the practice."

Heading west on Route 22 across the West Virginia Panhandle to Ohio, Jonathan enjoyed the rolling foothills and winding roads while Xavier extolled the virtues of a rural practice. "Carroll County has a population of about 28,000 people, so expansive countryside with plenty of opportunities to use all of your vet skills, as we have the standard rural animals—pigs, goats, cows, horses, and well," Xavier cleared his throat, "other animals. But believe it or not, there is a surprisingly diverse and exotic population of companion animals too."

Something about the way he said "other" sparked Jonathan's imagination. "Others? You can't mean that you have jackalopes in your practice?"

"Certainly not. They're a Western Plains animal, never migrated this far east," Xavier said. "Although, Elmer Stubb once told me he saw one on Hipster's Ridge. I think it was the summer of '96, maybe '97. That was around the time we had a spike in the local rabbit population, and well, Elmer was never one to say no to an afternoon libation."

"Hipster's Ridge?"

"Yep, it's on the way to Steubenville, the birthplace of Dean Martin. There's a lake nestled in the hollow below the ridge where men would go to drink and gamble during the first half of the twentieth century. Hipster's Ridge got its name when, one year, Dean came back for a fundraiser in Steubenville and brought a few of his Rat Pack buddies along. They came to the lake for some fun and spent part of the evening on the ridge singing and drinking under the full moon. It's been Hipster's Ridge ever since."

"What was it called before?" Jonathan asked.

"Pig Ridge."

"Pig Ridge?"

"Yes." Xavier moved left to pass a livestock truck carrying cows and waved to the farmer. "As you may know, William McKinley was from Ohio, where he was governor before he became president. While campaigning in this part of the state in 1891, some supporters took him turkey hunting on that ridge. Legend has it that a wild pig charged out of the woods toward him, and without thinking twice, he shot it right between the eyes. It was McKinley's Pig Ridge at first, but eventually, it was shortened to Pig Ridge."

Jonathan envisioned the sturdy McKinley standing his ground against a charging boar. *Or perhaps a bore of the political variety,* he thought and chuckled to himself.

Xavier continued, "Personally, I'd call it Flying Monkey Ridge."

"*Flying monkeys?* You mean like *The Wizard of Oz?*"

Xavier looked sideways at Jonathan. "Exactly! Only without the bellhop costumes. Seems every so often someone claims flying monkeys gather on the ridge—usually during a full moon. Most people think it's a committee of buzzards, and a few claim that it's a drift of gryphons."

Jackalopes? Gryphons? Jonathan stared out the window at the twisting road, sweeping fields, and green hollows. *Flying monkeys? What's going on here? Who talks this way? Is he nuts? Is everyone around here nuts?* He stole a glance at Xavier. *He doesn't look like he's delusional, but then, I don't know what madmen are supposed to look like.* Jonathan shook his head slightly. *Hmm, here's a thought. Maybe he's trying to see if I have a sense of humor?*

"Gryphons! Good one!" He gave a short laugh before asking, "What do you think?"

Xavier turned left onto Steubenville Road in Amsterdam and continued toward Carrollton. "I think it's time for lunch! Are you hungry? We'll be in Carrollton in about twenty minutes. We can grab a sandwich at Caroline's Deli before heading on to the clinic. She has great Reubens."

"Sounds like a plan," Jonathan agreed. He settled back to ponder why some people saw flying monkeys while others saw gryphons, and why that was so appealing to him.

"This *is* one of the best Reubens I've ever had!" Jonathan effused, then ventured a question. "If you don't mind me asking, I've been wondering, is Xavier a family name?"

Xavier smiled. "Not really. I was named for Xavier Cugat."

"The Rumba King?" Jonathan choked on his coleslaw.

"Yes! How do you know that? Not many people your age have heard of him." Xavier patted him on the back.

Jonathan cleared his throat and sipped his iced tea. "My grandmother was a ballroom dance teacher, and she always had Cugat playing. She would dance around the kitchen while putting cookies on a plate and pouring glasses of milk. She especially loved 'Sway.' It was her all-time favorite."

Xavier began to murmur the sultry tune while tapping the Latin beat on the edge of the table with his fork.

Jonathan joined in, then laughed. "You're not going to ask me to dance, are you?"

"Have no fear! I'm a terrible dancer. My wife won't even dance with me!" Xavier said. "'Sway' was also one of my parents' favorite songs. They met at ballroom dancing lessons when they were in college. The night the teacher introduced the cha-cha and the rumba, she paired them together. My dad was a total clodhopper most of the time—but somehow, he was a natural at the Latin dances, and it was love at first dance. When Cugat released 'Sway,' that became their song."

"That's a great story!" Jonathan paused. "You know Dean Martin did a decent version of 'Sway.' I wonder if he crooned that atop Hipster's Ridge…"

"Maybe!" Xavier laughed. He rose and turned toward the door, bumping into a tall, athletic blonde with startling green eyes. "Sorry, Anita. I didn't see you there!"

"Well, I won't sue if you introduce me!"

"This is Dr. Jonathan St. Roche. He's considering joining the practice. And, Jon, this is Anita Vandenberg, one of our animal control officers."

"Nice to meet you, Ms. Vandenberg," Jonathan said, extending his hand.

"You too, but call me Anita," she said, taking his hand and grasping it with both of hers. "I hope you'll like it here."

"I do too." Jonathan pried his hand out of hers.

"Just let me know if there is anything I can do for you!" Still smiling, she nodded at Xavier and headed to the counter to order.

Xavier shook his head. "Let's go meet Madge and Janice, eh?"

CHAPTER 2

The twelve-mile drive to the clinic wound through hilly countryside peppered with woods and well-kept barns. Sunlight filtered through oak and maple trees skirting rolling green pastures where cows and horses grazed. Chipmunks darted in and out of the forest edge, while squirrels chattered above them like supervisors on a road crew. Jonathan inhaled the spring-scented breezes and sighed. Snaking along a gravel drive, they arrived at the vet clinic, tucked in a heavily wooded hollow. Jonathan noticed a small barn and paddock at the far end of the parking lot. "That's for our large animal patients," Xavier said as he pulled Jonathan's bag from the backseat.

"And that," he said as he pointed to a large A-frame structure shaded by a thicket of birch trees that challenged the morning light's access to the two-story windows, "is our home, which doubles as the small animal clinic."

A short, trim woman with grey-highlighted auburn hair and an expansive smile burst through the red doors of the clinic, followed by a solid, wiry woman with equally wiry hair coiled for action. The auburn-haired woman gave Jonathan a warm hug. "Welcome, Jonathan. I'm Janice." She took a step back, examined him head to toe, and exclaimed, "You remind me of a golden retriever!"

"Janice sees everyone in terms of dogs," Xavier explained. "I, apparently, am an Irish setter, as my hair used to be red, and Madge here is a Jack Russell terrier."

Madge Guzman seized Jonathan's hand. "And I'm Madge. That's Madge with a *d*, not Marge with an *r*, and I'm so glad to meet you," she said as her grip intensified. "Not everyone finds rural Ohio to be their cup of tea."

"Speaking of tea," Janice interjected, "I know you stopped for lunch, but would you like some coffee or tea?"

"Coffee would be great." Jonathan rubbed his right hand as Xavier shepherded him into the large, inviting kitchen.

After putting his bag in the spare bedroom and refreshing himself in the bathroom, Jonathan helped Janice take the coffee out to the deck. Jonathan swirled cream into his coffee and almost drifted off into contemplating why one could read tea leaves but not coffee grounds, when Janice reappeared with some chocolate chip cookies. "Please help yourself," she said and set the plate down in front of him.

"So, Jonathan, why would a Cornell-educated vet come to rural Ohio?" Madge demanded.

Madge's bluntness startled him, and he half-choked on his cookie. Xavier leaned over and patted him on the back for the second time that day, while shooting a warning look at Madge.

Great! Xavier is going to think I don't know how to eat! Jonathan took a sip of coffee. "That's a good question! I always thought that I was destined for the horse world, but recently I realized that I want more than horses, and that a rural practice might be the right combination of farm and family animals."

"And what was it that made you decide to turn away from

the horse world?" Madge asked.

Xavier shot her another look, but she ignored it.

Jonathan took a bite of cookie. *What do I say? I am not sure she will stop asking until she gets the truth, the whole truth, and nothing but the truth.* "Well, I was standing at the counter of a coffee place in Wellington when a woman came up behind me, wanting to get to the condiments. She was beautiful, immaculately dressed, complete with a gold D-ring snaffle bit bracelet and Rolex watch." He ran his hand through his hair. "And she exuded all the arrogance and privilege that's endemic to the Florida horse set. She took one look at my University of Illinois sweatshirt and immediately dismissed me as a Midwesterner not worth her time or regard. It hit me that if I stayed there, I would have thirty years of dealing with people who thought more of themselves than they did of anything else, their animals included."

He hesitated a moment. "The more I thought about it, the more I realized that I wanted to come home to the Midwest." Jonathan rubbed the back of his neck. "There's something steady and serene about this part of the country. I really like the people here"—*that is, if they're not seeing mythological animals around every corner*—"and I want to work with owners who genuinely care about the welfare of their animals. I'd also like to try to make a difference in their lives, something that would be nearly impossible in the horse world."

Madge nodded. "No girlfriend?"

"No, ma'am! No time for that," he said. *Man, no wonder Janice sees her as a Jack Russell; she won't stop until she pulls the rat from its hole.*

"Now, Madge, Jon did not sign up for the Spanish Inquisition!" Xavier said. "And I'm sure he wants to know about the practice." He turned to Jonathan. "We have open clinic hours, set appointments, and on-site visits. Large animal clinic is Monday morning, small animal clinic Friday, and other animals on the second and fourth Saturdays of the month. Surgeries are generally scheduled for Tuesdays or Thursdays. And I schedule Wednesdays and Sundays off."

"Other?" *That word again! What is he talking about? A jackalope clinic? A gryphon vaccination day?*

"There are several vets in the area who specialize in either small or large animals, but I'm the only one who will do, um, more exotic species. Since some clients don't necessarily want to share the waiting room with snakes, lizards, monkeys, that sort of thing, we have an 'other' clinic."

"Monkeys? You have actual monkey clients?" Jonathan vowed to review his mammalian physiology notes from his zoo rotation.

"Well, we've been known to care for one or two in our time." Xavier chuckled.

Janice smiled, glanced at Madge, and asked, "Would you like to see the clinic?"

"Yes, I would!" Jonathan said, grateful to be freed from the inquiring mind of Madge Guzman.

Madge stood up, and everyone followed. "We've recently been certified fear free, and we are the only one in Carroll County," she announced, and led the way to the small animal clinic.

After touring the facilities and having dinner, Xavier spread out a map of Carroll County while Janice warmed brandy in the kitchen. "Here's Hipster's Ridge," he said as he smoothed the deep creases, "and Elkhorn Creek, which snakes through our property. And here's the clinic."

"Not a lot of roads in the county," Jonathan said as he remembered the drive along winding roads, through dense thickets and expansive green valleys. "This would be a good place to hide if you were a flying monkey!" He laughed.

"Indeed it would!" Xavier said and moved toward the massive stone fireplace that dominated the great room. "It's a bit chilly this evening. How about a fire to go with our brandy?"

Jonathan nodded and, looking around the room, he noticed a large collection of Bavarian decorative eggs. "You have quite a collection," he said, moving toward the laden shelves.

"We do. It started with my grandfather." Xavier piled a couple of logs on top of the fire-starter and looked around for a lighter.

Each egg seemed more magnificent than its neighbor. Vibrant colors and intricate designs entwined the eggs in serpentine vines, delicate flowers, and idyllic pastoral scenes populated with a bestiary of mythological animals such as unicorns, centaurs, and fauns. Impossibly complex details defied the imagination. *I've never seen anything like them—and yet—why do I feel as if I have seen these before?*

A truck backfired, and Jonathan looked out the large window to the east. He didn't see the truck, but a flock of geese was on the move, and the pink sunset reflected off a cluster of five birch trees. Turning back to the eggs, it hit him: *These are set here! These eggs are painted with scenes of Ohio!*

Xavier finished tending the fire and joined him at the bookshelf. "Here," he said as he handed Jonathan a jeweler's loupe, "take a closer look."

The scenes sprang to life as the details of grass, feathers, and foliage were amplified. The house in one scene was this very building, complete with the stone chimney, the red door of the clinic, and the five birch trees. Another was a tidy red barn overlooking an expanse of soybeans—*Soybeans! Holy cow, you can actually see that they're soybeans!*—with a stout little unicorn grazing in the adjacent pasture.

"Amazing, aren't they?" Xavier remarked.

"I've never seen anything like them. They're unbelievable, almost otherworldly." He looked at Xavier. "Did you make them?"

Xavier laughed. "Don't I wish! No, they're how one client pays her bills and has for years. Since Gertrude insists on giving one to us every time we see her, I insist that her bill is covered."

He turned to face Jonathan directly. "I said in the ad that there wasn't much money, but the clientele was varied and unique. If you're willing to work with them as they are and get your rewards in interesting ways, then you can thrive here. Take Gertrude, for example. She's very private, and she doesn't sell her eggs, won't even consider selling them. They are hers to give, and that's what she does. Some of these eggs were given to my father and grandfather—happily given, mind you, but always with the promise they would not be sold."

"Your family has been here a while, then," Jonathan said. *As has Gertrude.*

"We have. The practice was started in 1912 by my grandfather, Rupert. He started as a farrier in upstate New York but wanted to do more, so he headed to vet school." He punched Jonathan playfully on the arm. "He was a Cornell man! Graduated in 1910. He was one of the first students to go in horse-drawn vehicles to serve clients in situ, which was rather extraordinary at the time."

"The Cornell ambulatory clinic is still going strong! They treat over 45,000 animals a year, though they seldom use horse-drawn carriages," Jonathan said. "It's where I discovered how much I like goats and donkeys."

Janice handed the two men their brandy and went to get her own.

Xavier leaned against the bookcase. "Wow, that many? It shows the power of a good idea!" He swirled and sipped the brandy. "Grandad believed that providing vet care on-site was *the* best way to serve rural communities. In 1912, he and Nana were headed to Columbus for the wedding of a cousin, and they stopped around here to visit some of her relatives. They loved the rolling hills and decided this was the perfect spot to establish an ambulatory farrier and vet service. We've been serving this community ever since."

Jonathan sniffed then sipped his brandy. "My family has been rather transitory, and we've seen a lot of the country, especially the Midwest. My parents always made it a fun adventure, but I sometimes think that to be connected to a single place and a profession would add a certain depth to one's life."

"That's true, Jon, but on the other hand, it can make things a bit complicated and difficult as well!" Janice said as she gestured to the comfy sofas by the fire.

"How so?"

"Well, your clients are the people you see every day—at church, the grocery store, the PTA. They're your friends and neighbors in a way that you would never have in a large city. That makes it wonderful when you are celebrating the birth or sale of a prize heifer, but it can be very hard when you deliver bad news, ask for payment, or report a public health or safety issue. Intimacy has its drawbacks."

Don't I know it! Jonathan mused to himself. "It must be hard to find the appropriate professional distance," he ventured aloud, "especially if you've grown up with them. Do you find that it's hard for them to take your advice at times? Kind of like being a prophet in his own land?"

Jonathan's phone rang before either of them could answer. "Mind if I take this? It's my mother."

"By all means! We'll get some decaf started," Janice said.

As Jonathan moved toward the deck, Xavier and Janice took the brandy snifters to the kitchen.

"Xavier, what do you think of Jon so far?"

"I like him. Depending on how the next couple of days go, I hope to make him an offer. He seems to have the right disposition for the job, and he handled Madge well, which is saying something, if you ask me!"

"Very true! Madge can be a force unto herself!" Janice took Xavier by the arm. "But, more than that, I can't help but wonder when to tell him. I *know* it's a delicate subject to be handled with care, but shouldn't he know the whole truth before he accepts?"

Xavier sighed. "Janice, I hear what you're saying, and I don't disagree, but my duty to our clients takes precedence. I want to tell him, I do, but I've got to be sure. You need to trust me that all will be revealed in due course."

CHAPTER 3

BZZZ, BZZZ, BZZZ! The relentless buzz from the outside intercom jolted Xavier awake.

"Dr. Xavier, it's Salvador. Ven aca, por favor. Panachel hurt his wing."

"THAT'S RIGHT, DOC! HE'S MADE A RIGHT MESS OF IT, HE HAS."

"Gremsboc, por favor! There is no reason to shout."

"I AIN'T SHOUTIN', I'M BLOODY WELL TELLING 'EM WHAT'S WHAT!"

"I'll be right down," Xavier muttered into the intercom. Still drugged with sleep, he pulled on his clothes, grabbed his phone, and hurried out to meet the phalanx of flying monkeys. Retirement could not come soon enough.

"Hello, boys," he said, unlocking the door to the clinic. Six jolly fellows crowded into the lobby, chattering and laughing. They had obviously been celebrating something—Xavier could smell the alcohol. And there, in the center of the troop, stood Panachel with a bloody nose and his right wing drooping awkwardly to the side.

"What happened to Panachel?"

A flurry of explanations exploded from the tribe, and it took Xavier several minutes to get the story straight, or at least semi-intelligible. Apparently, it was Panachel's birthday, and he'd made chicha from his grandmother's treasured recipe. After several rounds of the Peruvian delicacy, Gremsboc, a London East Ender, opened a bottle of Cotswolds single malt whisky, and toasts were offered for the health of Panachel and his beloved grandmother. It was then proposed that Panachel, being the newest member of the squadron as well as the birthday boy, take a solo flight and show them what he could do. Bewildered but honored, Panachel climbed up a tree, took off, and promptly careened into an inconveniently located white oak atop Hipster's Ridge.

"Well, let's have a Butcher's, shall we?" Xavier winked at the delighted Gremsboc.

"THAT'S RIGHT, DOC! WE'LL MAKE A COCKNEY OUTTA YA YET!" the East Ender shrieked.

Xavier helped the moaning Panachel onto the exam table and gave an ice pack to Salvador, the Castilian troubadour. "Hold this on his nose while I take his vital signs and check over his wing."

Salvador nodded and gently pressed the ice to his friend's tender, bleeding snout.

"Vital signs normal," Xavier murmured, and moved on to the wilted wing. "This reminds me of the first time I met you, Salvador, and you too, Gremsboc! Seems as though you fellows are rather prone to minor wing tears and sprains—especially when attempting new aerodynamic feats."

"THAT WE ARE!" Gremsboc agreed. "BUT WE COME OUT RIGHT IN THE END, WE DO!" He punched his comrade in the arm. "DON'T WE, SALVY?"

Salvador winced but said nothing as he adjusted the ice pack on the groaning Panachel.

The Peruvian aerialist had clearly sprained the ligaments attached to the upper ridge bone of his drooping wing. Xavier reached into a nearby drawer and pulled out a bag of jumbo plastic straws. He slit two straws lengthwise, guided them onto the wing and taped them into place, thus creating the perfect lightweight splint. Panachel cautiously lifted his wing and found, to his surprise, that it was functional. Not fully functional, but good enough.

"Okay, Panachel, let's look at that nose of yours."

The ice had done its job. The swelling had lessened, and the bleeding had abated. A long gash ran the length of the rapidly bruising snout but could be closed with butterfly closures, and there was no indication that the nose was broken.

As he affixed the bandages, Xavier addressed the motley troop. "Listen up, all of you! You have to *promise* me that you will make sure Panachel leaves these bandages on his nose alone. They will come off on their own. Does everyone understand that?"

There was a great deal of nodding and crossing of simian hearts.

"Good." Xavier smiled at the earnest fellows. "Now, two more things: I need Panachel to come back in a week for a recheck and—this is important—no alcohol until he's healed!"

"HIS FACE'S A SIGHT, AIN'T IT, DOC?" roared Gremsboc. "I'LL MAKE SURE HE DON'T GET AFTER IT, I WILL."

"Thank you, Gremsboc. I am sure you will do a fine job. But I repeat: *no alcohol*, as I am giving him some pain meds to start once he's sober." He looked at Panachel. "Do you understand that you can't peel off the bandages on your nose, and that you cannot drink alcohol while taking these pain meds?"

Panachel nodded.

"I am also giving you an antibiotic to take twice a day for ten days while you rest your wing."

The macaque nodded again, but Xavier wasn't convinced he understood. He asked Salvador, the closest one to sobriety, to reiterate it to Panachel in Spanish and to help get Panachel to his feet. They supported him as he lurched around the exam table, folding and unfolding his wings, oblivious to the chatter going on around him.

"You can send a message to me during the day if he needs anything, and I can come out. I don't want him flying unless absolutely necessary." Xavier let go of Panachel's arm and gestured for one of the monkey's compatriots to take his place. "Also, two of you will need to hang on to him, one on each side, as you head home. He can fly, but not far, and he will be unstable."

Panachel looked at Xavier, tears pooling. "Muchas, muchas gracias, Señor Doctor," he slurred as he lurched toward the exit. The semi-sober crew formed a phalanx around their injured comrade and cast themselves into the fragrant night air.

"They're like simian marines," Xavier mumbled as they flew through the moonlight. "Leave no macaque behind."

Jonathan woke to the sound of heavy footsteps on the stairs outside his room. It took him a minute to realize where he was, and by that time the footsteps had descended into the darkness. He heard muffled voices and a door closing. *Has Xavier been called out in an emergency?* He didn't hear the grumble of the F350 starting, so if there was a problem, it had come to him.

He turned on the light by his bed and picked up his phone: 2:30 a.m. Now wide awake, he pondered what to do. *Should I follow Xavier and offer to help? I could call the clinic . . . if I had the number. Call Xavier's phone?* He settled on texting Xavier and offering his help.

Hi there. I heard you leave and assumed there was an emergency? Do you need any help?

Xavier replied: *Thanks, but I think everything is under control. I'll see you in the morning.*

Okay. See you then, but if you need any help, let me know.

Will do.

Jonathan turned off the light, but sleep remained elusive. He got up and wandered over to the window and slid it open. The birch trees shimmered in the silvery glow of the nearly full moon, while the desperate song of spring peepers and hints of hyacinths and awakening earth punctuated the cool night air. A sudden, intense desire to embrace this Buckeye Eden startled and unsettled him and stirred up memories he'd relegated to the mists of forgetfulness—a barely waning moon, the smell of spring flowers. He smiled. *I wasn't supposed to be out, but the night was perfect for a ride, still and silver. A splash! Chief startled, and I landed in a bed of Mom's prized daffodils. I thought Chief would bolt, but he didn't. He didn't leave me; he turned and nuzzled me until I got up.* Jonathan snorted softly. *My ever-faithful companion in mischief. God, I loved that horse.*

He stopped himself right there, lest any more carefully packed memories refused to be contained, and forced his thoughts back to the present. He genuinely liked Xavier, felt at home with him and Janice, and even enjoyed the nervy abruptness of Madge. *So, is that it? Is one day enough to know? Have I found what I've been searching for?* Resolving to learn more and to make the most of his time here, he turned back to bed, thereby missing the squadron of flying monkeys passing by a nearly full moon.

CHAPTER 4

Monday, April 1, 2013, dawned with a cerulean sky and a crisp forty-three degrees. *What sort of omen is it that my first day of work is April Fool's Day?* Jonathan wondered as he filled his travel mug and headed to the clinic. *I really hope Xavier isn't one for practical jokes. But, if he is, well, then I'm resolved to see it through with good humor.* He sighed. *At least to the best of my ability.*

He'd arrived back in Ohio with a "new" F250 packed with the few things he thought essential and the many things his mother deemed indispensable. Having encountered a few snags in the remodel of their retirement home, Xavier and Janice would remain in the house for another few weeks, and Jonathan would occupy the small apartment above the large animal barn. This was a secret relief for both Xavier and Jonathan, as it afforded a sharing of the after-hours emergency service. Xavier didn't want Jonathan to have to deal with an emergency before he was introduced to the "other" aspect of their practice, and Jonathan, for his part, wanted to get to know a few of the clients before he was thrust upon them in an urgent situation.

A pudgy beagle with pancreatitis, first shots for a litter of schnauzer puppies, a lab with an ear infection, three dogs needing physicals and heart worm tests, a spunky golden retriever with a deep puncture wound in his front paw from a romp in a nearby stream, and a cat who turned out to be pregnant not fat, kept him occupied until lunchtime.

They had two farm visits that afternoon for horse, sheep, and goat care, and Xavier suggested that they stop for lunch at El Pegaso Mexican Grill, where Jonathan encountered the startling blue eyes and jet-black hair of the woman who would revolutionize his existence. Fragments of a Celtic song about a Galway girl with black hair and blue eyes, and something about twirling at the Salthill Prom, reverberated in his head. He had no idea what the Salthill Prom was or if there was one around here—he highly doubted it—but if there were, he would want to whirl around it with *her*.

As he stood frozen in place at the checkout counter, the woman turned and smiled in his direction just as Xavier arrived at his side. Taking one look at his face, Xavier chuckled and said, "Hi, DeeDee, allow me to introduce Dr. Jonathan St. Roche, our new vet." He gestured toward Jonathan. "And this is Dr. Virginia Guzman, daughter of Madge and Lorenzo, and our newest family practice doctor."

Another radiant smile. "Nice to meet you, Jonathan. Please call me DeeDee." In response to what she thought was a puzzled look, she explained, "I couldn't say Ginny as a kid and called myself DeeDee. It sorta stuck." She extended her hand. "My mom has spoken quite highly of you."

Well, she never mentioned you to me, he thought, and finding his voice sputtered, "It's nice to meet you too! Call me Jon." He shoved his wallet into his back pocket and took her proffered hand, holding onto it a moment too long—its cool softness just felt so right in his hand. What was going on here? He never acted this way, or perhaps more precisely, he never *let* himself act this way, and certainly wouldn't allow his feelings to run amok in this fashion. *Get a hold of yourself, man!*

"Well, DeeDee, why don't you come by this week for a drink, and we'll catch up. Call your mom and ask her to set it up; she knows our schedule better than we do. Right now, we need to get going," Xavier interjected.

"Sounds like a plan!" DeeDee said. Smiling a goodbye at Jonathan, she turned to pick up her takeout.

Jonathan nodded farewell as Xavier steered him out the door.

Jonathan's head was ablaze. *What happened back there?* Convinced that his emotions were under strict control, this upheaval, even if it was quite pleasant—and somehow so familiar—completely and utterly unnerved him. But before he could fall deeper into this rabbit hole, Xavier's voice pierced his thoughts.

". . . known DeeDee all her life—she was the daughter we never had," Xavier said, then paused to look both ways at the stop sign and turned left. "I remember when she was about eight, she brought me a bird that the neighbor's Brittany Spaniel had caught. It only had one wing, but it was still breathing, and DeeDee begged me to help her. What could I say to that tear-stained face?" He glanced at Jonathan, who was listening intently.

"She nursed it for three days, but to no avail," Xavier said, shaking his head. "However, the next year, a mother cat had a litter of six in the Guzmans' front bushes. On the second day she moved her kittens to a new location, but left one behind, and DeeDee was *adamant* that this one would not die on her watch! And, due to her amazing diligence, Squeakers not only made it, but lived for seventeen years!"

"And you didn't encourage her to join the practice?" Jonathan smiled.

"I did, but"—Xavier cleared his throat—"things changed for her in high school."

"How so?"

Xavier slowed to a stop and put on his flashers. Harley Lapp was moving his flock of sheep across the road to pasture. "Well, DeeDee was diagnosed with osteosarcoma, and her best friend, Audrey, was by her side the entire time. Unfortunately, Audrey was not only helping DeeDee, but she was also helping herself to DeeDee's pain meds." Xavier waved to Harley and put the truck into gear.

"Really?"

"Yes," he said, his face hardening. "Audrey denied there was a problem, and well, to make a long and miserable story short, she eventually overdosed, and DeeDee was the one who found her."

Xavier sighed and turned onto the drive to the farm of Armstrong Clegg while Jonathan stared out the window, his head swirling with inchoate thoughts. *Oh my God! Poor DeeDee—I can't imagine what it would be like to find your best friend dead. Poor Audrey!*

The tidy red barn and soybean fields caught his fractured attention. Though he was certain that he had never been here before, the scene was familiar. *Where have I seen this?*

Xavier's voice once again pushed into his consciousness. "Jonathan," he said as he slowed the truck to a crawl, "I'm not sure why I told you all this—I probably should have let DeeDee tell you—but it's been a while since I thought about all this, and it just sort of spilled out. I hope you will keep it in confidence."

"You have my word," Jonathan said. He resigned the tragedy of Audrey and DeeDee, along with the nagging thoughts about the farm, to the back of his mind as they were greeted by the irrepressibly cheerful farmer and his retinue of geese, border collies, ducks, chickens, and the odd goat or two—or perhaps four.

Strong pumped Jonathan's hand. "So happy to meet you! I've been telling Doc Pratt for years that he ought to expand! Guess he finally listened to me, eh?"

"Armstrong is an unusual name. Are you in any way related to—"

"General George Armstrong Custer?" Strong interrupted. "Yes, I am! Truth be told, we've had someone serve in every war since the Revolution, the most glorious, of course, being the General." Strong waved his arm toward one of his barns. "As a matter of fact, my farm abuts New Rumley, the birthplace of Custer, and if you know where to look, you can see the monument to my second cousin thrice removed from the loft of that barn!"

Jonathan smiled, but before he could comment, Strong continued.

"But, enough of that! Do you like sheep? Cause I have some fine ones, if I do say so myself!" Helped by the work-obsessed border collies, Strong herded the vets into the sheep barn with honking geese, waddling ducks, and curious goats escorting them. The chickens, Jonathan observed, opted to peck for grubs in the uncut grass bordering the drive. One of the border collies, noticing him lagging behind, came round to nudge him forward.

"Leave off, Storm!" commanded Strong, and the dog backed off but stayed behind Jonathan, knowing that people can be tricky, and he just might wander farther afield. Worse than sheep sometimes.

"Stella, Story, come round," Strong bellowed, and two of the dogs zoomed to the front of the moving menagerie. A few whistles and the geese and ducks were herded into a stall, all except for one large soul with bridal satin feathers who glided alongside Strong with unusual grace. With surprising tenderness for a man still built like the defensive lineman he was in high school, Strong stroked her iridescent head and cooed, "That's a good girl, Gertrude."

"That'll do," Strong directed at Stella and Story, and the two dogs settled in the doorway of the stall. Jonathan knew, without a doubt, that the waterfowl were there for the duration. Before he could ask about Gertrude, Strong called out, "Stare, Strap, come round!" and two more dogs appeared in front of him. Another few whistles and the goats were also ensconced in a stall, with the dogs effectively thwarting any escape attempts.

One last border collie moved to Strong's other side, eagerly awaiting his instructions. Strong gazed down at the youngster and smiled. "That'll do, Wingus. Go lie down with Strap."

"Wingus?" Jonathan asked.

"Yup," was all the explanation proffered.

Jonathan glanced at Xavier, who smiled and shrugged, then asked, "Now, Strong, where do we start?"

After asking permission from Stare and Strap, Jonathan vaccinated the goats, and with the help of the amazing Storm, the sheep were quickly inoculated as well. Despite her initial uncertainty about Jonathan, by the time they were getting into the truck, Storm was wiggling and licking him as if they'd known each other forever. "She doesn't take to everyone like that," Strong observed. "Seems Dr. Pratt made the right choice!" He pumped Jonathan's arm again and promised to take him fishing the following weekend.

"Where you off to next?" Strong asked as he stroked the ears of several dogs at once.

"Calloway's," replied Xavier, putting the truck into gear.

"That's a grand wee farm, as my granddad Scotus used to say." Leaning in Jonathan's window, he laughed conspiratorially. "His timothy hay is nearly as good as mine!"

CHAPTER 5

The sign at the top of the tree-lined driveway read: *Lucash Family Farm, est. 1801*. The farm was indeed grand but hardly wee—at 320 acres it was one of the larger ones in Carroll County. Like the Clegg Clan, the Lucash family came to Ohio after the American Revolution. But, unlike the Cleggs, who arrived immediately after the war armed with land grants given for their heroic service to the new republic, the Lucash family had no military glory. They'd purchased their farm under the Harrison Land Act and had successfully retained all of their original land.

"There are two white clapboard houses on this side of the property," Xavier explained as they drove past fields being planted with spring wheat. "Calloway, the younger of the two Lucash boys, his wife, Connie, and their three little girls live in the larger one with the three barns. The other slightly smaller home is nestled in a copse of birch and maple trees. That's where Montgomery Jr., the older son, lives. A third house tucked behind a small hill is the summer residence of Louise and Montgomery Sr. And, just so you know, while Montgomery Sr. calls his older son 'The Deuce,' he prefers Monty."

Jonathan thought about Strong's comment and asked, "Seems like there's a rivalry between Calloway and Strong?"

"Not a serious one. Cal and Strong have been best friends since they were defensive linemen on Carrollton High School's 'glory team.' As co-captains they led the Fighting McCooks to the class C regional finals for the first and only time. They lost to Youngstown by *three* points." Xavier sighed. "Believe it or not, people still talk about that game—that whole season, if truth be told."

"I bet! That's the stuff of legends."

Xavier smiled.

"So what happened after that?" Jonathan asked.

"Well, Cal went to *The* Ohio State University, graduated with a degree in agriculture, married his high school sweetheart, continued the family dairy business, and has become a very successful quarter horse breeder."

"Sounds like a great guy. I'm looking forward to meeting him. You said he has an older brother. Does he farm too?"

Xavier laughed. "Monty? Noooo. Like Cal, he was reared to love farming, but somehow missed out on any aptitude for it. He is, oddly enough, an exceptional apiarist, and teaches beekeeping at the farmer's co-op the first Saturday of the month.

"According to Cal, when Monty was in high school, their father sat him down and said, 'I'm sorry to say this, son, but you are all brains. We know you love farming, but it just doesn't love you. Your mother and I think it's best if you choose something else, like law or medicine or even astrophysics. You'll always have a home on this farm, you just can't farm it.'"

Jonathan laughed. "So what'd he do?"

"Well, he earned a law degree from OSU after graduating *cum laude* with a degree in entomology." Xavier parked the truck under a mammoth sycamore tree. "And lately, his practice is increasingly focused on helping locals negotiate mineral rights with oil companies eager to frack their way to fortune."

They got out of the truck, and Jackson, Calloway's Australian shepherd, ran up to greet them before darting back to the nearest pasture where some horses were grazing. One round palomino mare was wearing a light blanket with a loose belly strap that delighted Jackson. The pup tugged and played with impunity as the horse moved through patches of tender spring grass.

"Hello, Dr. Pratt," boomed Calloway, coming out from the barn. "Jackson, leave off, will you?" Jackson zoomed over to his person, but he kept his focus on the temptation at hand.

Jonathan extended his hand to the farmer while nodding toward the pasture. "That palomino is certainly a calm one. I don't know many horses who would be so tolerant of that sort of canine attention."

"Delta's a special one, that's for sure," Calloway said and guided them into the barn. Jackson followed a few steps behind, then snuck off for another round of belly strap tug.

With the help of Calloway and his farmhands, Seth and David, the dairy herd was quickly vaccinated. One heifer was isolated and treated for mastitis, and the others waited contentedly as Seth and David readied the barn for the evening milking. As Calloway led them to the horse barn, he noticed that Jackson wasn't with him. "That dog! When he gets an itch, there is no stopping his scratching!"

Just then, Seth called Calloway over, and Xavier's phone rang. With both men occupied, Jonathan walked to the doorway to see what Jackson was doing and enjoy the stirring of the late afternoon breezes. Sure enough, Jackson was tugging on the belly strap and had the blanket pulled almost to the point of no return. Jonathan noticed that the horse was plump, and before he could expound upon this thought, Jackson won the tug-of-war and wrestled his worthy opponent off the back of the palomino.

Delta did a full body shake, releasing the blanket from her neck and lofting her iridescent mane. Jonathan stared, transfixed, as it wafted down onto her neck. "Holy cow! I've never seen anything like—"

Delta shook again, sending her mane aloft once more, while her plump belly rolled left to right and pearlescent wings unfolded, radiant in the golden afternoon light. Jonathan, still trying to make sense of the opalescent mane, shook his head in an attempt to reboot reality. *What in the world is going on here? This can't be for real, can it? Is it an April Fools' joke?* Delta sauntered over to the fence line and folded her wings as she reached her head through the rails toward a particularly tender clump of clover. He snapped his fingers. *That has to be it!*

"Good one, guys!" He laughed and turned to congratulate Cal and Xavier, expecting them to be guffawing, but one look at their taut faces told him this was no joke. Jonathan's stomach lurched. *No! It can't be.*

Bracing himself against the barn door, he looked at the bucolic pasture with the grazing equines and Jackson barking at a squirrel scurrying along the four-board fence. He closed his eyes tight, took a deep breath, and opened them. Delta was still there, still standing with her wings folded and her mane resting against her neck, still placidly eating clover.

Xavier stepped toward him. "Jonathan, I—"

Jonathan waved him off. He paced in the doorway of the barn, running his hands through his hair and scratching the back of his head. With another deep breath, he turned toward the unreal scene. *What is this?* He exhaled. *She looks like a horse—albeit a fat horse with sparkly things on her back—wait a second—she's fat?* Jonathan, grasping for a hold on reality, stared at Delta's belly, then turned back to the men. "You do know she's probably pregnant?"

"She's what?" Calloway and Xavier cried, hustling over to Jonathan. They stared at the peacefully grazing mare while Jackson busied himself with subduing the troublesome blanket into a final and definitive submission.

"Pregnant." Slipping into clinical mode helped Jonathan to momentarily regain his composure. He cleared his throat. "I managed pregnant mares for three years in Spain, and I'm ninety percent sure this mare is pregnant."

Calloway beamed while he fidgeted with his Cleveland baseball cap. "I-I-I don't know what to say!"

You don't know what to say? What about me? Jonathan groused to himself. "Well, since I am only familiar with *horses*, I could be wrong about a . . . a . . ." His voice trailed off.

"Pegasus," Xavier said. "Delta is a Pegasus. I don't know if the gestation period is similar to a horse's, but then, I don't know anyone who does!" He smiled at Jonathan. "But how about we do an ultrasound? That should give us some more information."

Jonathan nodded. "I'll do it," he mumbled as he started toward the truck and the portable ultrasound. *Just focus on the task at hand,* he repeated to himself while setting up the machine and the supplies needed for an internal exam.

Calloway and Xavier brought the mare to the barn and cross-tied her in the breezy hallway. Jackson wrestled the bedraggled blanket into the barn and lay down on it to watch the proceedings. Xavier gave a deep sigh and said, "Jon, I can only imagine what a shock this must be—I've been struggling with how to tell you about our *special* clients and hadn't planned on it happening this way."

Jonathan felt heat rise on the back of his neck. *Was I supposed to somehow infer from all this talk about "other" clients that you meant* actual *mythological beasts?* He wrapped Delta's tail then pulled on an examination sleeve and lubricated it thoroughly.

"I wanted to be sure that you were right for this practice before the 'great reveal,' but sometimes fate has its own agenda," Xavier continued.

"Really? *That's* the reason you didn't tell me before I took the job?" Jonathan clipped as he finished Delta's rectal exam. "Didn't it occur to you that this might make a difference in my decision?" He gritted his teeth and reached for the ultrasound probe.

"Actually, Janice brought up that very point and urged me to disclose all this before I made an offer." Xavier rubbed the engorged vein throbbing in his temple. "These animals are free and independent beings who *allow* us to share their lives. I'm committed to keeping their existence as secret as possible because they don't survive—much less thrive—in captivity. Our obligation is to protect the few of them that remain, as well as defend their right to live free of fear and distress. So, I'm sorry if I made a mistake in not telling you, but I wasn't quite sure how to proceed. Since we were unable to have children, I faced a decision that neither my father nor grandfather had to: how to bring someone into the business who wasn't born to it."

Jonathan inserted the lubricated probe. He unclenched his jaw. "Okay, I can see that. I'm not sure how I would've handled it either, but I can't help but think you probably owed it to me to fully disclose." His face flushed again.

"You may well be right. I don't know. My hunch was that you'd be a good fit, so perhaps I should've plunged ahead. But my fear was that you'd decide that you didn't want to be here, and I would've exposed these creatures unnecessarily." Xavier paused and looked at Jonathan. "What I do know is that your response today shows that you are more ready for this than I thought."

Jonathan adjusted the probe and optimized the image. The three men watched in silence as a foal with a strong heartbeat and what appeared to be tiny wings appeared on the screen.

"This explains a lot," Calloway said as he watched Xavier clean and pack up the ultrasound. "She's been hesitant to fly lately and slow on her takeoff when she does. And she's been balky at jumps. But holy cow, who is the father, do you think?"

Jonathan unwrapped Delta's tail. When he finished, the mare caught his eye and inclined her head in his direction. He reached out and scratched her ears. She leaned into his touch and moved her head so he could stroke her silky mane. Jonathan inched his hand down her neck to the pearlescent wings gracing her back.

Delta nickered softly and unfolded her wings in an elegant, honey-scented swoosh that ruffled his hair and cooled his sweaty brow. Amber light danced through the golden gossamer wings, full sails ready for flight. As light and airy as the wings appeared, they were nonetheless remarkably strong. The lustrous fibers of the wings reminded him of spider's silk, flexible but eminently strong and resistant to rips or tears.

Delta furled her sails as Calloway unhooked the cross ties and led her back to the pasture. Xavier and Jonathan headed to the truck, where the farmer joined them. "I bet you could use a beer, eh?"

"Yes!" the two vets said simultaneously.

"Maybe two," Jonathan added.

CHAPTER 6

Calloway disappeared into the rambling farmhouse and quickly reappeared with a local IPA and his brother, Montgomery, who had stopped by on his way home. Jonathan sank into a patio chair, took a long draw from his beer, and exhaled. "I'm not sure what to say or do. This is, as you can imagine, the definition of unbelievable, and I've a million questions."

Xavier also took a long draw from his beer, and Calloway and Montgomery followed suit. Connie Lucash, watching from the kitchen window, realized that it was likely to be a long evening, and soon emerged with a cooler of beers and some snacks.

"I'm sure you do, and I'm not sure where to begin," Xavier said, "which, of course, was one of the stumbling blocks for me in the first place!"

"Well, then, um . . . how many of these creatures are we talking about, and who knows about them? Was I the only person left out of this secret?" Jonathan asked.

"Good questions. Let's start with who knows." Xavier cleared his throat. "It's very few, actually. Carroll County, where the majority of them live, has a population of about 28,000, so there is a lot of room for them to hide and not a lot of people to find them. The few who live with people reside with the families that have been here for several generations: the Burgetts, Haskins, Woosters, Lucashes, Cleggs. Outside of them, I can't think of more than a half dozen people who know."

"Like whom?" Jonathan asked as he reached for some chips and guacamole.

"Umm, let's see, Morgan Carter, our sheriff of twenty-six years, knows, as does Lodi Wooster, the fire chief. But I don't think anyone else on the squad knows, and I'm fairly certain the animal control people don't know anything." Xavier pointed at Jonathan. "You met one of them, Anita Vandenberg."

Jonathan nodded.

"They may well suspect," Xavier continued, "but they have no confirmation that we know of." He grabbed a handful of chips. "And of course, DeeDee knows, her mom having worked for us for thirty years, but I'd be surprised if her boyfriend knew anything."

Jonathan snapped to attention and shot Xavier a look. The older vet smiled sadly and shrugged. Calloway, rummaging in the cooler for the bottle opener he'd dropped, missed this exchange, but Montgomery did not. He was sorely tempted to comment, but his lawyerly instincts kicked in to restrain his tongue. Clearing his throat, he said, "I think Madge would personally take her out if she told the esteemed orthopedic surgeon *anything*. So, my advice, Jonathan, especially if you wish to avoid the wrath of Madge Guzman, would be to assume that the person you are talking to has no knowledge—wouldn't you say, Xavier?"

"I would. But I would also add that you check with me first before you say anything to anyone, even if you are pretty sure they know. We don't want to expose or jeopardize these beings unnecessarily."

"Got it. I will proceed with utmost caution." Jonathan shook his head and shoulders as he watched Delta and a couple of quarter horses saunter toward the barn. "So, besides Delta, who else is there?"

Xavier leaned back into his chair. "Well, let's see. There's the flying monkeys, and Gertrude, the goose at Strong's farm that lays the Bavarian eggs you admired. Strong also houses a lovely little unicorn by the name of Bluebell. In fact, I suspect we'll get a call in a few weeks for Bluebell's hooves. She tends toward laminitis, despite my warnings to Clegg to limit her sweets . . . but I digress."

Jonathan stopped mid-sip. "Unicorn? Seriously? This I have to see!"

"And you will," Xavier continued, "along with the lovely miniature gryphons that Florence Burgett and her family have bred for years." Xavier turned his attention to the Lucash brothers. "Cal, how long would you say the Burgetts have been at it?"

"Hmmm. That's a good question. Let's see . . . I remember granddad talking about Eustace Burgett's new barn having a heated part for the mothers and babies, and Eustace was old at that point. Was he Florence's great-grandfather?"

"No," interjected Montgomery, "Eustace was the bachelor brother of Florence's grandfather. But they've been here longer than that. Florence told me that her great-great-great-something grandfather was one of the Revolutionary War veterans who settled in this area, and that he'd brought along a pair of chicks given to him by *his* grandfather, Manfred Von Burgett. Legend has it Manfred's gryphons were direct descendants of the ancient Assyrian gryphons of Nineveh." Montgomery took a swig of beer. "But the relevant point here is that this area has been a safe haven for these animals for several generations, going back at least to the early nineteenth, if not the eighteenth, century."

"That's right," Xavier chimed in, "and we've had an interesting array of animals over the years, including a phoenix, a thunderbird, and the centaurs, of course."

Of course! Who could forget the centaurs? Jonathan wondered as he drained his beer and reached for another.

"The flying monkeys . . . and Monty, remember the white hart that ate all your white roses?" Xavier chuckled. "He was only here for about a year, wasn't he? I wonder where he went?"

"Maybe he went to visit Philomena and Ahusaka in the Caucasus Mountains," Calloway interjected.

Xavier and Montgomery laughed, but Jonathan ran his hand over the stubble on his chin and through his hair. "Who are Philomena and Ahusaka, and why the Caucasus Mountains?" He sputtered, "I am so confused."

Calloway warmed to the subject. "Philomena was the phoenix, and she lived in Pitchfork Hollow with Luckey Haskins. She'd been there for years, even immolated once! Scared the heck outta Luckey. He was making breakfast one day, and Philomena was sitting on her perch, preening herself. All of a sudden, there was a loud *whoosh!* Luckey turned just in time to see her go up in flames and smoke." He paused and pointed his beer at Jonathan. "Luckily for Luckey, his brother-in-law is the fire chief!"

Jonathan nodded. Calloway continued. "There's still a black spot on his ceiling, by the way—in any event, a small worm crawled from the ashes and stopped in one of the sunbeams streaming into the room. Next thing he knows, there's another *poof,* and a young Philomena flies to her perch and starts preening herself as if nothing had happened. But I, too, digress," Calloway said in response to the exasperated look of his brother. "So, sometime after the immolation, Philomena was out with the chickens when they suddenly dive for cover as a huge, bird-shaped shadow glides overhead, and a thunderbird lands on the roof of Haskin's barn. Now, Luckey hears the thud, sees the chickens scurrying, and goes out to see what's happening. There's Philomena, gazing intently up at the roof, while this huge bird stares right back at her, and neither one breaks the eye lock. Finally, the thunderbird drops down to the yard, and he and Philomena start pecking around the grass as if this is an everyday occurrence. After that the thunderbird, whose name is Ahusaka, takes up residence with Philomena. They move into the barn loft and seemingly, this is now the new norm."

"Hold it!" Jonathan interjected. "How does he know their names?"

"Ah, well, with Philomena, he asked her what her name was, and he didn't quite understand what she said and thought it was Philomena. I guess that after several attempts to correct him, she gave up and left it as is. As for Ahusaka, apparently, he came to Luckey in a dream and told him—which I kinda believe—as Luckey would never have come up with that name for him."

"Yeah, it more likely would have been something like Duke or Butch if he'd named him," Monty chimed in, picking up the story. "So, all seems to be going well, except the chickens stopped laying for several weeks, stressed by having a giant predator living overhead. Ahusaka starts getting restless and comes to Luckey in another dream, telling him that he and Philomena are going to go to the Caucasus Mountains because, apparently, he's 1/32 Vishap, a type of Armenian dragon, and his great-great-great-grandmother was from the Armenian part of the Caucasus Mountains. Besides, he thinks the mountain air will help him with his chicken feather allergy. So, three days later, off they go, and no one has seen them since."

Jonathan ran his hand through his wavy brown hair again and rubbed his temples, as if massaging the unbelievable into his brain. "Let me get this straight: Currently, there's a pregnant Pegasus, a unicorn, flying monkeys, some miniature gryphons, a goose that lays Bavarian eggs, and some centaurs? Am I missing anyone?"

Calloway paused then said, "Well, I can think of two others. There's Tyrone, the faun—or is he calling himself a satyr these days? I never know what he prefers. All I know is that I always get it wrong and must suffer his wrath."

"Well, if you'd stop calling him Tumnus, maybe he wouldn't be so touchy with you," Monty retorted.

"At least *I* don't call him Ty-Ty!"

"That is a perfectly acceptable nickname for Tyrone—look it up, little brother."

"I will!"

Jonathan interrupted the banter. "What's the second one?"

"Second one what?" Calloway asked.

"You said you could think of two others. One was the faun—what's the other?"

"Ah, yes. Well, to be honest, I am not sure what it is or even *if* it is. Strong has a small dell near the back of his property." Calloway nodded at Xavier. "You know the one, it's near the road to Luckey's farm."

"Yeah, there's a low spot and a stand of pine trees and a small hill, right?"

"Exactly!" Calloway continued. "That low part becomes

a pond with heavy spring rains. Geese like to gather there, and Strong says that on more than one occasion he's come across three or four dead ones, just lying there. Then, in the summer, when he's grazed sheep there, one will go missing and never be found or, like the geese, will just be lying there dead. He's convinced that there's something killing them."

"I still maintain it's coyotes," said Monty.

"Yeah, I thought that too, or maybe something about the water, but Strong had the water tested, and it was fine. And the weird thing about the dead animals is that there's never any mark on them—*none*. It's as if they all had heart attacks and dropped dead, and it only seems to happen in that dell," Calloway replied. "I'm beginning to think that Strong is right: something is out there that has amazing killing power."

"Well," Monty replied, "Strong has signed an oil lease, and they plan on drilling in that dell. So, that might solve the problem, especially if there is some environmental reason like a poisonous plant or snake."

"Or it might just displace the problem to a new location," Calloway countered.

"We don't know what the cause is, and a mythological killing machine is not the most reasonable explanation, even for these parts! It's probably a lot simpler," Monty said.

"I will grant that we have poisonous snakes and plants here, but when was the last time a copperhead or a rattlesnake killed three geese, or a sheep, for that matter? How would it even do that? It's not like snakes hunt in packs."

"Okay, so maybe it wasn't a poisonous snake, but what about a poisonous plant?"

Jonathan looked at Xavier, quietly sipping his beer and enjoying the Lucashes' banter. Xavier's love for these creatures and commitment to them was obvious. Even though it still bothered Jonathan that he had been left in the dark, he couldn't help but wonder, *What would I have done in his shoes?*

Jonathan caught Xavier's eye, smiled, and lifted his beer to him. "I'm in," he said.

After leaving the Lucash farm, Xavier had invited him over for dinner, but Jonathan declined. He was restless and knew that movement would help him to process the day. When he was young, it was galloping Chief full out, and when that option vanished, running became his preferred way to clear his head. And, indeed, this evening's run had helped to focus his thoughts and coalesce his unruly emotions. Disbelief, irritation, and confusion, as uncomfortable as they were, at least made sense to him. What he hadn't counted on was the fear inching its way to the surface. His run had ended an hour ago, but he still couldn't relax.

He suspected that the fear was related not just to the job, but to the question that had hung around him all day, overshadowed by the revelation of the "other" animals: *What had happened back there in the restaurant?* At the thought of DeeDee's shining black hair and cornflower-blue eyes, his heart raced. On an impulse, he dialed Nathan. Maybe he couldn't tell him about the flying horse, but if there was one thing Nathan understood, it was women.

"Hey there, how was the first day on the job? Interesting?"

"You have no idea…" Jonathan launched into a description of the two farms and mentioned the Pegasus as an April Fools' joke, not explaining that it was real, but needing to get it out in some way. He paused.

"Did something else happen today? I've known you for a long time, and honestly, you sound like you're holding something back."

Jonathan took a deep breath and let it out slowly. "Um, yeah. There was . . . is a girl."

"I knew it!"

Before Nathan could say anything more, Jonathan described his nearly mute introduction to DeeDee and the tumult of emotions that engulfed him. "The whole thing really unnerved me, reminded me too much of Piper."

"Uh-huh. I get that." Nathan paused. "But you know—Piper is ancient history, and it might be wise to consign her to the history books. But more to the point, how long has it been since you—I don't know, say, took a woman out for coffee?"

"Um, longer than—"

"Exactly!" Nathan interrupted. "You are out of practice on the woman front, so I wouldn't take this encounter so seriously. Let it go—smile and wave when you see her again, and focus on the new job."

"Good advice," Jonathan said. *Especially since there's a boyfriend.*

"Hey, I have to go. I've got another call coming in, and since I'm on call, I've gotta take it. You're gonna be fine. Just take it one day at a time, and call me whenever, okay?"

Jonathan tossed the phone aside, rolled his head to loosen up his neck and shoulders, and headed to the shower. *This has been one unbelievably weird day.*

CHAPTER 7

Anita Vandenberg looked in the mirror of the restroom at Caroline's Deli and sighed. Pulling a small brush from her purse, she attacked the tangled mess that was her hair and contemplated, not for the first time, her unfortunate luck of being from around here but not *from* here. This fact kept her more or less on the outside, despite her attempts to infiltrate the close-knit Carroll County community. In high school she'd attended Canton Central Catholic and had competed against Carrollton High School as a football cheerleader and a volleyball player. She'd even dated Jim Peterson, the star center of the Carrollton basketball team. But that inroad was cut short when he headed off to Heidelberg University on an athletic scholarship.

When she took the job at the Carroll County Animal Control Office four years ago, her outstanding organizational skills and quick wit made her much sought after for the social committees of the local Jaycees, Rotary Club, and the young adult group at Our Lady of Peace. Nonetheless, there was still a sense that as welcome as her talents may be, she was not truly one of them.

She thought about the time that Luckey Haskins dodged her question about the giant vulture his neighbor reported on the roof of his barn, and when Morgan Carter dismissed her concerns about the "gang of wild horses" that Mrs. Lapp declared were "rampaging through her property" along the Harrison/Carroll county line. Then there was the fact that Strong and Calloway *always* stopped talking when she was around. It just felt as if the whole of the community was hiding something. "But what is it?" she demanded of her reflection. "And, exactly how long does one have to live here to be let in on this big secret?" Shoving her brush back into her purse and exiting the bathroom, she saw Jonathan St. Roche. He'd only been here a few months, but he seemed to be making remarkable inroads into the community. Perhaps he was her next best hope.

Jonathan was third in line at the deli, right behind Calloway Lucash, debating between a Reuben or trying a Rachel for the first time. He was grateful to have a few minutes to weigh the pros and cons but, unable to make the decision, his mind switched gears. *Why do the little things seem to be more difficult to decide than the big ones? Is this a universal phenomenon? Is it related to decision fatigue? How would you test that?*

He was jerked from this contemplation by the sudden appearance of Anita at his side. Her green eyes smiled at Jonathan, but she spoke to the farmer. "Calloway, so glad I caught you! I have the tickets for the Cleveland game on Sunday, and I emailed everyone with the details, but yours bounced back."

"Sorry about that. We got a new server. Connie sent out an email with the updated address, but apparently not everyone got it. You aren't the only one to tell me this. Here's the new one." He pulled a pen from the inside pocket of his jacket and wrote the email address on a napkin. "By the way, if you haven't heard from Monty, he can't go. He's got some last-minute legal thing due on Monday, but he said he'd pay for his ticket."

Anita silently thanked St. Paula di Rosa, the patron saint of opportunity, and seized the moment. "Well then, Dr. St. Roche, would you like to join us?" She gave him her most flirtatious smile. "They're playing the Yankees. There's a group of us from the Jaycees going, and I promise it'll be fun."

"Jon. You can call me Jon. And sure. Especially since you *guarantee* it will be fun." He smiled back.

The farmer stared at the vet.

Jonathan reached for his phone to check his calendar and added, "But let me check with Xavier to make sure that he's on call that day. Can I call you this afternoon to confirm?"

"That'd be perfect! Here's my cell number, but I might be out of cell range; you know what rural Ohio is like. So here's my home number as well." She handed Jonathan one of her cards and scribbled her personal numbers on the back.

Jonathan pocketed the card in the breast pocket of his shirt, and before he knew what he was doing said, "Have you eaten yet? Would you like to join me?"

"I would, really, but I have eaten and need to get back to work." She touched Jonathan on the arm. "Can I have a rain check?"

"Sure, anytime." Jonathan smiled once again. She squeezed his arm and left.

Calloway chuckled softly. "Jon, do you like to fish?"

Jonathan turned away from watching Anita leave the deli. "Fishing? Uh, sure, why?"

"Because, in case you didn't realize it, you're the big fish that Anita plans on reeling in this weekend."

Jonathan recalled Nathan encouraging him to move on from Piper. *Besides, DeeDee's not available, so why not Anita?* He astonished even himself when he said, "And that's a bad thing how?" He smiled and stepped up to the counter. "I'll have the Rachel, please."

CHAPTER 8

On a bright Saturday morning, a month or so after the ballgame, Jonathan stood at the railing of his porch swirling cream into his coffee and musing over the fact that he now had a girlfriend. Anita was fun, funny, and not demanding—exactly what he needed to jumpstart his love life. His rumination was interrupted by what sounded like a cry for help. *There it is again! But from where?* He called to Madge, who'd come in to inventory the clinic's supplies but was currently in the kitchen getting coffee. "Did you hear that?" he asked as she stepped onto the porch.

"I did. It sounds like it's coming from across the road—*there*." She pointed to the small meadow used to pasture recovering hoof stock.

Jonathan left his coffee swirling on the railing and, with Madge close behind, hurried down the lawn, across the road, and into a small copse of trees. A plaintive moan drifted through the shade. "There he is!" Madge puffed, pointing to a shadowy figure by a tree.

A black dog stood on his hind legs, his left front leg pinned between the trunks of two dogwood trees while a noisy squirrel chattered from high in the branches. It seemed the pup had chased the miscreant up the trees, only to get his leg stuck where the trunks crossed. "Easy, fella, we'll get you out," comforted Jonathan. He looked around the copse. "First of all, we'll need a strong branch to pry the trunks apart. Then, as one of us levers the trees apart, the other one has to lift the dog up and out."

"Got it. I'll hold the dog; you go to the horse barn and get the crowbar. It's under the sink. That will be quicker than trying to find the right stick," Madge replied.

Jonathan shot off to the barn while Madge turned to the trembling dog. He wasn't wearing a collar, but his shiny black coat and feathery tail had fewer burrs than Madge would've expected from a feral dog. Liver highlights glistened in the intermittent sunlight dancing off his long, velvety ears, crimped from the humidity. "It's okay, sweetie," she cooed as his chocolatey, almond-shaped eyes begged her for relief. Even in pain, his tail swept softly to and fro, and he gently licked her proffered hand. "I think you're a flat-coated retriever." Was it her imagination or did he perk up when she said that? She inched closer. "We don't see many of those around here. Who is your person?" Madge asked as she gently stroked the dog.

Jonathan sprinted back across the meadow, and Madge waved to him to slow down, not wanting him to burst into the thicket and scare the dog.

He caught her signal and quickly but quietly approached, carrying a horse blanket as well as the crowbar. "Are you ready?" he asked, dropping the blanket at the base of the trees.

Madge nodded. Jonathan put the crowbar between the trunks and pushed hard to the right. The trunks groaned and separated just enough for her to lift the dog up and away from the tree.

JULIE FUDGE SMITH

Jonathan dropped the crowbar and helped lay the moaning pup down on his right side.

"Did he just say thank you?" Madge asked.

"It kinda sounded that way, didn't it?" Jonathan replied while examining the wound. There wasn't much blood from the scrape on the leg, but it was tender to the touch and starting to swell.

"I think his leg might be broken, so when you're ready, let's use the horse blanket as a stretcher to get this fellow back to the clinic."

Jonathan unfolded the blanket next to the dog, and before he and Madge could get into position, the dog squirmed his way onto the blanket and settled in for the ride.

"What's your name, buddy?" Jonathan chatted as he gathered the supplies needed to cast the broken leg. "I doubt it's something like Luke or Duke or Hank. You're far too elegant a fellow for that."

"Bnngllyy," muttered the dog, woozy from the preanesthetic meds.

"What's that?"

"Bnngllyy," the dog replied.

Jonathan stopped talking to concentrate on what he was doing and to clear his head. *Was this dog really talking to him? Did he respond to questions? Most dogs respond to voices, but this dog . . .*

"Okay, fella, here we go. I just need to get Madge in here to help." He walked to the door leading to the reception area. "Madge! We're ready for you!"

Jonathan gave the pup a general anesthetic, and he snuggled close to Madge before drifting into unconsciousness. Jonathan slipped a stockinette over the injured leg while Madge expertly steadied the limb. He wet a strip of plaster of Paris and wrapped it around the leg. He applied a few more, then swore under his breath as a strip bunched up in an inconvenient spot.

Madge kissed the top of the dog's head. "You really need to hire a vet tech," she reminded him for the thousandth, ten thousandth, millionth time. "Did I mention that you should talk to Florence Burgett? I know Xavier trusted her to do all sorts of procedures with her gryphons that he would never let another client do."

Jonathan paused. "Right. Yes, of course, you're right. And yes, you did, but I don't really know her." He took a deep breath and resumed the sticky process of applying, drying, and perform-ing the ceremony of four-letter words to create an elegant and tidy cast.

They gently moved the dog to a bed of towels on the floor and waited for him to come out of the anesthesia. Jonathan stretched and sighed. "You know, when I was prepping, I idly asked him his name, and he answered me—twice!" He reached for the disinfec-tant and a cloth to help Madge clean the stainless-steel work area.

"Really? Because as I was waiting for you, he looked me right in the eye when I mentioned that he looked like a flat-coated retriever, just as if he understood every word I said." Madge scrubbed at a particularly stubborn lump of plaster. "What did he say his name was?"

"Bnngllyy."

"Bnngllyy?"

"Yes. Bnngllyy. I've no idea what that means. Maybe he was just making noises. But he said it exactly the same way both times."

Madge mulled this over, suddenly standing up straight. "Bingley! I believe he was saying Bingley!"

Jonathan stared at her.

"Oh, you know, from *Pride and Prejudice*!"

"Ah. Yes, of course, how could I have missed *that*?"

"Mr. Bingley is such a happy fellow. I do believe he is my favorite character."

Jonathan was stunned. He had never heard the ever-practical Madge fawn about *anything*, including her daughter the doctor. Moreover, she was slipping into some sort of British accent. "Oh, really?" he razzed.

Madge ignored his sarcasm. "Yes, *really*. Bingley is the only one of the main characters who sees the best in everyone, and I think that is why he is so very happy." Madge threw the cleaning cloths into the appropriate hamper.

"Um, okay then," Jonathan stuttered.

"You," Madge replied, "are like every other man I know. You could be a Bingley, or a Darcy, but you bumble your way along like Mr. Collins!"

"Mr. Collins?" Jonathan asked.

"No—Bingley. My name is Mr. Bingley," said the dog.

The following morning, Jonathan sat on the sofa nearest the fireplace drinking coffee and watching the sleek black dog dream. *Of all the things I've encountered here, this has to top them all—a talking dog! I'd say I'd imagined it, but Madge heard him too. Hmm, I wonder—could we be having a shared auditory hallucination?*

Mr. Bingley let out a soft groan as he stretched himself awake, his cast making it hard to get a full extension on that leg.

"Good morning, Mr. Bingley. How're you feeling today?"

The dog whipped his head around and lurched himself into a sitting position. He stared wide-eyed at Jonathan but didn't make a sound.

Jonathan smiled. "I bet you need to go out, and then you'd probably like some breakfast, huh?" He rose, put his coffee mug on the mantel, and reached for the sling and the leash he'd left on the couch the night before. "Let me help you get down the steps and into the yard, just until you feel steady on that leg."

Bingley struggled to a standing position and didn't protest as Jonathan helped him into the yard and back. By the time they returned to the kitchen, he was beginning to get the hang of moving with an immobilized limb.

"Here you go, some water and some breakfast," Jonathan said as he placed a bowl of kibble topped with a scrambled egg and some Greek yogurt in front of the smiling flat-coated retriever.

Bingley tucked in and licked the bowl clean. Then, he walked over to Jonathan, leaned in close, and sighed.

Jonathan reached down and massaged the dog's ears. "You are most welcome. Now, let's get you back on the bed and off that leg."

He got another cup of coffee while Bingley settled into the dog bed. "Do you want to know how I know your name?" Jonathan asked.

Bingley raised his head and looked at the vet.

"Well, you aren't wearing a collar with tags, you aren't microchipped, and no one has called the clinic about a lost dog," Jonathan said and sipped his coffee. "Madge called the local shelters and rescues, checked social media, and contacted other vets in the area—no one has reported a lost or missing flat-coated retriever, by *any* name."

The dog lowered his head, but he watched Jonathan as he paced.

"Now, I can tell you that of all the names I would consider for a dog, *Mr. Bingley* isn't even close to being considered, much less put on that list." He stopped pacing, set his mug on the coffee table, and sat on the floor next to Bingley, stroking his neck and side. "So how would I know your name," he said quietly, "if you didn't tell me?"

Bingley blinked several times, but he remained perfectly still.

Jonathan felt the dog stiffen slightly, so he stopped petting him. "You might not remember telling us your name because you were coming out of the anesthesia, but both Madge and I heard it quite distinctly," Jonathan said as he leaned back against the sofa. "But, have no fear, your secret is safe with us—and we are very good at keeping animal secrets—just ask Gertrude, the talking goose." Jonathan reached for his mug.

"You have a talking *goose?*"

Holy cow! He really can talk! Okay, stay calm! Don't spook him! "Well, *I* don't. She lives on a nearby farm, along with a plump unicorn named Bluebell."

"Can the unicorn talk too?"

"No, but the centaurs and the faun can."

"Well, of course they can! They have human bodies. Everyone knows that!"

Jonathan stared at the dog. "How do *you* know that?"

Bingley pushed himself into a sitting position and shook his head. "Well, it just so happens that I am a direct descendent of the talking dog in Aesop's fable *The Dog and His Master,* so I'm familiar with the legends from the ancient world—I just thought they were myths. I had no idea these beasts actually existed."

Jonathan shook his head. "Wait—*what?*" He rubbed his forehead and ran his hand through his hair. "How, how, how . . . is any of this possible?"

"Look, *very* few dogs can talk, but flat-coats have a small gene pool, so the ability to talk pops up every now and again. Dalmatians and Pharaoh dogs can also talk, but they have really heavy accents and are prone to mumble, so that's why Aesop chose the black dog who was the ancestor of our line."

"So mumbling Dalmatians aren't a mystery to you, but talking geese and centaurs are?"

Bingley nodded and shrugged. The two gazed at one another for a long moment.

Jonathan broke the silence. "So, how is it that you ended up here?"

Bingley's shoulders slumped as he looked at the cast on his leg and sighed. "Well, Walter—he was my person—was put into a home by his son, which I don't understand, because we had a home, so why does he need a different one where I can't go?" Bingley raised his chin and howled. The mournful longing reverberated around, in, and through Jonathan. He put down his coffee and wrapped his arms around the wailing dog.

Bingley took a deep breath and leaned into Jonathan's chest. "Eugene, that's Walter's son, took me to his house and put me in a pen in the yard. He said that dogs don't belong in houses and that I was a hunting dog now and better get used to working for my dinner. I ran away that night."

Jonathan stroked the silky ears and pressed his cheek to the top of the dog's head. "Well, I think dogs belong in houses, on furniture, and, if they don't snore, on the end of my bed at night. So, as far as I am concerned, this is your next home—if you'll have me."

Bingley licked Jonathan's face then grunted, stretched, and drifted off to sleep, firmly ensconced in the arms of his new person.

PART II

CHAPTER 9
The Dog

Heading into his second year, Jonathan was grateful to feel settled. Xavier had retired, Anita remained surprisingly undemanding, he had the best dog ever, and work that was satisfying and interesting. His biggest concern seemed to be the lack of squash opponents. These halcyon days, however, would be not only the best of times, but the worst.

But first, the dog.

Storm, Armstrong Clegg's best border collie, was hunkered down in the back of the Silverado's cab, eyes tightly closed. She'd developed crusty, dry eyes, seemingly out of the blue. The farmer's eyes were also itchy, and Strong wondered if he might be developing allergies of some sort. Or maybe it was the meds he started this week. One of the "more common side effects" listed was dry mouth; maybe he got dry eye instead? He'd call Dr. Guzman later, but that wouldn't explain the fact that he and Storm had developed eye issues at the same time. Strong sped down the gravel drive and skidded into the parking lot of the vet clinic. He lifted Storm from the car, nestled her head inside his jacket to shield her from the sun, and carried her inside.

After recording Storm's weight and offering her a biscuit she uncharacteristically rejected, Madge ushered them into an exam room. She lowered the shade and turned off the overhead light. "I'll tell Dr. St. Roche you're here."

"Thanks, Madge." Strong sat down on the washable loveseat and patted the cushion next to him. Storm jumped up and rested her chin on his lap. Shuddering, she sighed and snuggled close. Strong buried his hand in her soft black mane and gently massaged her neck and shoulders. "It's okay, girl, you're gonna be just fine."

Jonathan stood in the hallway outside the exam room reading Storm's file while reflecting on the border collies he had seen in Andalusia, Spain. The first time he'd witnessed those magnificent dogs in action, he'd come close to becoming a sheep farmer rather than a vet. Bingley waited patiently by his side, occasionally leaning into him and rubbing his muzzle on the seam of the vet's jeans. The stiff edge of the seam scratched the dog's cheek with just the right pressure, and the nuzzling served to remind his person of the reality at hand.

"What's up?" he said, glancing down at Bingley, who stopped and stared at him. "Right, then! We've got a border collie waiting for us, don't we?"

Entering the exam room, Bingley greeted Storm, sniffing her muzzle and caressing her with soft kisses, which she returned. Jonathan shook Strong's hand then sat down next to the border collie, who turned and licked his face. He massaged her neck and shoulders. She grunted and leaned into the ministrations. "So, what's up with Storm?"

The farmer rubbed his right eye. "Well, just yesterday she was fine, but this morning, when she woke up, her eyes were crusted shut. I washed them with warm water, and she opened them, but she was blinking a lot, and when I let her out to pee, she did her duty then ran into the new barn. She hid in the shadows and wouldn't come out until I covered her eyes with a fly mask. Even with it, she's really uncomfortable." He blinked and rubbed his left eye.

"Is it one eye or both?" Jonathan asked.

"Both."

"Well, let's take a look." Jonathan loosened the neck strap and carefully removed the fly mask, noting the mucus discharge, excessive blinking, and red-rimmed eyes. "Poor girl, I bet you're uncomfortable, and I don't want to cause you any distress, but I need to examine your eyes a bit more closely and do a tear test." He turned to Strong. "Can you hold her steady while I look in each eye, or do I need to get Florence to help?"

Strong swallowed and blinked. Repeatedly. He knew full well that he could hold Storm, but the chance to see Dr. St. Roche's pretty vet tech was too tempting. "Umm, let's get Florence in here. Storm responds so well to her."

"Pfff!" Bingley snorted. Strong flushed.

"Bing, go get Florence, will you, please?" Jonathan opened the door just wide enough for Bingley to slip out. He reached for a magnifying lens as well as his otoscope. "How's Bluebell?"

"Aye. She's great. She's kept the weight off and hasn't shown any soreness in a while, and I've been really good about limiting the toffees."

Bingley trotted back into the room, followed by Florence. Strong sat up straight, smiled, and ran his hand through his hopelessly mussed hair, to no avail, as Florence focused on holding his dog. Jonathan examined Storm's eyes and, not finding anything unusual, he had Florence numb the border collie's eyes before doing the tear test. Bingley lay down next to Storm. She settled her head on his withers to wait the interminable minute needed to complete the test.

"This is surprising," Jonathan said as he checked the results. "The last time I saw numbers this low, I was treating a dog for cancer who reacted to an antibiotic with severe dry eye—and that developed over a three-month period." The vet turned to the farmer. "You said this happened overnight? She had no symptoms until this morning?"

Strong blinked and closed his eyes for a long moment. "That's right. Yesterday morning she was right as rain. Last night, come to think of it, she started rubbing her eyes and stayed in the darkest corner of the living room all night, but they didn't get crusty until this morning."

"Did anything unusual happen yesterday? Did she get into something? Chase something into the woods, go anywhere she might have scratched her eye?" Jonathan noted that Strong rubbed his eyes for the umpteenth time. *What's up with his eyes?*

Before he could ask, Strong spoke up, "Yesterday, early afternoon, one of the lambs wandered off and into the old barn, you know the one." Jonathan did indeed. The lumbering structure was dark and cluttered with broken equipment, belying Strong's best intentions to resurrect them.

"I sent Storm in to get him, and then I heard a yelp, and Storm flew out of the barn without the lamb. I figured she'd been spooked by one of the broken threshers, so I went in to get the lamb myself. It was pretty dark in there, so I pushed my sunglasses onto the top of my head. I remember this because when I bent over to pick up the lamb, they fell onto my face, and I didn't see whatever it was I bumped into. I just held onto the lamb like it was a Ming dynasty vase and moved toward the door, but he was jumpy and kicked me in the knee." Strong gestured at his leg and smiled at Florence. She busied herself with taking notes. Strong continued.

"So then, I stumbled backward a few feet, there was a scuffling noise, a flash of light, and then it was quiet. I didn't know what was going on, but I knew this little guy needed to get back to the flock, so I headed out of the old barn and over to the new one. I figured maybe a squirrel or raccoon was hiding in the barn, and the flash came as he darted through a loose board." He paused and dabbed at his eyes. "Strange . . .but my eyes started to itch today. Nothing like Storm's, but still . . ."

Jonathan had stained Storm's eyes and looked closely for any scratches on the cornea. Both eyes showed superficial scratches, but he did not think further testing would be needed, at least for now. He prescribed three medications for Storm and showed Strong how to apply each of them while he mulled over what he'd been told. As the lubricating gel soothed her tender eyes, Storm leaned into Jonathan and exhaled.

"Strong," Jonathan said as he stroked her ears, "you look pretty miserable yourself. Have you seen Dr. Guzman about your eyes?"

"Not yet. I was gonna call her when I got home. I was wondering if it was allergies, or maybe a side effect of my meds?"

"Or maybe it's an irritant that you both encountered in the barn. Let me know what she says and keep us posted—I wanna hear how both of you are doing."

CHAPTER 10

There is one week every spring when the moment the sun rises it strikes Jonathan's pillow with laser-like precision. The first day of this week always catches him by surprise, and this sunny Saturday in late April, three days after Storm's visit for her eyes, was that day. It was also a rare weekend with no clinic hours. Jonathan had planned on a lazy morning spent reading and drinking coffee, but when Bingley heard him groan from the blinding brightness of the new day, he seized the moment. Standing on Jonathan's chest, his tail waving in a typical flat-coat salute, Bingley nuzzled and licked him until there was no option but to rise and face the dawn. As Jonathan stretched in front of the sunny window, Bingley trotted to the closet, emerged with a pair of running shoes, and deposited them on the bare feet of his favorite person.

"You don't quit, do you?"

Bingley smiled, his tail and rear end wiggling, his front legs shifting left, right, left, right, left, right.

"Got it. You are ready for a run. Okay, just give me a sec to get dressed."

As Jonathan laced up his running shoes, Bingley said, "Let's go out along clinic road and then back through the woods, okay?" The road crossed several streams, and Bingley loved to run through the culverts that went under the road, noisy, wet agility tunnels that emptied into pools of cold, clear water. What more could a dog ask for?

"Fine with me, Bing. Let's go!" Jonathan did some perfunctory stretches and flipped the switch on the coffee pot as they headed out the door, wishing he could be sitting on the deck with a steaming cup of joe, but also knowing how much better it would taste after having exerted himself.

As Jonathan loped down the gravel drive on this brisk morning, Bingley raced to the first culvert and disappeared over the left bank. As he approached the stream, a happy, wet dog popped up the right embankment and jogged alongside him.

"Feels good, eh?" he called after the slick black shadow dashing toward the next stream.

Once again, Bingley plunged down the left bank, emerged up the right, and sprinted through the grove of pine trees to the next corrugated tunnel. Jonathan chuckled as Bingley predictably tore down the left side of the road to enter the culvert. *Why always the left? Is it because that's the way the stream flows? But why would that matter? Note to self: ask dog why always left to right.*

As he neared the culvert, he was surprised that Bing was not coming up the right side. He whistled and called, but no dog, no answer, and no sign of him on either side of the road. A small groan rose from below him. Racing down the embankment, Jonathan looked inside the culvert and saw his beautiful boy with a rusty weasel trap clamped onto his back leg. Trembling, Bingley's wide almond eyes begged for help.

"Easy boy, I've got you." Jonathan waded into the frigid

water and found the post next to the entrance where the trap was wired into place. He detached the trap and eased it and Bingley out of the culvert and onto the sandy creek bank.

"Hold still, buddy, and I'll get it off, I promise."

"Hurry," Bingley whimpered.

Jonathan carefully pried the trap open and released the dog's leg. Bingley immediately plunged the leg into the stream and continued to tremble as the cold water numbed his tender, swelling appendage.

"Who the hell set this thing, and when?" Jonathan fumed as he threw the trap up onto the road. He lifted Bingley from the water and struggled up the slope to the road, muttering, "I never gave anyone permission to trap on this land!"

He laid the pup in the grass and wrapped him in his hoodie. "You stay here. I am going to get the truck to take you back to the clinic. I don't want you to put any weight on that leg until we can get an X-ray. I won't be more than a few minutes."

Bingley nodded and closed his eyes. Jonathan sprinted toward the clinic, fear and anger gripping his heart like a second rusty weasel trap.

X-rays showed that somehow the fates were with them that day, as the trap did not crush or break any bones. The leg was scraped, bruised, and clearly tender, but Bingley could bear weight on it. Jonathan gave the pup some pain medication and settled him by a sunny window with a water buffalo horn to chew, then set out to check the remaining culverts for any additional traps. He found three: one empty; one with a snarling weasel that he managed to release; and one with Janice's orange tabby cat, who was no longer alive but still warm. As he stroked the silky matted fur, his nose dripped, and his shoulders hunched. He wrapped Scotty in a clean towel, laid him on the passenger seat in the cab of the F250, and whispered, "I'm so sorry I didn't get here sooner."

He hurled the last trap into the back of the truck where it clattered into the others, rattling his nerves as well as his truck. Not wanting to get in the cab with the cat, Jonathan paced and pummeled his fist into the palm of his other hand. "I didn't know anyone still used these things. What are they hoping to trap here in Ohio? It's not like there's a booming fur trade."

He stopped pacing. Suddenly, his skin went clammy, and the hairs on his neck stood up. "Maybe there is a market for trapped animals, just not the kind most people think of . . ." He pulled the keys from the front pocket of his jeans and jumped into the truck. *I need to talk with Xavier.* He looked at the small figure lying next to him on the seat. *And Janice. But first, let's see what we can do to prevent another incident like this.*

He picked up his cell phone and dialed his girlfriend. "Hey, Anita. Jon. Could you give me a call as soon as you get this? I need your help with something."

CHAPTER 11

Anita sat at the second table from the window on the left-hand side of the deli because it was the best place to see everything that happened in this social center of Carrollton as well as everyone who walked by. The whole town, from oil field workers to lawyers, seemed to come in at least once a week, which is why Anita was here, in her spot, almost every day of the workweek, as well as many a Saturday. She, unlike Jonathan, did not lose herself in contemplating abstract ideas. She was too busy watching and evaluating her surroundings and could not understand what possible value there was to wondering why honeybees were attracted to caffeine when there were so many local enigmas to mull over.

On this particular Saturday, she'd wandered into the deli a bit early and was staying a bit late. The weather was sunny but slightly chilly, so the hot coffee, which she enjoyed strong and black, was particularly satisfying. Why Jonathan added cream to this heavenly elixir was beyond her—as was the fact that things had lasted this long with him. It had been close to a year since the Indians game (which they agreed was the "opening day" of their relationship), and if this had followed her usual relationship trajectory, she would have gotten bored by now and ended it. But

things with Jonathan were different—easy, and mostly uncomplicated. She still suspected that he knew more about the community than he was letting on, so she remained convinced that he
was her best chance to get in on the big secret.

A woman in her early thirties, with a Burberry trench coat
and a heavily laden, somewhat worn Coach messenger bag, caught
Anita's attention as she entered the deli and strode to the counter.
The woman's brown hair was pulled back in a sensible ponytail,
and she had red-rimmed glasses poised on the top of her head.
Anita couldn't catch her name when she gave it for her order,
but something about her seemed familiar. Determined to learn
more, Anita made her way to the counter to refill her coffee and
intercept the woman. The deli was filling up, and tables were at a
premium. Maybe if she offered the woman a place to sit—but she
veered off to the bathroom, leaving Anita to refill her mug or stalk
the woman outside the restroom. She chose coffee.

Anita returned to her table to consider her next move. The
woman emerged just as her name—"Connolly!"—was called out
from the counter. Anita nearly choked as it dawned on her that
this must be *the* Connolly Davis from *Ohio Monthly* magazine.
That's why she recognized her; though if truth be told, she looked
a lot older than her byline picture. Anita stood up and walked
straight to the counter. "Excuse me, are you Connolly Davis, the
journalist?"

"Um, yes, I am. And you are?" Connolly took a small step
backward.

"Anita Vandenberg. Sorry if I startled you." Anita smiled. "I just
wanted to tell you how much I've enjoyed your work over the years."

"Thank you," Connolly said, letting her shoulders relax as

she picked up her tray and looked around for a seat. Anita seized the moment.

"There aren't a lot of open seats; would you like to join me?"

"Sure, that'd be great. Thanks."

"I think one of your best pieces was the one about the big cat collector in Zanesville," Anita said as Connolly hung her coat on the back of her chair. "It was just bad luck, if you ask me, that the *very* next week, he let all his animals go and committed suicide."

"Yeah, that was a bummer, especially since I was on vacation and couldn't cover *that* story." Connolly sighed as she slipped her coffee and sandwich off her tray and put a napkin in her lap.

"But your piece last year on Ohio puppy mills was amazing! I'm an animal control officer for the county, so that's something I really care about."

Connolly swallowed. "Actually, that was three years ago, but I'm glad it resonated with you."

"Really? That long? I could have sworn it was just last year." Anita paused. "So, ah, what brings you to Carrollton?"

"I'm doing a story on oil fracking in this part of the state and the new millionaires it's creating. There's been a lot written about the environmental concerns, but *my* editor decided that *I* had to write about how a sudden, large influx of money affects a rural community." Connolly's phone buzzed with an incoming text. She frowned at the phone. "Yes, Jack, I *know*," she growled at the phone while stabbing out a response. "Bosses! What ya gonna do?"

Anita shrugged as she offered a half-smile. "So, I guess you and your boss, uh, disagreed on this story?"

Connolly nodded and rolled her eyes as she tucked into her sandwich.

"I mean, your boss is right. Historically, there hasn't been a lot of money in Carroll County, so the sudden influx has some unintended consequences—but that's just today's headline. I suspect there's a much bigger story here."

"Such as?" Connolly interrupted.

Anita kept her voice low and steady as she leaned in and whispered, "One reason why your article on puppy mills resonated with me was because there are other animal stories beneath the surface out here. Things may look normal, but . . ." She looked around to see if anyone was listening. They weren't.

"*But?*"

"But . . . they aren't normal, at least some farms aren't." Anita shook her head and took a sip of coffee.

"Not normal? This is your big story?"

Anita pinched her brow together as she tamped down her irritation with Connolly's condescension. "What I mean is, there's something going on that's been going on for a *long* time. I grew up close to here, knowing most of these people, and I have long suspected that they were hiding something, some oddity or oddities—"

"What sort of oddity?" Connolly interrupted.

"That's just it, I don't know *exactly*—but I do know that it has something to do with both the remoteness of this area and the people who have lived here for generations." Anita leaned in. "I suspect that if you figure out what they're covering up, you will have the real story, maybe even the story of the century."

Connolly didn't say anything as she finished half her sandwich, but she no longer looked patronizingly at the animal control officer. Anita took this as a positive development. She snapped her fingers. "*What* if you used the excuse that you're looking at the impact of fracking as an *in*, and then maybe you can find out what's really going on!" She sat up straighter and jabbed her finger at the reporter. "Strong Clegg has a fracking lease, and I know there's some odd stuff going on at his farm, including a goose that has lived for *years,* I mean forty to fifty years!" She leaned back and crossed her arms over her chest, nodding.

"A long-lived goose? This is your story of the century?"

"Well, fifty years is really long, even for a domestic goose. Okay, explain this: why is it that we get calls *every year* about flying monkeys?"

"You mean like in the *Wizard of Oz*?"

"Exactly! Only, no one ever reports that they're wearing hats—but it's always a visitor to the county, never a resident, so there's that."

"There's what?"

"I think the locals know something, but they're covering it up. I mean, how is it that not a single Carroll County resident ever reports a sighting or backs up a visitor's claim? They *always* insist the visitor was drinking. But, really? Every visitor who gets drunk has the same hallucination? I find *that* hard to believe. And then, there's the beagles."

"Beagles?"

"In rural communities—all over the country, by the way, not just in Ohio—there's a problem with beagles being abandoned when they don't hunt well. Shelters like ours are overrun with them, especially during hunting season. But, in the last year, the surplus beagle population has dropped to nearly zero, *for no apparent reason*. It's not like all these hunters have suddenly stopped using beagles or grown consciences. So where are these dogs? What is happening to them?"

Connolly sipped her now-cold coffee. "Look, I have to say that I'm skeptical about the flying monkeys, and your hunch about some hidden mystery." She paused as she nestled the mug on the tray precisely one-half inch from the plate. "But the beagle problem intrigues me, and the fracking story does give me a good excuse to meet these people. So if there's something to any of this, I'm in the perfect position to find out, especially since I'm rather adept at getting people to open up, particularly when they claim there's nothing to say!" She folded her napkin into a perfect rectangle and tucked it under the edge of the plate opposite the mug. "Now all I need is a list of people to contact."

"Montgomery Lucash. He's the local attorney who negotiated oil leases for most of the farmers. He'd probably know who would be most willing to talk, and his office is just two doors down, next to the Fighting McCooks Museum." Anita pointed in the direction of the nearly famous landmark. Anita's phone vibrated in her pocket, but she ignored it. "I'd be happy to introduce you if you'd like."

"Thanks," Connolly said as she gathered up her briefcase and coat, "but let me do some research first. I've found that it pays to be well informed when talking to attorneys."

Anita handed the reporter one of her cards and wrote her cell number on the back. "Call me anytime."

As she walked to her car, Anita listened to her voicemail. The message from Jonathan was uncharacteristically abrupt, and he was clearly upset—anxious? Annoyed? She wasted no time in calling him back. "Jon? I got your voicemail. Is everything okay?"

"No. It's not! Bingley got caught in a weasel trap someone put—*illegally, I might add*—at the end of one of the culverts on my road!"

"Oh, Jon, I'm so sorry! Is he okay?"

"Yes, miraculously, he has come out of this with only some abrasions and bruising." He paused, then added, "I found one of Janice's cats dead in a trap, though, and I released a weasel from a third." Before Anita could respond, Jonathan added, "What can be done about this? This was not a humane live trap. This was an iron, spring-loaded thing. Are these traps even legal? Can I press charges against the person who did this without my permission?"

Anita took a deep breath and cleared her throat. "Jon, I'm really sorry about Bingley and Janice's cat. But people have been trapping weasels and raccoons in this area forever, and honestly, weasel traps are pretty far down on my list of things to be concerned about."

No reply.

She went on, "The guy who set the traps has probably been doing this for years. And even if you did find out who he was, what're you gonna charge him with besides trespassing?" The silence continued, though she thought she detected him pacing and swearing under his breath, so she veered in another direction. "Have you told Janice yet?"

Now it was Jonathan's turn to take a deep breath. "I was just about to call them when my phone rang, and it was Xavier. Apparently, they hit a moose yesterday just outside of Calgary. Unfortunately, Janice was standing when it happened, and she was thrown to the floor, breaking her arm in two or three places. So she's in the hospital, and the RV is in for extensive repairs, and they don't know when they'll be back. I didn't want to add to their burdens, so I didn't say anything. I figured more bad news could wait a bit."

Anita took a moment to absorb this information and changed tack again. "Jon, you need to remember that outdoor cats are at a higher risk for injury and death, including being caught in a trap. If it wasn't on your property, it could have happened elsewhere, and then you never would have found it. Now, at least, Janice won't have to wonder what happened to her cat." She paused slightly before adding, "I know we disagree about this, Jon, but now maybe you'll see why I think it's important to keep Bingley on a leash?"

"So let me get this straight: You don't think this is important, and you won't help me figure out who put these traps on my property? And somehow you also think this is a good time to lecture me about how I manage my own dog on my own property? Have I missed anything, Anita?"

Anita was not one to back away from a challenge, but then again, she'd never experienced this side of Jonathan St. Roche. "Jon, I'm sorry if I said anything to upset you. That was not my intention."

"I appreciate that, but I *am* upset. Look, I don't want to argue, and I have to check on Bingley. So we'll talk later, okay?" He hung up.

Anita threw her phone onto the passenger seat and jerked her car into reverse, very nearly hitting Montgomery Lucash's office cat. "Stupid animal," she groused as she sped off.

CHAPTER 12

On Sunday morning, the light once again seared the eyelids of Jonathan, who'd forgotten to close the shades on that particular window. "Ugh," he groaned and rolled to the left, surprised to find Bingley lying next to him. "What are you doing here, buddy? I thought you'd stay on your bed with your sore leg."

"Hmmpf," the canine groaned, ignoring the question. "You're hogging the bed, you know." He shifted his weight to nestle closer to Jonathan, and the two drifted into a hazy morning slumber.

Forty-five minutes later, Bingley was wolfing down his breakfast while Jonathan sipped a latte from his new cappuccino machine and watched the red and gray squirrels scamper around the yard. *Why aren't flying squirrels diurnal like their cousins here? Were they ever diurnal? What would be the advantage of being nocturnal?*

Having licked every molecule from his bowl, Bingley now interrupted Jonathan's pondering by rubbing his face on the seam of his shorts.

"Need to go out?"

Bingley nodded and trotted over to the door, tail waving, front legs shifting left, right, left, right.

He's too eager, Jonathan thought. "Let me get your leash. I don't want you to overdo it on your leg. I *know* the game you play with the squirrels!"

After a leisurely perambulation around the yard, Jonathan showered and dressed and settled Bingley once again in the enclosure by the window. "Look, just rest while I am gone, and when I get back, maybe, *just maybe,* we can go for a real walk."

"I will hold you to that." Bingley sighed and stretched out on his bed.

Jonathan headed out the door, amazed that he would be on time for Mass.

Jonathan squinted from the brightness of the noonday sun as he left the narthex of Our Lady of Peace. He pulled his sunglasses from his shirt pocket as he approached his truck, frowning at the presumed familiarity of Anita leaning against the driver's side, scrolling through her phone. He brushed the annoyance aside and smiled.

"Hey there, I didn't see you inside." Jonathan gestured over his shoulder to the church.

"I got here late and sat in the back," Anita replied. She eased her weight off the truck and stepped toward Jonathan, who stopped walking. "Can we talk?"

"Sure."

"Look, I'm sorry if I came across as unsympathetic or gruff about Bingley. I *do* care that someone was trapping illegally on your property, and I wish there was something I could do to help." She paused, unwrapped a cherry Jolly Rancher, and popped it in her mouth. "How is Bing?"

He flinched at her use of his dog's nickname and the clicking of the candy against her teeth. *What is wrong with me? I shouldn't be this annoyed with her. She is trying to be nice.* He took off his sunglasses and started to clean them with his shirt. He forced another smile.

"He's okay. Luckily, there were no broken bones." Jonathan finished polishing his sunglasses. "But I should get back to check on him." He blew one last speck of dirt from the left lens and paused for a split second. He stepped toward her and brushed a lock of hair from her face. "How about we go out to dinner tonight? I'll pick you up at six, and we'll go to the Hunt Club."

Anita relaxed her shoulders and closed the gap between them. "That sounds great." She lifted her face. He tucked her hair behind her ear, leaned in, and kissed her. He stepped away from her and opened the door to his truck. *Yuck,* he thought, *I hate cherry Jolly Ranchers.*

Dressed in a seafoam green halter dress with a lacy cream wrap and imitation Jimmy Choo sandals, hair piled in an artfully arranged messy bun, Anita waited at the entrance to the Minerva Hunt Club while Jonathan parked the car. She hoped that he'd reserved an outdoor table but vowed not to say anything negative should they be seated indoors. Holding her tongue was not one of her virtues.

"That sounds perfect," Anita said when the maître d' suggested they get a drink while they waited the twenty minutes for an outdoor table. She steered Jonathan into the expansive bar, complete with oak paneling and a boar's head over the massive fireplace. She left him to order the drinks and went to find seats on the brick terrace overlooking the pasture where three palomino ponies grazed.

"What can I get for you, sir?" the bartender asked while Jonathan glanced at the drink menu.

"A dirty Grey Goose martini and a Jameson and ginger ale, please."

"Very good, sir."

A comforting earthy smell exuded from paneling colored from years of cigars and roaring fires. Jonathan noted that while there were many pictures of men and their prizes, the only actual hunting trophy was a rather mangy boar's head. As he put the menu back on the cherry and oak bar, he noticed a brief history of the building on the back:

> The Hunt Club was originally the elegant home of James Fuller McKinley, favorite nephew and ward of President William McKinley. James built the house in 1905 and furnished it with locally handcrafted furniture. He also hung above the fireplace in the library (now the bar) the head of the boar that McKinley shot during his gubernatorial campaign in 1891.
>
> The current owner, Marmaduke Langdon, began restorations in 1992, painstakingly recreating wallpaper, carpets, and many pieces of furniture. He even located the original boar's head!
>
> The Hunt Club opened as a restaurant and banquet facility in 2000.

Jonathan smiled at the description, remembering when Xavier told him about the turkey hunt resulting in the ancient boar now staring down at him. He put a couple of dollars in the tip jar and headed to the terrace, where he found Anita seated with DeeDee and her boyfriend, "the esteemed orthopedic surgeon," Marcus Daniels. DeeDee's ebony hair, usually pulled back in a practical ponytail, flowed gracefully over her shoulders and played with the black stitching on the top of her jonquil-yellow sundress. Sunflower earrings caught the reflection of the garden lights, causing shafts of light to dance in her hair and Jonathan to stop in his tracks.

Anita waved and gestured to him. Jonathan swallowed hard and made his way to the table. He deposited the drinks, shook hands with Marcus, and sat next to Anita on a bench by the railing. "Good to see you," he lied. "It's been a while, eh?"

"I suppose it has. I haven't been to Carrollton lately. Tweedle Dee here usually comes to Pittsburgh, as there is *so* much more to do in the big city." Marcus squeezed DeeDee's upper arm. Jonathan noticed her flinch and found his neck growing hot despite the evening breeze.

Anita slid closer to Jonathan, took his arm in hers, and drank deeply from the martini. Marcus popped several peanuts into his mouth and gazed over the railing at the palominos now loping through the field. "Beautiful horses!" he sputtered, then took a deep pull on his Guinness. "Do you ride, St. Roche?"

"Use to. Not much time for it now, and I don't currently own a horse. How about you, Daniels?"

Marcus chuckled. "Nope, not unless I'm visiting my folks." He took another long drink. "They have a horse farm in Maryland.

I get there on holidays if I'm lucky." He glanced around the terrace. "I play squash now—have since my Princeton days."

Anita squeezed Jonathan's arm and inched closer. "I haven't been riding in *forever*. What about you, DeeDee? You used to compete, if I remember correctly?"

"Really, you rode competitively? I had no idea. What in?" Jonathan freed his arm from Anita's grasp and leaned his elbows on the table.

"Hunter/jumper, then jumping. But I had a bad fall my sophomore year in high school that broke my leg and subsequently revealed early-stage osteosarcoma. I stopped riding and became interested in medicine instead. It's when I decided to become a doctor," DeeDee said and blushed.

"Really? My twin sister broke her arm our senior year, and the only thing it inspired her to do was party with her friends!" Jonathan grinned.

DeeDee smiled and laughed.

Anita looked back and forth between them while Marcus drained his glass and said, "Now, *that's* my kinda gal! Anyone need another drink?"

"*I do!*" Anita finished off her martini. "A dirty Grey Goose martini, please."

"Be right back," Marcus said and disappeared into the bar.

Anita sat up. "DeeDee, Marc said he plays squash, right?" She didn't wait for a reply. "Well, it just occurred to me that a good fundraiser for the upcoming Millionaire's Ball might be a squash tournament! Everyone would pay a fee to play, and the winner, or winners, would get a 50/50 prize. I'd be happy to organize it!" She smiled at Jonathan. "What do you think?"

"Sure! I love squash," Jonathan said.

"The vegetable or the game?" Marcus asked as he put Anita's drink on the table.

"The game, of course!" Anita giggled. "I suggested that we have a squash tournament as a fundraiser for DeeDee's Millionaire's Ball."

"You have a facility for squash here in Boondocksville?" Marcus asked.

"We do. At the new YMCA, supported, by the way, by many of the same people who are sponsoring the Millionaire's Ball," DeeDee said.

"I stand corrected!" Marcus smiled, patted DeeDee's hand, and disentwined a strand of hair that the evening breezes had tossed across her eyelashes. He turned his attention to Anita. "So, are you and Dr. Doolittle here any good?"

"I don't play, but Jon was the intramural doubles champion three out of his four years at Cornell," Anita bragged. She took a drink from her martini.

"Only three of four? What happened?" Marcus asked.

"Well, if I understand it correctly," Anita said as she suppressed a giggle, "Jon stopped to tie his shoe, and his partner tripped over him and twisted his ankle, so they had to drop out." She smiled and gazed at Jonathan. "But I'm *positive* they would have won otherwise."

Jonathan furrowed his brow and, Anita noted, finished his drink.

"That makes two of us who play, not really enough for a tournament. You may have the courts, but does anyone else around here actually play squash?"

"I do."

"Connolly!" Anita squeaked. The reporter was standing next to their table holding a large glass of red wine.

"There's actually a facility for squash around here?" Connolly said.

Marcus pointed both his index fingers at DeeDee. "See, I'm not the only one!" He turned to Connolly. "Would you care to join us?"

"Thanks," Connolly said and slipped onto the bench by the railing. "You should have told me this was the place to come to," Connolly chided Anita while smiling at Marcus.

Anita ignored the remark and introduced Connolly. "And," she concluded, "she's doing a story on the impact of fracking money on our community—"

"Anita's planning a squash tournament," Marcus interrupted. "You interested?"

"Absolutely." A waiter in a starched white shirt and pristine black pants motioned for her to follow him. "Ah, my table awaits." She stood up and waved her wine at Anita. "Give me a call, and we'll talk about this tournament, okay? It was great to meet all of you."

Another young man in a crisp white shirt and perfectly pressed black pants approached. "Dr. Daniels?" He looked from one man to the other. "Your table is ready, but it's only for two. Did you need a table for four?"

"No," both men replied at the same moment DeeDee and Anita each said, "Yes!"

No one moved or spoke. The waiter broke the uneasy silence. "Do you need more time?"

"No," Marcus declared, taking DeeDee's arm and guiding her toward the retreating server. "We don't want to make things difficult for you." Nodding at Jonathan and Anita, he added, "See you on the court, St. Roche."

"So *where* did you meet Carol Davis?" Jonathan asked. He swallowed his bruschetta topped with goat cheese and locally grown yellow tomatoes.

"Her name is *Connolly*, and I ran into her at the deli. There were no open tables, so I offered her a seat, and we got to talking." Anita sipped her third martini and shook her head when he offered her the last bruschetta. "She usually does animal welfare stories, but I got the sense she was pressured into doing this story, and I offered to introduce her to Monty since he brokered so many of the oil deals." She placed her hand on his forearm. "But it occurs to me that you know several of the farmers as well. Maybe you could suggest some she could talk with?"

Jonathan shook his head. "I'm sorry, Anita, but I can't—won't—do that. These are very private people—you know that." He sipped his water before continuing. "Not to mention the fact that I don't talk about my clients to anyone at any time. Besides, it's really none of my business, and I don't want them to feel like I'm violating their trust by pushing them to talk to a journalist." He looked at Anita biting her lower lip and slipped her hand in both of his. "Look, I think having her talk with Monty is a much better idea. There's no doubt in my mind that he's more likely to know who'd be willing to talk to a reporter than I am."

She smiled weakly. He pressed his lips to the back of her hand before releasing it and reaching for his water glass. "So you're going to organize a squash tournament, eh? Think I can beat Dr. 90210?"

"I most certainly do!" A third waiter in a spotless white shirt set their dinners on the table with a flourish. As Anita described how she'd organize the tournament and what she thought the T-shirts should look like, Jonathan caught sight of DeeDee and Marcus headed for the exit. Marcus slipped his arm around her waist, pulled her close, and kissed the top of her head while he winked at Connolly now swirling a brandy at the bar.

What a jerk! I'd never do that! Holding her while flirting with another woman? DeeDee deserves so much more. He shook his head, which allowed Anita's words to break through his mental fortification. "What? You don't like red? I thought that was your favorite color?"

Jonathan's head reeled. *She sounds what? Annoyed? Exasperated? Hurt? Oh man! What did I miss?* He took a stab at what he hoped was an appropriate response as small beads of sweat broke out on his brow. "Red? Well, yeah, I do like red, but I think that is an over-done color. Why not be bold and go for something more daring?"

"Hmmm, maybe you're right. I'll ask DeeDee what colors they're using for the ball and tie the shirts to that theme."

"There ya go! Great idea! Will you excuse me for a moment? Nature is calling." He stood up and pushed his chair back. "Why don't you pick out a dessert for us to share? And could you order some coffee for me?" He put his hand on her bare shoulder and leaned over to kiss the top of her head at the very moment DeeDee Guzman turned and scanned the crowd.

Jonathan held his breath.
DeeDee caught his eye and held his gaze.
He winked.

CHAPTER 13

"So, what's with Lucretius and dogs?" Jonathan asked as he and Calloway drove the backroads to the hollow that lay on the border between Harrison and Carroll Counties.

"I don't think anyone knows for sure, but here's what I've pieced together: When Lucretius and his cousin Cassius were young, they were playing in a stream and apparently didn't notice that some feral dogs were watching them. The pack sprang out of the reeds and grabbed the two young centaurs by their back legs. Lucretius, being somewhat bigger, was able to shake them off, but Cassius was pulled under water and drowned. Lucretius wasn't strong enough to help his cousin and couldn't get help there in time to save him. He's hated dogs ever since."

"Can't say as I blame him. How long ago was this?"

"About a hundred years or more."

"You're joking, right?"

"No. Centaurs live a really long time."

Jonathan thought about this. "And he still holds a grudge? You know, my mom used to say that being cranky and bitter was the key to longevity! She had a grandmother who lived to 102 and apparently was a piece of work right up to the end. So, maybe it's true for centaurs as well."

Cal smiled. "Well, at least Lucretius no longer kicks a dog to death whenever he sees one. But it's probably best to keep them away from him, and him away from the subject, especially if he's been at the mead."

Jonathan motioned to the bag next to him on the seat. "Speaking of mead, do you suppose that's what this is? Madge gave it to me as I was leaving and said to tell Lucretius it was from Lorenzo."

Cal pulled the bottle from the bag. "I bet it is. He's been known to dabble in wine making." He slipped the bottle back into the paper bag. "Xavier once told me that he found it helped to make the centaurs more receptive to his *suggestions*." He reached into his own bag and pulled out a black wine bottle with a medieval-looking label. "Connie sent this along just in case."

"Just in case of what?"

"You need to make a *suggestion*." Cal tucked the two bottles of mead into a leather satchel and cinched the top.

Jonathan parked the truck under the large pine obscuring the trailhead to Tangled Hollow. He reached for his medical bag in the backseat, and his hand landed on a wet snout emerging from the folds of a horse blanket.

"Bingley? What are you doing here?"

The dog stood up and shook himself. "Napping—well, I *was* napping, but now I am awake." He hopped to the front seat that Calloway had vacated. "And coming with you."

Jonathan stared at him. "I don't think so!"

"Why not?"

"Because Lucretius—" Calloway started to say.

"*Hates dogs.* I know, but I have a plan for that," Bingley interrupted.

Calloway and Jonathan looked at one another. "And what would that be?" Jonathan asked.

Bingley's tail waved enthusiastically. "I will be the bearer of the wine! He can't hate anyone who brings him mead." He leapt from the cab and parked himself next to the farmer.

Jonathan looked at the afternoon sun, still high in the sky. *I can't leave him in the truck. It'll be way too hot, and if I leave the windows down, he'll just follow us—so, I guess we take our chances.* "Okay, Bing, you win. But stay close, be respectful, and don't speak unless spoken to."

Bingley nodded, picked up the leather satchel, and they hiked the half mile through the hilly pine forest and across Rocky Fork Run. The centaur encampment centered around a large fire pit in the middle of a clearing edged with enormous pines, which shaded the shale caves forming three sides of the hollow. Calloway whistled "Volare" loudly to signal their approach, and as they rounded the corner, they saw Lucretius showing a young centaur how to bank the embers of the fire. Jonathan stopped. Even after everything he'd seen, he could not believe that these magnificent half-men, half-horse creatures of myth and legend truly existed, and he was amazed and delighted by the sight.

"Calloway Lucash, dear friend, good to see you!" the centaur bellowed, grasping his hand and kissing him on both cheeks. He turned to Jonathan. "Dr. St. Roche, thank you for coming to—" Lucretius stopped mid-sentence when he saw Bingley standing a step behind Jonathan. He stretched to his full height, his tone icy as he demanded, "You brought *a dog* to my camp?"

"His name is Bingley, and he wishes to give you a gift,

Lucretius," Calloway said, as he put a restraining hand on the shoulder of the centaur.

Lest he anger the temperamental beast and risk being kicked, Bingley avoided making eye contact. He placed the leather satchel in front of Lucretius and backed away two feet before offering a deep bow.

Lucretius glared at the dog, then pointed to the satchel. "And what's in there?"

"Mead, milord," Bingley answered, still bowing.

Lucretius softened almost imperceptibly. "Septimus! Come here and take this to the table!" The young centaur walked by Bingley, and the dog caught a scent that concerned him. He tried to catch Jonathan's eye, but Lucretius was addressing the vet and had his full attention. So, Bingley took the opportunity to retire to the entrance of a seldom-used cave and curl into a tight ball. Jonathan watched him retreat and only relaxed when the dusty shadows swallowed his black dog.

"As I was saying, thank you, Dr. Roche, for coming to see me. Please, have a seat," Lucretius said, pointing to the logs encircling the fire pit.

"Please, call me Jon," he said and moved to where he could keep an eye on his dog.

Flavia, Lucretius's sister, made a point of coming over. "Dr. St. Roche, how good to see you again. It's been a while now, hasn't it?"

"About a year, I believe. How are you doing? I take it you haven't had any more bouts of laminitis?"

"I haven't, thank you for asking. You remember my son Septimus."

Jonathan smiled warmly as he shook hands. "It's nice to see you again, Septimus. What was your uncle showing you when we arrived?"

Just then, Lucretius ordered Septimus to gather ox horn cups and the other centaurs to bring tables, wine, and food. After chatting with Lucretius, Calloway moved to Jonathan and said, "He says that there has to be a toast first, then you can do the exam. You don't have to drink much, but you need to at least lift your glass and take a sip."

"Got it, can do." He accepted a cup of the burgundy liquid and waited for everyone to be served.

Lucretius cleared his throat. "Ahem. May I have everyone's attention, please?" He paused as the group turned its attention to him. "First, let us welcome Calloway and Jonathan." With great ceremony, Lucretius picked up a small piece of toast off a silver tray, dropped it in his glass, and proclaimed, "To the Good Spirit! To Zeus! To health!" He raised his glass high, then drank deeply from the translucent horn goblet. The centaurs cheered and drank heartily. Jonathan took a sip of the full-bodied wine and closed his eyes as the silky elixir glided down his throat.

"This is the best wine I think I've ever had," he exclaimed and lifted his cup to Lucretius. "But I'd be derelict in my duty if I drank any more before I examined you."

Lucretius frowned but placed his goblet on the table and pointed to the entrance of a cave next to the one hiding Bingley. Jonathan picked up his bag and followed, caught Calloway's eye, and nodded toward the cave.

Lucretius was sweating profusely, even though the temperature was in the mid-seventies, and Jonathan noticed he hadn't shed his shaggy winter coat. "So, tell me, have you been feeling lethargic or fatigued lately?" he asked as he pulled his stethoscope, otoscope, and blood pressure cuff from his bag.

"I have, but I thought it was just because my middle-aged paunch was expanding," he chortled, then grew serious. "But, honestly, I haven't changed my diet or decreased my exercise, and yet I have gained weight, especially around my midsection." He jiggled his belly, and Jonathan noticed the beginning of pink stretch marks on his skin, as well as a buffalo hump between his shoulder blades.

Calloway spoke up, "Lucretius, I don't remember you having that hump on your back. Is that new?"

"Yes! It started a couple of months ago, about the same time I started to balloon in the front. I feel as if I am inflating on both sides!"

"Did the lethargy start around the same time?" Jonathan asked as he finished taking the centaur's vital signs.

Lucretius furrowed his brow. "Maybe. It seems as though I have always been tired." He sighed. "After the spring solstice bacchanalia, I thought perhaps I'd overdone the celebrating, and the fact that I am no longer young made it harder to recover." He paused to wipe the sweat from his brow. "But that was three months ago! And the symptoms have not abated. So, I thought it best to see if there was something more than old age wrong with me." He looked around the opening of the cave. "By Zeus, I'm thirsty!"

"I'll get you some water," Calloway said. He grabbed a bucket and headed to the communal spring, stopping for cups on the way.

Jonathan cleared his throat. "Well, Lucretius, I have some good news for you. First, your temperature, pulse, and respiration rate appear normal. Your blood pressure is within the accepted range for a horse, but elevated for a human, so I am not sure how to interpret that. Do you have any idea what your normal blood pressure is?"

Lucretius stared at Jonathan for a split second before answering, "No, I'm afraid I don't."

"Well, I didn't think that you did, but it was worth asking." He cleared his throat again. "I don't think that your fatigue and weight gain are age-related, per se." He paused. Lucretius relaxed a bit and nodded for him to continue.

"I think they're much more likely to be the result of an endocrine disorder called pituitary pars intermedia dysfunction— PPID, more commonly known as Cushing's disease. This syndrome occurs more frequently in horses nineteen years of age or older, so age can be a factor, but not a cause."

Lucretius nodded again. Calloway arrived with the cool water. Lucretius drank three full cups. "Continue!" he ordered.

"Well, you're exhibiting the classic signs of Cushing's— except most horses lose weight, not gain it—and I'm not sure what to make of the buffalo hump and the pink stretch marks. But people get Cushing's too, so I suspect those are symptoms as well, especially since they're on your, um, torso." Jonathan stuttered and began to sweat, not knowing how Lucretius would take the next part.

Calloway stared at him and handed him a glass of water.

Jonathan drained the cup. "The problem is, at least for horses, it's *not* curable, only treatable."

Shadows descended over the centaur's face. He stomped his left hoof, startling Bingley in the adjacent cave. The dog crept into a shadow closer to the entrance of the cave, ready for a quick escape, if needed. Lucretius began pacing, and Jonathan noticed a slight limp. "You are sure, Dr. St. Roche? Incurable is not acceptable!"

"Well, I understand this isn't what you wanted to hear, but I have an idea. Since you seem to have both human and equine symptoms, I'd like to get a second opinion before deciding on a course of treatment. So, would you object to me bringing Dr. Guzman to see you?"

Lucretius stopped pacing and relaxed his brow. "Is this person related to Lorenzo Guzman, who makes the finest mead in all the land?"

Jonathan seized the moment. "Yes, she's his daughter! In fact, her father's mead is one of the gifts Bingley brought for you!"

"His nectar would make Dionysus jealous!" Lucretius sighed. "And this *Bingling dog* is a friend of Lorenzo's? Who would have guessed?" He resumed pacing, then stopped and shook his head. "Yes, *yes*—I remember her now, a pretty child—black mane, startling blue eyes." He looked up at Jonathan. "You may bring her here, but now we feast!" He trotted out of the cave to the fire pit and called for food, wine, and music.

As Jonathan repacked his bag, Bingley padded over and whispered, "I need to tell you something important about Septimus."

But before Jonathan could reply, Calloway moved closer and murmured, "Well done! When he stomped his hoof and started pacing, I thought for sure we'd be on the receiving end of his wrath. But you recovered quite nicely!" He put his hand on

Jonathan's arm and looked him in the eye. "Look, I understand why you need to bring DeeDee here, but whatever you do, *don't leave her unattended with him.* He is a Lothario of the first order."

Jonathan felt the heat rise on the back of his neck. "Got it. Maybe you should come too? Just as an insurance policy?"

"Nah. I think you can handle it, and besides, I don't want to be the third wheel." He laughed and slapped Jonathan on the back before he headed toward the revelries.

Jonathan turned to Bingley. "What did you want to tell me?"

Bingley's beautiful almond-shaped eyes brimmed with tears. He was shaking as he leaned in and whispered, "I smelled . . ."

Jonathan squatted down and stroked his silky ears. "What?"

Bingley slipped his head onto Jonathan's left shoulder. His tears slid down the cheek of his person as he whispered, "Septimus—there's something wrong. His blood smells funny."

"Funny? Funny how?"

"It's, um, it's sour, like it needs sugar."

Jonathan kissed the top of his dog's head and stood up. "Thanks, Bing." He looked around and saw Flavia headed to the feast. He beckoned her over, and as she trotted to the vet, Bingley slinked to the mouth of the cave. "Flavia, um, I have reason to be concerned about Septimus. My dog has the ability, apparently, to smell health issues, and he just told me that Septimus's blood smelled sour."

"Sour? What does that mean?"

"I'm not a hundred percent certain, but it could mean that Septimus has low blood sugar and may be insulin resistant. Since you have had laminitis, and Lucretius appears to have Cushing's, then it's more likely that Septimus could be developing pre-diabetes."

"Diabetes? But he seems so normal. I haven't noticed any-thing different."

"Good! That's good, but I think, as a precaution, we should do a urine test and a blood panel, including an A1C test, to start with. That will help us decide how to proceed."

Flavia's face fell. Jonathan put his hand on her upper arm and gently squeezed. "Flavia, the good news is that we're lucky. I think Bingley detected this quite early and, at least with horses, it's easily managed with diet and exercise. Septimus should be fine."

Flavia smiled and patted his hand. "Where is this dog? I should thank him."

Jonathan glanced over at the cave. Bingley shook his head and curled into a tight ball. "I think he's asleep. I'll tell him you said thank you."

Flavia smiled, took Jonathan by the arm, and pulled him toward the festivities.

CHAPTER 14

Jonathan woke with a start and a pounding headache when the alarm went off at 6:00 a.m. the day after the visit to the centaurs. *Who knew that wine so robust and smooth could cause this much distress?* He groaned and lay back down, praying for another hour of sleep, but willing to settle for five more minutes. He got three. At the sound of the alarm, Bingley threw himself onto the bed and laid his head on Jonathan's chest, wuffing softly in his ear. Then, ever so gently, he nuzzled and licked his person into an unsteady consciousness.

"Urrrgh," Jonathan muttered as he pushed himself vertical. Bingley nudged his back until he stood up. "Too bad you don't have opposable thumbs," he murmured to the dog. "Then you could go down and make coffee while I shower." He took two shuffling steps. "My only hope is that Lucretius is in just as bad a state."

"I doubt that," replied Bingley. "My understanding is that centaurs can hold their liquor quite well."

"And how would you know that?"

"Everyone knows that," Bingley said and pushed past the woozy vet and down the steps to the kitchen door, where he waited to be let out.

"There you go, smarty-pants." Jonathan opened the door and breathed in the warm, fragrant air. *I'll make some coffee, take some ibuprofen, shower, and then maybe, just maybe, I can face the day—and Madge!—she'll want to know everything, and I can barely remember anything.* "Well, first things first." He sighed.

Thirty minutes later Jonathan was standing at the railing, dressed in jeans and a white shirt, watching Bingley chew on a buffalo horn beneath the trees reflected in his coffee. He was startled out of his reverie by his phone buzzing in his pocket. He answered with excessive cheeriness. "Cal! How ya feeling today?"

"Not as good as you, apparently. I just wanted to be sure you were okay. I don't know about you, but some of the details from yesterday are a bit fuzzy, like who drove us home?"

"According to Bingley, Tyrone did, though I don't know how he got home after that."

"Why was he there?" Calloway asked. "Did we invite him?"

"No, he was there to borrow a book from Lucretius, *A Natural History of Pigeons* by Pliny, or something along those lines. I just remember he arrived right in time for dessert and mead." Jonathan's stomach turned at the thought of the honey wine. "Did we really drink the entire bottle of mead?"

"No, no, we didn't—we drank two." Calloway groaned and laughed at the same time.

"No wonder I thought the world was coming to an end this morning! How could I forget two bottles of mead? Makes me wonder what else I might have forgotten!"

"That reminds me! I promised to remind you to call DeeDee

about Lucretius and . . . Addison's disease, was it?"

"Cushing's, actually, but they are both endocrine issues, so close!" Jonathan could feel himself blushing. "Thanks, but it's already on my to-do list."

"I bet it is! But still, I wanted to be sure you didn't forget, you know, for Lucretius's sake." Jonathan could hear the smile in Calloway's voice.

"How very thoughtful of you."

"I am nothing if not a thoughtful guy!"

"All righty then, Mr. Considerate, I am sure you have many others awaiting your thoughtful attention, so I am going to hang up now."

Jonathan checked the time: 7:30. "Too early to call DeeDee?" he mused.

"No, she's an early riser," Bingley responded.

He turned to look at his dog. "And how do you know this?"

"Duncan told me. She gets up when the crickets stop and the birds start. She does floor stretching, gives him a bone, and leaves. So, if I were you," he paused and stretched in a down-dog pose, "I'd call now." He moved into an up-dog stretch before adding, "But that's just me." He shook from head to toe and trotted to the yard to retrieve his buffalo horn from the ivy at the base of the birch trees.

"Okay, then," Jonathan said to the retreating retriever, "I'll do that."

DeeDee answered on the first ring. Jonathan inhaled deeply. "Hey there, I need your advice and help with two clients. One, I suspect, is insulin resistant, and the other likely has Cushing's. Is this an okay time to talk?"

"Yeah, I have a few minutes before I need to leave. So, who are these clients?"

"Lucretius and his nephew Septimus. I think that Septimus is suffering from insulin resistance. Bingley smelled something off with his blood. He said it smelled 'sour, like it needs sugar.'"

"He smelled it? Wow. I'm pretty sure that's way beyond Duncan's pay grade!" She laughed. "And you suspect Cushing's in Lucretius?"

"Yes, but he has a mixture of human and equine symptoms, so I'm undecided as to a course of treatment. I asked Lucretius if I could bring you in for a consult, and he was . . . well, delighted, actually."

DeeDee laughed. "Really? I wonder why?"

Jonathan grinned at her melodic chuckle. "Well, he did mention that he remembered you as a beautiful child with a black mane and startling blue eyes."

"You're joking, right?"

"No, seriously, that's what he said! You can ask Cal."

"Let me guess, my mom suggested you take him along, and I bet she sent a bottle of my dad's mead too?"

"Yes, to all of the above, and honestly, she was spot on. I am not sure it would have gone as well without both of them."

DeeDee laughed again.

She has such an easy laugh. I could get used to that. Jonathan pulled himself back to the conversation. "So when might you be available to go out there with me?"

"I have Wednesday afternoons off." He could hear her flicking through some pages. "And it looks like I don't have anything planned for a week from tomorrow. Would that work?"

His heart crashed against his chest wall. "Yeah, that would be great! I have Wednesday afternoons off as well, so we could go right after lunch." He swallowed. "Maybe we should meet beforehand to discuss these?"

"Good idea, but I don't think we should talk about this in public." Jonathan heard more papers rustling. "I don't have anything the Saturday before we go—and it occurs to me that it's been a while since Bingley and Duncan played—so maybe I could bring Duncan over, and we could take the dogs for a run or a swim and discuss the centaurs?"

"That would be great! I'm sure Bing will be delighted." Jonathan paused as the dog, hearing his name, trotted over and rubbed his face on Jonathan's jeans. "How about you come for lunch—say around noon?"

"Sounds like a plan! I gotta run—see you Saturday."

Jonathan hung up and planted a huge kiss on the top of his dog's head. "Gotta love Saturdays, eh, Bing?"

CHAPTER 15
The Goose

Jonathan entered the exam room and set the customary cup of dandelion tea next to Gertrude on the exam table. She nodded gratefully but didn't take a sip. "What brings you in today, Gertrude?"

Tears welled in her eyes and slid down her silky cheeks as she nudged a wicker basket toward Jonathan. Nestled inside was a Bavarian egg decorated with detailed country scenes of bunnies, rolling hills, and bees darting between daffodils and forget-me-nots. One detail that caught his attention as he picked up the egg was an odd animal standing in the doorway of Strong's barn. Even so, the egg itself was exquisite. It was also black and white.

Jonathan stared at the monochromatic masterpiece and said softly, "Gertrude, are you trying to create black-and-white eggs?"

The goose shook her head and honked softly. Her shoulders heaved in rhythm to her sobs. "It's okay, Gertrude. Take a moment to let it all out, have your tea, and we'll figure out what's going on." He patted away her tears then sat quietly as Gertrude struggled to regain her composure. He remembered the first time he'd seen her eggs and how astonished he'd been by their exquisite detail and beauty. *Was it really just last year?*

Gertrude slurped the last of her tea and cleared her throat. "Vhen I got my wormer last month, everything was fine." *Honk.* "It's just been in the last veek or so I felt off, and my vision was verwischt for a few days. I tought I had a cold, so I vaited to see if it vould clear up." *Hissss. Sniffle. Honk.* "The blurring vent away, but now I see only black and vhite, and, and, and, now dis!" *Honk honk!* She pointed at the egg as if it were emitting radioactive isotopes.

"Any other symptoms?"

"No, not really." *Honk.* "Except my eyes feel a bit dry and itchy."

Jonathan froze. "Gertrude, I know you were staying with Florence while you were being treated for aspergillus, but have you moved back to the Clegg farm yet?"

"Jah. I moved back about two weeks ago. Vhy?"

"Did anything happen out of the ordinary in the last seven to ten days?"

Gertrude thought for a minute as Jonathan took her vital signs. "The only ting that I can tink of is a moment in the barn about a veek ago." *Hiss.* "It was very hot, so I step inside the old barn to get shade. Someting rustled in the back corner, and I tought the goslings had vandered back there, so I went to shoo them out before they got hurt." *Honk, hiss.* "I heard more scuffling, but it sounded more like a rat dan a gosling, so I turned to leave. But I run into someting, saw a flash of light, und it vas dark again. I didn't tink anything of the light at the time, as I tought a loose board had swung open ven the rat or vhatever ran out of the barn. It was a day or so later that I felt under the veather and the verwischt started. I didn't tink of the incident in the barn until now."

Jonathan made a mental note to call Strong and make a farm appointment for the next day or so. *What the heck is going on in that barn?* "You do know that Strong and Storm have irritated eyes as well?" He turned off the overhead lights and turned on his otoscope. Gertrude's eyes were normal, but dry.

"Jah. Storm seems to be doing better, and mine vere never as crusty as hers." *Hiss, hiss, honk.*

"Well, Gertrude, the good news is, there doesn't seem to be any physical damage to your eyes. I want to put you on some meds for dry eye, and I suggest that we add in some supplements to your diet that support eye health. I'll have Florence go over everything with you."

He picked up the black-and-white egg. "Gertrude, may I keep this for a day? I want to look at it more closely."

"Please don't show it to anyone!" Gertrude honked.

"I won't, I promise. I will bring it back to you in a day or so, and I can check on everyone's progress at that time."

While Bingley worked on his dinner, Jonathan poured himself a neat scotch and sat down to examine Gertrude's black-and-white egg, specifically the animal in the door of Clegg's barn. *What is that thing? An iguana? But where would Gertrude have seen an iguana?* The one thing he knew for sure about Gertrude's eggs: every one of them reflected her world. Jonathan's favorite, and the first one that Gertrude had given to him, was an exquisite night scene with several flying monkeys silhouetted against a full moon. Aspen trees shimmered in the moonlight, and you could almost smell the lilies of the valley perfectly situated amongst the tulips at the base of the trees. Even though that one was a night scene, it was not black and white. The sky was midnight blue, the tulips were red and yellow, and the tender leaves on the silver birches were a luminous spring green.

This egg, though just as finely detailed as any of her creations, was truly black and white. *This must be how Gertrude is seeing things at the moment, solely in black and white, but why?* His instincts told him that the eye problems at the Clegg farm—Storm, Strong, and Gertrude—were related. But what could cause dry eye in one species, black-and-white vision in another, and allergy symptoms in a third?

Using his surgical magnifying glasses, Jonathan focused on the creature in the doorway. It had four legs and a ridge along its side that looked like folded skin. *Or folded wings?* Its tail was ridged, serpentine, and split at the end. And it had pointed ears and a dewlap. *Ears? On a reptile?* Moreover, it appeared that the animal was squinting, and one of its front legs was raised as if it were scratching at its face, or, more precisely, at its eyes! "Holy cow!" Jonathan set the egg carefully on the desk and took a long draw of his scotch as he paced the room, trying to comprehend what this thing might be. Bingley trotted over and nudged him toward the door. "You can go out, but no ball playing for a while. You don't want to overdo it just yet." Dog and human went into the garden, where Bingley checked his pee-mail, and Jonathan continued to pace.

Let's try to look at this rationally. From what I remember, iguanas have dewlaps, and there is an Australian frilled lizard, which might explain the fold along the side. But Strong has never mentioned any reptiles to me. Jonathan put down his scotch to play tug-of-war with Bingley. "Ouff, ouff, ouff! You win. When did you get so strong?" he panted. Bingley pranced off with the stick and settled down in the ivy to chew his prize to smithereens.

But, even if it is a frilled lizard with an eye infection, that doesn't explain anything, really. Reptiles can get conjunctivitis, but I don't think it can spread to humans. But what about to dogs or birds? Dogs can get pink eye from people, but it generally doesn't go from dog to human. Moreover, why did their symptoms appear almost simultaneously rather than serially, if it spread from one to another? And why is it causing such diverse symptoms? Maybe this thing is something else entirely? But what?

Jonathan pulled his phone from his back pocket and made two phone calls: one to Strong and one to tell Madge that he was going to Strong's first thing and should be back before clinic hours started. Then he called to Bingley, "Stop doing your imitation of a woodchuck and let's go for a walk."

CHAPTER 16

"Gertrude brought this to me yesterday," Jonathan said as he handed his jeweler's loupe and the egg to Strong. "She was very upset that it was in black and white and told me that she started to see only in black and white, just about the same time that you and Storm developed eye problems. I'm convinced there is a common cause to all this, but I can't figure out what it is and why it would cause such disparate symptoms."

Strong sat down on a bench under the ancient oak shading his back porch, propped his sunglasses on the top of his head, and examined the egg. "I thought it was a night scene, but it's really just black and white, isn't it? Does this mean that is how she is seeing things now?"

"That's what she told me."

"Huh." Strong turned the egg around and paused. "What's the animal in the door of the barn? I don't recognize it. It looks sorta like an iguana, but there aren't any iguanas around here that I know of. And why would it be in my barn?"

"My questions exactly! Did you notice his eyes?"

Strong took another look at it and gasped. "Holy cow, it's squinting . . . and it's scratching at its eye! Why? An infection, maybe?"

"That's what I was thinking, but I wanted a second opinion. Do you think whatever this thing is could be hiding in your barn and maybe infecting all of you?"

Strong gathered some straw into a milk pail and gently laid the egg in it. "You know, some odd things have been happening around the barn. I had a bucket of peaches that I left just inside the door of the barn when I ran to get the phone in the house. When I came back, the bucket was knocked over and several of the peaches had been bitten into. The dogs were nowhere to be found, and the birds were all in the paddock with the pond, so I just thought some daring squirrels had been having fun. But other things have been disturbed, like bags of feed ripped open, vines of green beans stripped bare, and straw scattered in odd places." He pointed to the errant pile of straw at the end of the bench. "Maybe something *is* living in the barn!"

"I have some live traps in the back of my truck. Do you have any?" Jonathan asked. "I was thinking that we should try to capture it. At least if we can figure out what it is, we might be able to get some answers about the eye problems you all have been having."

Strong went to collect the traps he'd used to capture a raccoon and her kits, while Jonathan got three traps of various sizes out of his truck. "I wasn't sure the exact size of this creature, so I brought an assortment. Any ideas of what to bait them with?"

Strong produced an aluminum foil package. "I thought we might use the zucchini bread my neighbor brought over. Lord knows I have enough of it—she gave me six loaves! And, we can add some duck feed, peaches, and/or green beans."

They tested each trap and baited them. Each man grabbed

two traps, and they headed into the barn. Once they were out of the light from the doorway, Jonathan realized he should have removed his sunglasses, but he, as fortune would have it, had no free hand to remove them. He banged his knee on some unknown hazard and was startled by something rushing past him and crashing into the barn wall. A flash of light, and Jonathan saw whatever it was dash underneath a broken wheat thresher.

"Strong, I think we scared it. I saw it run under the old thresher." Jonathan put down his traps and kneeled on the floor, trying to see if the animal was still there. It was, and it was staring right at him. He felt his eyes begin to water and was about to lift his mirrored glasses to wipe his eyes, when discretion told him it was the better part of valor to keep his eyes shielded.

Strong joined him but remained standing. "I heard a crash and saw the flash, and I wondered if it had escaped through a loose board. I think I'm glad we have it cornered."

Jonathan stood up. "He's still under the thresher. I suggest we place the traps as quickly as possible and close the barn door, with one trap just inside it." He picked up his traps while Strong started toward the other side of the barn. "And, Strong, keep your sunglasses on."

"Roger that."

Strong latched the barn door, and they made their way around the barn, nailing any loose boards into place. Convinced they had done their best to contain and hopefully capture the elusive critter, the two men each had a cup of coffee and some zucchini bread and made plans for checking the traps.

"I think it's best that no one knows about this guy until we've captured it," Jonathan said.

Strong nodded. "I see no reason to alarm anyone until we know more."

Two days later, the sun was just rising as a mix of growling and what could only be described as satanic emanations reverberated through the old barn. The hairs on the back of Jonathan's neck stood up like soldiers of the Grand Old Duke of York, and his blood ran as cold as a Canadian ice melt. He looked over at Strong. The usually ruddy man was the color of new milk.

Their plan was to throw fishing nets over the live trap as a second line of defense against escape, then cover it with burlap bags to provide a visual barrier that might help to calm the animal. Then, if they could get to its haunches, Jonathan would deliver a sedative.

Neither man was, in any way, optimistic that this plan would work, but such elementary equipment could be manipulated while wearing leather work gloves, heavy coats and overalls, and protective eyewear. The imitation Michelin men inched toward the beast past broken threshers, rusty mowers, and other disused farm equipment.

The blood-chilling lamentations quieted as the animal sensed their approach. Hunkering down at the back of the trap, it resumed hissing and wailing like a serpentine mermaid trying to lure a sailor to his death. It sang louder, then softer, higher and lower, until it let go with an agonizing shriek.

The men hurled their nets over the trap. Despite the dim light, Jonathan could see that its eyes were closed, and it had folds of skin along its side, just like the creature on Gertrude's egg.

The undulating wail prevented them from hearing one another, so Jonathan signaled Strong to toss his burlap over the front of the animal, while his bag would cover everything except where the beast's haunches were pressed against the bars. Not knowing the weight of the animal but guessing that it was likely twenty-five pounds or so, he gauged the dose of the sedative and plunged in the hypodermic.

The creature shrieked even louder, if that were possible, then slumped down in the cage, its breathing becoming shallow but steady. After five minutes of no movement or sound from it, Jonathan gently shook the cage. Whatever this thing was, it was out for the time being.

One of the first things they both noticed as they moved the trap to the doorway of the barn and lifted the animal from it, was the pus and crust around its eyes. Even though it was tranquilized, it closed its eyes tighter when they laid it in the sun. Strong pulled the extra fly mask he'd made for Storm from his back pocket and strapped it into place, securing it in front of the creature's perky ears and behind its colorful dewlap. The animal visibly relaxed with the fly mask in place.

It was approximately the size of a large raccoon but longer, shaped like an iguana, and much lighter than its size would suggest. Its skin was tough and scaly, and its four legs were stubby and powerful with long, razor-sharp claws. Jonathan imagined that it could run not only fast but for long distances, and he wondered if it rose up on its hind legs like the Australian frilled lizard. The tail was twice as long as its body and had two small spikes on the end, one straight and one curved. It was whiplike, and the men agreed that it probably had a vicious sting.

The most extraordinary feature, however, were the skin folds along its side, which were actually neither skin nor folds, but wings! Moreover, these were not limbs adapted into wings, like those of birds or bats, but silky, membranous appendages with sturdy, flexible ribs and iridescent blue-and-green markings that formed a rose-like mosaic. Jonathan carefully pulled a wing open as Strong snapped pictures and videos. "I've never seen anything like this," Strong whispered.

"Me neither," Jonathan whispered back. "But I think we have to assume that it's dangerous until we can determine otherwise."

"Agreed. So, what do we do now that we've captured it?"

"I think that we have to keep it isolated, for one thing. If it's truly dangerous, then we'll want minimal access to it. And it seems to have an eye infection. Since you, Storm, and Gertrude all have eye issues, and all of you have been in the barn, then it's probably a safe bet to assume that it's contagious." He paused. "But how it infected you when none of you had direct contact, that I don't know."

The animal stirred and started to kick its legs and thrash its tail. Jonathan and Strong quickly swaddled it in a towel, secured the bundle with self-adhesive tape, and secured it in a sturdy wire crate. A thick canvas cover blocked the light. Jonathan calculated the next dose of sedative. "Strong, I don't know where we—I— should keep this animal. I suppose we could put it in a crate in a horse stall at the vet clinic."

"That might work—but how many people go into your barn? Maybe not the best place if we're trying to isolate it."

"Good point. Owners come to see their animals, and Florence goes out there most days." He scratched the back of his head. "There're some kennels in the storeroom in the clinic, but what if it got loose during office hours?" The two men shuddered.

"Look, Jon." Strong had never called him by his given name, but then, they had never had to capture a dangerous mythological creature together, and formalities no longer seemed necessary. "I think we can rig up something right here. I don't have a lot of visitors, and I think we can fix it so the animals can't get to it. There is a storage closet in the far corner. The door is crooked, but replacing the hinges should do the trick, and I have an extra-large crate we can put in there. Then, we put a padlock on the door that only you and I have keys for."

"Hmmm. That might work."

Strong warmed to the idea. "I'm a bit nervous about keeping it contained, and those claws scare the hell out of me. But it occurs to me that, for whatever reason, it chose my barn. We might find that it's easier to handle if we keep it in an environment it likes."

"Hmmm," Jonathan repeated. "You might have a point, but—"

The animal shrieked. Strong grabbed a pitchfork and lifted the corner of the canvas cover. The swaddling was, fortunately, holding fast. Jonathan administered a second shot of tranquilizer, and the animal soon quieted.

"Man, I hope it stays sedated long enough for us to secure it in the closet," Strong said.

"Me too," Jonathan said. He looked at the slumbering animal. "What *is* this thing?"

CHAPTER 17

"ON YOUR LEFT!" Strong shrieked. Jonathan swerved to the right, only to jerk once again to the left as a trumpeter swan and her five adolescent cygnets emerged from a massive clump of irises. Though they had an airy barn and spacious barnyard, the swans frequently traversed the gravel road to get to the marsh and pond abutting the Lucash estate. As a result, it was a heart-stopping endeavor to negotiate the winding drive to the non-descript house of Tyrone Edmund Athanasiou, resident faun and historian.

Jonathan slowed to a pace that even a geriatric snail could outrun and scanned the horizon for bush, flower, rock, cow—*anything* that might conceivably hide a wayward swan—while Strong returned to flipping through his pictures of the creature. "Man, they just don't show the details of the creature like I hoped. The colors in the dewlap look dull, and the iridescence of the wings didn't come through."

"I think they are FINE!" Jonathan shouted as he slammed on the brakes to avoid an angry male emerging from the ditch on the right. Glaring at the truck, the swan blasted what was probably a curse, turned, and reentered the ditch. Jonathan shook his head, blew out the breath he had been holding, and turned *ever so slowly* into the driveway. "We can fill Tyrone in on the details, but at least we have pictures to show him," he remarked as he parked in front of the garage.

"True that." Strong closed the door of the pickup, took off his ball cap, scratched his head, and ran his fingers through his thinning hair while glancing in the side mirror. He shook his head, sighed, and threw his hat onto the passenger seat.

Jonathan was already halfway to the front door when Strong jogged up to join him. The vet tucked his sunglasses into the front pocket of his shirt and rang the bell next to the freshly painted forest-green door. Mozart's Serenade No. 13 in G Major echoed down the long central hall. Strong tapped his left foot in time with the music and hummed along. Jonathan looked sideways at him, shaking his head slightly. "What?" Strong replied. "I played the viola in a string quartet in high school, and this was our signature piece."

"Seriously?"

"Yes, *seriously*."

"The *viola?* Why the viola?"

"All the violins were taken."

Click, click, click. The faun's hooves beat a tattoo on the parquet floor in time to the serenade. The front door flew open. "Jonathan, Strong, welcome! Come in, come in, come in! I was just sitting down to tea. Would you care for some?" Tyrone hustled them in the door and hung their jackets on the antler rack alongside his impressive collection of umbrellas. He guided them through the meander of cozy rooms brimming with books, maps, globes, and various paraphernalia amassed by the faun and his ancestors for longer than anyone could recollect. Having the largest library of books and articles relating to "so-called" mythological creatures outside of Bavaria, Tyrone was highly respected for his extensive knowledge of all things fabled and fabulous. If anyone could identify the mysterious inhabitant of Strong's barn, it would be the faun.

"I also have some lemon ginger scones just out of the oven. I'm so glad you're here so that I don't eat all of them!" Tyrone showed them into the airy, plant-filled sunroom just off the kitchen. Orchids and gardenias bloomed in profusion on a shelf along the eastern window, and the intoxicating scent of gardenias mixed with the homey aroma of the scones. The two men were quickly settled into comfortable garden chairs with bone China mugs of steaming Lady Grey tea.

Tyrone scurried into the cozy kitchen and could be heard whistling the overture to *The Marriage of Figaro* as he burdened the ivory inlaid tea tray with scones, Irish butter, clotted cream, homemade strawberry jam, mini blueberry mint muffins, strawberries, delicately painted plates, filigree teaspoons, and butter knives. Embroidered tea napkins were piled on top as Tyrone expertly balanced the tray on his left hand and gathered another teapot with his right.

"Here we are," he sang as he slid the tray and teapot onto the glass-topped table in the sunroom. "Please help yourself!"

"Is that clotted cream? I *love* clotted cream!" Strong's eyes lit up.

Jonathan stared at Strong for a second time. *First Mozart, now clotted cream? Who knew?*

"It is, indeed! I remembered that you enjoyed it the last time you were here, and I just got some in from Harrod's."

Strong sighed deeply, nearly groaning, as the buttery jam-and-cream-laden scone melted in his mouth. "Wow. This beats zucchini bread *any* day of the week . . ."

"And twice on Sundays!" Jonathan chimed in.

"Thank you! You are very kind," Tyrone said as he popped a muffin, paper liner included, into his mouth. "Now, what is this all about? You sounded so mysterious, not to mention urgent, on the phone."

Having just crammed another scone into his mouth, Strong nodded at Jonathan, who was about to put a muffin into his own. Jonathan sighed, set the buttery delight down, and handed Gertrude's egg to Tyrone. He told the story of the egg, the eye problems, and pointed out the creature in the doorway of the barn. Tyrone pulled a magnifying glass from the writing desk nestled amongst a forest of ferns in the corner of the sunroom. As he looked more closely at the scene, Strong took over the story and told him about capturing the creature and securing it in the closet of the old barn. He opened the pictures on his phone and handed it to Tyrone.

The faun put down the magnifying glass and the egg and scrolled through the photos before reaching for a golden scone. As he buttered it, he said, "I think it is one of three things: a dragon, a cockatrice, or a basilisk—though some classify the cockatrice as a basilisk. Personally, I think there are legitimate arguments on both sides, but I tend to think that they are separate animals, with the cockatrice being more bird-like than the basilisk." He added a large dollop of strawberry jam to the scone and paused before popping half into his mouth. "Let me get my bestiary," he said and trotted out of the room. He returned with an antique leather-bound book, which he carefully removed from its linen wrapping. "Okay, let's see what we have here. The size of the animal could make it any of the three, especially since we don't know if it's a juvenile or an adult. So, let's start with the dragon."

He opened the book, revealing an illuminated manuscript with elaborate Latin script. "Now, the reason I think it might be a dragon rather than, say, a wyvern, who tend to be smaller than dragons, is because wyverns have two legs; dragons have four. This fellow has four legs. That said, it also has talons and two very distinct spikes on the end of its tail." Tyrone looked up from the text. "Most dragon or wyvern tails are arrow- or diamond-shaped, and their feet are reptilian."

The faun turned to the page on the cockatrice. "Now, the feet may indicate a cockatrice, but the head of our fellow makes me think it isn't one, because it doesn't have feathers or a beak like a rooster, and its wings are membranous." He flipped to the basilisk page and held the book out to Strong and Jonathan. They looked at the page and then at one another, and said in unison, "That's it."

"That's what I suspected," Tyrone said. "But when you mentioned the eye problems, I was confused as to why you two were still alive. One glance from a basilisk kills a man."

Silence, one might even call it a deadly silence, insinuated itself across the room.

Tyrone pinched a dead blossom from one of the gardenias. "But I suppose the eye infection must have diminished his power somehow." He pointed at Jonathan's mirrored sunglasses tucked in the front pocket of his shirt. "Were you wearing those when you captured it?"

"Yeah, why?"

"Well, that might have helped to defray the deadly glance. But. . ." Tyrone paused, tapping his index finger to his lips, "interestingly, according to many of the ancient stories of the basilisk, looking at its reflection in a mirror will kill *it*. The *Codex Alexandrinus* states that Alexander the Great killed one using a shield polished to a high sheen, like a mirror. So I'm a bit surprised your mirrored glasses didn't kill him." He paused a second time. "I wonder if the eye infection worked the other way as well."

Jonathan shook his head. Strong furrowed his brow.

"What I mean is that the eye infection not only prevented the full power of his glance from killing you, but it also prevented the mirror from killing *him* by clouding his eyesight or gumming up his eyes so he couldn't see his reflection. So, I speculate that not only are his powers to kill diminished, but the traditional means of killing him may not work either."

Silence once again engulfed the sunroom.

"Well, this is a conundrum," Tyrone said, "but at least be glad you have him contained for now. The bigger question is, what'd you plan on doing with him?"

Jonathan looked at the picture of the creature with the icy stare and said, "That's a very good question."

CHAPTER 18

"Hang on, there's another book I want to find." Tyrone scurried off and returned with a modern hardcover book. "This," he said as he held up the well-worn tome, "contains an account of the Warsaw basilisk of 1587, and I think you will find it very interesting. It's a bit long, so I will try to condense it." Tyrone sat down, cleared his throat, and began to read from *The Feejee Mermaid and Other Essays in Natural and Unnatural History* by Jan Bondeson: "*The 5-year-old daughter of a knifesmith named Machaeropaeus had disappeared together with another girl. The wife of Machaeropaeus went looking for them, along with the nursemaid. They found the children lying motionless in the cellar of a ruined house. When the children did not respond to the women's shouting, the nursemaid courageously went down the stairs. Before the eyes of her mistress, she sank to the floor beside them and did not move. The wife of Machaeropaeus wisely did not follow her into the cellar but ran back to spread the word about this strange and mysterious business. The rumor spread like wildfire throughout Warsaw. Many people thought the air felt unusually thick to breathe and suspected that a basilisk was hiding in the cellar.*"

"Because a basilisk is the first thing you would think of when the air is thick? Not fog or smoke or, I don't know, a volcanic eruption? Even that seems more probable," Strong groused.

"Remember, we are talking about *1587*, Strong." Tye glared at the farmer. "Now, where was I? *The local senate consulted an old man named Benedictus, a former chief physician to the king, since he was known to possess much knowledge about arcane subjects*—sort of like me!" Tyrone chuckled and dabbed his eyes. *"The bodies were pulled out of the cellar with long poles that had iron hooks at the end, and Benedictus examined them closely. They presented a horrid appearance, being swollen like drums and with much-discolored skin; the eyes 'protruded from the sockets like halves of hen's eggs.' Benedictus, who had seen many things during his fifty years as a physician, at once pronounced the state of the corpses an infallible sign that they had been poisoned by a basilisk.*

"The senate called on the burghers, military, and police but found no man of sufficient courage to seek out and destroy the basilisk within its lair. A Silesian convict named Johann Faurer, who had been sentenced to death for robbery, was at length persuaded to make the attempt on the grounds that he be given a complete pardon if he survived the encounter with the loathsome beast. Faurer was dressed in creaking black leather covered with a mass of tinkling mirrors, and his eyes were protected with large eyeglasses." Tyrone paused. "See? Mirrors and glasses!" He continued, *"Armed with a sturdy rake in his right hand and a blazing torch in his left, he must have presented a singular aspect when venturing forth into the cellar."*

"A rake?" Strong exclaimed. "Seriously?"

"Yes, a rake." Tyrone sighed and shivered. *"After searching the cellar for more than an hour, Faurer finally saw the basilisk lurking in a niche of the wall. The populace ran away like rabbits when he emerged from the cellar in his strange outfit, gripping the neck of the writhing basilisk with the rake. Dr. Benedictus was the only one who dared examine the strange animal further, since he believed that the sun's rays rendered its poison less effective. He declared that it really was a basilisk: it had the head of a cock, the eyes of a toad, a crest like a crown, a warty and scaly skin 'covered all over with the hue of venomous animals,' and a curved tail, bent over behind its body. The strange and inexplicable tale of the basilisk of Warsaw ends here: none of the writers chronicling this strange occurrence detailed the ultimate fate of the deformed animal caught in the cellar."*

The enormity of the situation, their incredible luck at capturing the beast, and gratitude for his mirrored sunglasses, left Jonathan stunned. The uncharacteristically silent Strong nodded at the book, which Tyrone handed to him just before he let loose with a tirade of sneezes. Strong put down the open book and handed the faun a tissue.

"Tye, are you okay?" Jonathan asked.

"Yes, I have seasonal allergies to certain pollens, and to mohair. It's a curse, really." He patted his nose and watery eyes. "But back to the task at hand: What are we to do with the basilisk? Will you treat its infection? Release it? Relocate it? Euthanize it?"

"Good questions, Tye, and I don't have any answers," Jonathan said.

"Well then, if you're not going to immediately euthanize it, you're going to need a twenty-four-hour guard, and that means weasels."

"Weasels?" the farmer and the vet replied in unison.

"Yes, weasels. According to the Oxford M. S. Bodley 764 bestiary, they're the known enemy of the basilisk, and for some reason are not affected by its look or breath."

"It's breath?"

"Yes, Strong, some subspecies of basilisks have a hot or fiery breath that can kill people. Others claim the noise they emit can cause deafness or death—"

"*That* I can believe!" Strong snorted.

"But that is not as well documented," Tyrone continued. "Mongooses are also considered the enemy of basilisks, but they are harder to come by, and the literature is not particularly clear on this point. Thus, I suggest we recruit a small squadron of weasels to guard the basilisk."

Just then, the door to Tyrone's first-floor guest room flew open, and Gremsboc roared into the kitchen. "BLIMEY, TYE, YA DIDN'T TELL ME WE 'AD COMPNEY, OR I WOULDA GOT UP A LOT SOONER! 'ELLO, DOC, HOW THE 'ELL ARE YA?" He grabbed Jonathan's hand and vigorously pumped it, while slapping Strong on the back with his other hand and nearly sweeping the tea set to the floor with his wings.

"Oh, for heaven's sake, have a care, Gremsboc!" the faun sputtered as he tucked the tea set into a corner. "He stopped by last night, and we stayed up late drinking and playing cribbage."

"AND EATIN' DORITOS!" Gremsboc guffawed.

Tyrone turned a remarkable shade of crimson at this comment. "I suggested he avail himself of the guest room rather than try to fly home in his altered state."

"ALTERED STATE, MY ARSE! I WAS JUST WARMING UP!" Gremsboc bellowed. "AND I WON THE BEST OF FIVE, I DID!" Gremsboc moved toward the scones. "IS THAT CLOTTED CREAM? BLIMEY, I LOVE THE STUFF, I DO!" He stuffed two of the scones into his mouth, followed by heaping spoonsful of clotted cream and jam. "NOW, WHAT'S THIS I 'EARD 'BOUT WEASELS?" He spit the words out amidst a shower of scone crumbs. "SEEMS TO ME THE ONLY THING GOOD ABOUT 'EM IS THEY CAN KILL A BASILISK."

Jonathan and Strong stiffened. Tyrone sighed and summarized recent events, while Gremsboc devoured three more scones and several cups of tea.

"CAN AMERICAN WEASELS DO THIS? I MEAN, THEY 'AVEN'T THE EXPERIENCE THAT ENGLISH WEASELS DO," Gremsboc thundered when Tyrone mentioned needing a contingent of them.

"My thoughts exactly," the faun said. "Do you think we need to bring over a whole battalion or just a few to train the locals?"

Jonathan glanced at Strong, who looked as dumbfounded as he felt. "Hang on a second. We haven't even decided what we're going to do with this animal. If he's as deadly as you say, as legend seems to say, shouldn't we be worried about the public and seriously consider euthanasia?"

Tyrone turned to Jonathan. "You're right to be concerned, but effective containment, for any length of time, requires weasels. You were lucky to trap it and to anesthetize it. But it's smart, and I highly doubt you'd catch him again if, or when, he gets out." Tyrone leaned toward the men. "If you can't contain him, you can't treat him, anesthetize him, *or* euthanize him."

Jonathan ran his hands through his hair as he paced the cozy kitchen. Strong bit his lip and tapped his foot. "You know, one thing that we haven't discussed is whether there might be more than one of these things. Should we be looking for a flock, or pack, or I don't know . . . a murder of basilisks?"

Jonathan paled.

"*Highly* unlikely," Tyrone said. "First of all, as far as I can tell, there is no historical account of more than one at a time. And secondly, they arise from the egg of a twelve-year-old cock that is incubated by toads. And this, I can assure you, does not happen very often."

"Especially since a cock is a male chicken—how could it lay an egg?" Strong asked.

"Some hens can have an abundance of male hormones, so they look more like males, including having a comb. That might be why it was mistaken for a cock," Jonathan said. "But this reassures me that it's rare and we're not dealing with a flock, murder, pride—whatever—of these guys."

Strong nodded, then furrowed his brow. "Look, I also wonder what Xavier would say about this. He's been caring for this, um," he glanced at the faun and the flying monkey, "*population* all his life, and I think he'd know what to do."

"I don't disagree." Jonathan sighed. "Xavier's opinion would be invaluable, but I just talked with him a few days ago, and they are stuck outside of Calgary. They hit a moose, Janice is in the hospital with a compound fracture, and they don't know when they'll be back. Xavier is *really* worried, and I don't want to add to his stress right now." He took a deep breath and slowly released it. "I'm sure he would want us to think about the 'natural order of things' and how we can best reestablish or protect that. This beast may have lived among us for years with no fatalities—"

"That we know of."

"You're right. We don't know if it's killed anyone or anything—nor do we know why it suddenly took up residence in your barn—or if we can restore the previous balance. But I'm sure Xavier would want us to carefully consider all options before making any final, irrevocable decision."

"If I may interject," Tyrone said, "I *know* this animal is very dangerous—deadly actually—but I'm loath to sentence it to death and thus into extinction. I mean, smallpox was a terrible scourge on humanity, but the CDC still keeps a stock of *it*."

"I have an aversion to euthanizing animals too." Jonathan renewed his circuit. "So, perhaps we need to consider if there's some medical," he nodded at Tyrone, "or historical benefit to the public that's greater than the risk."

"Okay, I can see that," Strong said. "But if we're not going to euthanize it, are we going to try to cure his eye infection? 'Cause *that* makes me uncomfortable. I mean, how could you possibly give eye meds safely? And won't curing him make him even *more* dangerous?"

Jonathan ran his hands through his hair again. "Two thoughts. First, eye infections in reptiles—and he seems to resemble a reptile more than a bird—can be treated effectively with systemic antibiotics rather than eye drops. So, hopefully, we could hide any meds in his food. And, secondly, I read, not long ago, about contact lenses that deliver eye medications, so that might be an option if he won't take oral meds."

Jonathan snapped his fingers. "Hold on! Some of these lenses are permanent—so what if we modified them somehow—like, um, polarizing them—so his gaze could no longer kill?"

Strong, Tyrone, and Gremsboc exchanged looks. Strong cleared his throat. "How do you plan on holding him still, opening his eyes, and dropping in contact lenses? Sounds a bit like the mouse trying to bell the cat . . ."

An illustration in *The Feejee Mermaid* caught Jonathan's eye. He stared at the drawing of a man with a tamed basilisk sitting next to him. "Gremsboc, could the weasels, in addition to subduing the basilisk, I don't know, train it, using food or some other reinforcement, to enter a cylinder so that its head pops out one end?"

The farmer, the monkey, and the faun stared at Jonathan as if he were stuck in a tube with only his head emerging. "You want to use positive reinforcement to train a deadly animal to stick its head into a tube so that it can't move its limbs? Do I have this right?" Tyrone asked.

"Yes! Exactly! We set it up so the basilisk crawls through a PVC pipe, sticks its head out, and is rewarded with its favorite food. And we add a bell or a whistle, so it associates the sound with the treat at the end of the tunnel. Soon enough, the bell will elicit the response to enter the tube and pop his head out the top. The weasels can make sure he doesn't back out, and we can put the contact lenses in. That is, provided I can get them, and they will fit the eye of a reptile." He paused. "Gremsboc, what do you think? Could they do this?"

"IT MIGHT TAKE A BIT O' CONVINCIN', BUT I THINK IT COULD WORK. ME BROTHER IS GOOD FRIENDS WITH A PACK O' NOTTIN'HAM WEASELS WHO 'AVE A LONG 'ISTRY OF GUARDING DANGEROUS THINGS. THAT'S 'OW I KNOWS THEY DO BASILISKS. I COULD ASK 'IM."

"Great! That sounds like a start—what's next?" Jonathan asked.

"I can build a wall around the closet with the basilisk that's wide enough to hold the squadron of weasels and whatever they need to be comfortable," Strong suggested.

"And I'll contact the local weasels and research food while Jon does the contact lenses. That leaves the training protocol. Who wants that?"

"I'll take it," Jonathan said. "I know a woman at the Tennessee aquarium who created a training program for ermine that taught them to happily accept medical treatment such as blood draws. I bet she'd have some tips." He tapped his fingers together. "I also think we need a code name for this guy so that we can discuss it and not worry if someone overhears."

"Good idea. Any suggestions?" Tyrone asked.

"Cowper, we'll name him Dean Cowper," Jonathan stated.

"COWPER? WHO THE 'ELL IS DEAN COWPER?"

"He was one of the many bullies in my eighth-grade class, and the basilisk reminds me of him. If you don't like that, we could name him Marcellus 'Pink Eye' Giancarlo, Cowper's minion."

"Well, there you have it, a name and a plan. We'll call this the Cowper Plan. Who wants to come up with a backup Plan Giancarlo?" Tyrone asked.

"I think that one thing we need to consider in any plan is what to do not only if the plan *doesn't* work, but what if it *does*? Then what?" Jonathan said.

CHAPTER 19
The Woman

Saturday dawned overcast and humid with ominous thunderclouds, but Jonathan was determined that it would be a great day no matter what the weather threatened. So, in an attempt to outmaneuver the heat and rain, he went for an early run through the pine trees and along the path skirting Elkhorn Creek, arriving home just as the skies opened. He put on coffee, took a shower, and spent more time than usual picking out a shirt to wear.

"Why don't you wear the dark blue one. It makes your eyes stand out," Bingley said from the doorway.

"What?" Jonathan started.

"You are trying to impress DeeDee, so wear the shirt that makes you look the best. It's simple, really." Bingley jumped onto the unmade bed and curled into a sleepy ball.

Heat creeped up the back of Jonathan's neck as he reached for the khaki shirt next to the blue one. *He's right, you know,* the little voice in his head said. *Just put on the blue shirt.* "Okay, fine," Jonathan grumbled, and he pulled the shirt from the closet.

Bingley sighed and burrowed deeper into the covers, content with a job well done.

Bingley and Duncan blasted into the yard during a lull in the rain. "Apparently, there are serious squirrel games to be had and no time to lose!" Jonathan said as he closed the door. DeeDee poured her tortilla soup into a saucepan on the stove while he retrieved the chicken salad he'd made as well as the melon he'd cut up that morning. He'd gotten the recipe from his sister. She'd given it to him without question—unlike their mother, whose third degree was legendary. Then he'd made chicken salad three times in the last week, finally got it right, and vowed never to make it again.

DeeDee pulled a ladle from a drawer next to the stove and hummed as she stirred the soup.

"You seem to know where everything is," Jonathan remarked, surprised at the ease with which he and DeeDee worked in the kitchen, especially in contrast to cooking with Anita, who had a right way of doing everything, including cleaning up.

"Hmm . . . I didn't think about that. My family spent a lot of time here with the Pratts, so I knew where Janice kept everything. I hope I wasn't being presumptuous!"

"No, not in the least." He smiled. "Ready to eat?" He glanced out the window, hoping to eat on the deck, but the skies remained openly hostile. Changing course, he put the dishes on a small table nestled in a corner of the living room with windows on both sides and motioned for her to sit down at one of the two chairs. "Maybe the weather will clear by the time we finish, and we can get the dogs out for that run."

DeeDee edged her way to the table, balancing two bowls of steaming soup and a basket of tortilla chips. Jonathan let Bingley and Duncan in and dried them off. He placed an old blanket on the sofa, where they settled down to enjoy the water buffalo horns he presented to them.

"Duncan can chew that on the floor, if you prefer," DeeDee offered. "I'm afraid that he doesn't understand that not every couch is his domain."

"Not a problem," Jonathan said. "Bingley's domain is pretty much every piece of furniture, and he'd consider it rude if I didn't allow his guests to take full advantage of his hospitality."

DeeDee laughed. "I see our dogs have the same philosophy. No wonder they're best buds." She paused. "I find it hard to understand why people value sofas over dogs. I can't imagine sitting on the couch and reading or watching TV without Duncan curled up with me. He also sleeps at the end of my bed, and there's nothing more comforting to me than to hear him sigh and drape his head over my ankle. I suppose there are dogs who shouldn't sleep on the bed because they guard it, or maybe because the person has allergies, but in general, I don't see the problem."

Jonathan nodded in agreement. *Wow, Anita would flip if she heard that! "Dogs do not belong on furniture, especially not beds!"* "I'm not sure that I even have a say! From the day I took off his cast, he's been sleeping on the bed, and he's always made himself comfortable on the couch, or the leather chairs in front of the fire."

He looked at DeeDee pushing her dark hair behind her ear so it wouldn't fall into her soup, and he had an almost irrepressible desire to help her. Instead, he reached for another tortilla chip and said, "I think that what we owe our pets is to make them happy. I find that when I provide for Bing the things that enrich his life, like long walks in the woods, or the chance to sniff as much as he wants on a walk, or a water buffalo horn on the couch, then my life is enriched too." Jonathan chuckled as he added, "Plus, I don't have to work so hard on obedience training." He swallowed the last spoonful of his soup. "Though it must be acknowledged that having a talking dog is a bit different from having your run-of-the-mill mutt. Nonetheless, he's still a dog and needs a life built around his needs as a dog."

Bingley trotted over and nuzzled his person's thigh. Jonathan reached down and scratched behind his silky ears. DeeDee smiled at the unrehearsed affection, set her bowl to the side, and reached for the chicken salad. "I couldn't agree more. I don't have as much time as I'd like with Duncan, but the time I do have, I want to spend doing things we both enjoy. After all, isn't that the point of a companion animal?"

Duncan, not wanting to miss out on either affection or chicken, squeezed himself next to Bingley and leaned into his person. DeeDee, like Jonathan, instinctively reached for the soft spot under his floppy ear.

Just then, lightning flashed, and thunder boomed directly above. Two trembling dogs leapt into the laps of their owners, sending the table and its contents crashing to the floor. Jonathan turned to DeeDee. "Coffee?"

Laughing so hard she could barely answer, DeeDee hugged her dog, nuzzled his head, and said, "I'd love some!"

When the dogs had quieted, DeeDee settled them in front of the fireplace with stuffed Kongs and classical music, while Jonathan finished cleanup and started the coffee. The afternoon slipped away as they sipped coffee and talked. Maybe it was conferring about the centaurs, or maybe it was just the ease with which the conversation flowed, but he found himself telling DeeDee about capturing the basilisk.

"Thank goodness for Tyrone, or we'd never have known what it was—not that I'm thrilled to have a basilisk in our midst—but at least we know what we're dealing with," he said.

DeeDee listened without interrupting, then asked, "So, if I understand this correctly, you're using English weasels to contain him so you can treat his eye infection with either systemic antibiotics or contact lenses?"

"Ummm, yeah, that's a pretty good summary."

"Then what? You can't release him back into the community. What if he encounters a person?"

"We've thought about that, and we don't have a final solution yet, but I'm not eager to euthanize, especially if I can figure out a way to prevent him from hurting anyone. I've been wondering if polarized lenses would be the solution." He contemplated this while stirring cream into his coffee.

After several moments, DeeDee coughed softly. Jonathan jerked back to the conversation at hand. "We talked about what Xavier would say about trying to restore the natural order, at least to the best of our ability. All I know is that I can't rush into a solution from which there is no return. That's why I want to cure the infection and then prevent him from killing anyone or anything with permanent lenses. Containing him in a large enclosure, say half an acre, that is guarded by weasels, allows me, us, to keep track of him and periodically check his lenses." Jonathan smiled, took a sip of coffee, and added, "Which is another reason why I insisted we train him to enter a tube and lie quietly—so we can easily check whether his lenses are in place."

DeeDee furrowed her brow, nodded, and set down her empty coffee cup. "Okay, I can see the reasoning in all that. My parents once had a recurring population of flying squirrels in their attic. They expended *a lot* of effort to humanely trap and relocate them because they didn't want to needlessly exterminate them. But flying squirrels don't kill you by looking at you—so promise me you'll be careful!" She smiled broadly. "And please let me know if I can help with anything, especially the lens insertion. It might be handy to have smaller hands for the procedure, and I have excellent small motor skills—if I do say so myself."

Jonathan smiled, delighted to hear her offer of help. "I will *definitely* keep that in mind."

"Good. Hey, look! The sun!" She pointed past him toward the yard, where the afternoon light was streaming through the trees. "I could use a walk! How about you?"

The dogs were already at the door when he replied, "Great idea!"

He grabbed a leash and a treat bag, and they headed out the door to DeeDee's truck, where she got a leash for Duncan. "Which way?" she asked.

"This way." Jonathan gestured toward the right. As they set off, dogs springing with excitement, it hit him how comfortable this whole day had been, and how grateful he was that, for once, the person he was walking with not only enjoyed dogs as much as he did, but also did not seek to harness their enthusiasm.

Yes, this has been a very good day, indeed!

CHAPTER 20

O n Wednesday afternoon, Jonathan parked his truck under the pine tree hiding the trailhead to the centaurs. He was grateful that Flavia had contacted him earlier in the week about treatment for Septimus and told him that Lucretius was "begrudgingly grateful to *that* dog" for catching the insulin resistance early. Still, he wasn't going to take any chances and made sure Bingley was in the house when he left. He also hoped that it was early enough in the day to avoid drinking heavily. He did *not* want a repeat of that massive hangover.

"Do you know how long they've been at this encampment?" DeeDee asked as she got out of the truck and shouldered her medical backpack.

"No, I didn't know they moved around," he answered as he grabbed a couple of bags from the back of the F250.

"They do, but it seems to me they've been at this one for a while. I haven't been out here for several years, but I think this is the one I visited with my dad. I recognize the big pine."

"How old were you the last time you were out here?"

"I don't know—eleven, twelve or so. It's been a while."

Jonathan remembered what Calloway had said about Lucretius being a Lothario. He looked at DeeDee's shiny black hair and trim figure. *Does she know about him? Should I say something?*

She interrupted his train of thought. "My mom called last night to warn me about Lucretius. She was concerned that he might try something 'unseemly' as she put it." She smiled at Jonathan. "But I told her that I was a big girl armed with scary-looking medical equipment, and I had backup!"

"That you do, but I was counting on you to back *me* up!"

DeeDee laughed.

"By the way, can you whistle a tune? Um, specifically 'Volare'?" he asked.

"Well, Lucretius," DeeDee began after Jonathan finished checking his vital signs, "looking at your physical symptoms as well as your high blood pressure, I agree with Jonathan that the most likely explanation for your symptoms is Cushing's disease. If we want to be more certain, then we could do more tests to analyze cortisol levels. What do you think, Jon?"

"I agree that it's probably Cushing's and that further testing might confirm high cortisol levels. But do we even know what high cortisol levels are for a centaur? Would we gain any useful information?"

DeeDee nodded with a frown.

Jonathan continued, "On the other hand, we might want to do them anyway, along with some basic bloodwork, so we have something to compare future tests to."

DeeDee unfurrowed her brow and turned to Lucretius. "Would it be okay with you if we did some lab work? I promise we won't reveal your identity."

Lucretius thought about this for a moment and nodded. DeeDee smiled at the centaur and continued, "Good! The question remains, where do we send the samples, to a human or an animal lab?"

"I think that our best chances of keeping Lucretius's anonymity would be with an animal lab. I'll send the samples in as a horse, and if they come back odd, then we can compare them to the reference range for an adult human male, aged . . . um, how old are you, Lucretius?" Jonathan asked as he made notes on the centaur's chart.

"One hundred and twenty-five, next Tuesday." He winked at DeeDee and leered. "You'll come help me celebrate, won't you?"

Jonathan's head snapped up at the centaur's lusty tone, and he glanced at DeeDee, who was growing crimson. Before he could speak, DeeDee managed to squeak out, "That's a lovely offer, Lucretius, but I have evening clinic that day. Though I am sure my father would love to join you. He has a new mead he wants you to try."

"A new mead, you say?" Lucretius was momentarily diverted from lust to gluttony.

Jonathan took advantage of the pause in Lucretius's libido to add, "Well then, if necessary, we will look at the reference range for a geriatric human male. As it is, I'll definitely specify that this is a thirty-year-old horse, which is comparable to an old man of eighty-six."

Lucretius stopped dreaming of drunken debacles and glared at Jonathan. "Hmmpf! I may not be as young as I once was," he insisted as he looked toward DeeDee, "but nor am I preparing for my trip to the Elysian Fields." He stomped his hooves, causing them all to choke on a cloud of dust.

DeeDee was the first to recover. "Lucretius, I'm sure Jon didn't mean anything derogatory by his comments; he was just trying to determine what to tell the lab so they can reference the correct range." She walked to the centaur and took his hand. "I'm sure you are quite healthy other than the Cushing's, and we want to get you back to your robust self. So, please, let us get the blood and urine samples."

Lucretius grumbled what Jonathan took to be consent. As the vet gathered the equipment for blood and urine collection, it occurred to him that DeeDee would have to collect the blood, as it would come from the centaur's arm, not the jugular vein in his neck. "DeeDee, I can do the urine sample, but I am going to ask you to do the blood sample. I don't know how to collect blood from an arm."

DeeDee nodded, drew the blood, and bandaged Lucretius's arm.

"Thank you, my dear. You were so very gentle, and what soft hands!" Lucretius reached for her arm, but Jonathan stepped between them as DeeDee moved toward the small cooler they'd brought for samples.

"Time for the urine collection," he announced and waved a clean Ziploc bag on the end of a telescoping pole. "Whenever you're ready, you start urinating, and I will collect some of the urine midstream. I am assuming you'd like some privacy?"

"Over here." Lucretius jerked his head toward a small grove of trees and turned to DeeDee. "We will be right back, and then we feast!"

When Lucretius was finished, Jonathan put the Ziploc bag of urine into another clean Ziploc and added it to the cooler. He removed his exam gloves and wiped his hands and forearms with several antiseptic wipes followed by copious amounts of hand sanitizer. He didn't know if Lucretius had or had not been careful in aiming his urine stream.

While Jonathan disinfected himself, Lucretius sidled up to DeeDee, took her by the arm, and led her toward the center area filled with tables of food and buckets of wine. DeeDee glanced over her shoulder and mouthed, *Hurry up!*

Jonathan needed no further inducement. He hurried toward the gathering herd and caught up to Lucretius and DeeDee just as the old lech asked, "Would you care to see my cave drawings? Tarquin has just finished the most delightful rendition of Dionysus and Ariadne. It rivals Titian's, if you ask me."

"Sounds great, Lucretius," Jonathan said, "but DeeDee and I need to get those samples off to the lab as soon as possible." He put his left hand on Lucretius's wrist and slipped his right arm around DeeDee's waist. Turning slightly to the right, he disentangled her from the centaur's grasp but not from his, and kissed the top of her head.

As DeeDee leaned into Jonathan's shoulder, the look on Lucretius's face turned from irritation to acknowledgement. "Ahh." He sighed and bowed to Jonathan. "My apologies for any misunderstanding."

Jonathan removed his arm from DeeDee to shake the centaur's hand. "Thank you, Lucretius."

As soon as Lucretius let go of Jonathan's hand, DeeDee entwined hers into Jonathan's and held his arm with her other hand. "I think we might have time for one toast, don't you think, Jon?"

"I suppose we do."

An hour later, DeeDee and Jonathan finally bid adieu to the centaurs and set off through the fragrant pines, their footsteps softened by the thick carpet of needles.

"So, Jon, I'm pretty convinced that Lucretius has Cushing's or—what did you call it for horses?"

"Pituitary pars intermedia dysfunction, or PPID."

"Right. How is it treated?"

Jonathan pointed to a nuthatch careening headfirst down the trunk of a nearby pine. "Most commonly with pergolide. I actually talked with my buddy Nathan about this."

DeeDee snapped her head around. "What?"

"I told him I had a horse that I suspected has PPID and that I was wondering if it was ever treated with metyrapone, and no, it isn't . . . but, interestingly, PPID in horses seems to be more like Parkinson's in humans. Seems they're both associated with dopamine neuron degeneration."

"Hmm . . . that is interesting. I know that pergolide has been used in the treatment of Parkinson's, so maybe that's why it's effective in horses!" DeeDee mused.

"My thoughts exactly. Moreover, since we know that pergolide is safe for both humans and equines, I think it might be the drug to start with for Lucretius. If it doesn't work, we can consider other options." He put everything except the cooler in the back of his truck and went around to unlock the door for DeeDee.

"I agree," DeeDee said.

"Okay. As soon as I get the test results, I'll order the pergolide. Will you want to come with me to deliver his meds, or have you had enough of centaur hospitality?" Jonathan queried as he started the truck and backed out onto the dirt road.

DeeDee chuckled. "I suppose I have." She turned toward Jonathan. "But seriously, thank you for what you did back there. I wasn't sure how to get out of that without enraging him."

"My pleasure," he replied automatically, but it dawned on him that it really had been a pleasure.

"I expected him to be a bit amorous, but the strength with which he was moving me toward the cave kinda scared me." She paused, looked down at her hands, and added quietly, "I don't think Marc would have recognized what was happening, or if he did, it would have been either an over-the-top response or a joke to him."

"Well, one look at your face told me it was no joke. If Marcus had been there, I don't see how he could've taken it any other way."

Jonathan turned onto the paved road and sped up, wind whipping through the cab of the truck. He started to roll up the windows, but DeeDee stopped him. "Can we leave the windows down? I enjoy the wind."

"Sure thing. I like it too, but most people find it to be too much." He turned onto State Route 151 toward Jewett before adding, "Funny thing, despite knowing Lucretius's inclinations, your mom seemed pretty excited to have you join me."

DeeDee laughed. "Yeah, I think she was disappointed when I didn't go to vet school. I'm pretty sure she had visions that I would take over Xavier's practice and that somehow, I settled when I chose med school. She may see this as my opportunity to get into real medicine!"

"Well, I'm all for keeping Madge happy, so anytime you want to dabble in real medicine, you let me know."

He pulled into the parking lot of the Carrollton clinic. DeeDee jumped out of the truck and leaned toward the open window. "I will! Despite Lucretius, that was fun." She paused. "And thanks again, Jon, for saving me back there."

"Anytime," Jonathan said, and knew that he had never meant anything more.

CHAPTER 21

"A re you sure I can't get you another cup of tea?" Strong asked.

"No, thank you, three is my limit." Florence smiled and put down her mug next to the plate piled high with goodies, most of which contained significant amounts of zucchini. "And I think it's time we head back."

With the help of Natalie, the trainer at the Tennessee aquarium and former flame of Nathan, Jonathan had devised an elegant training protocol that, in theory, would teach Cowper to grow comfortable and happy with putting his head into the tube. Jonathan was skeptical that the weasels would or could adhere to the plan, so he asked Strong and Florence to implement it. Tyrone suggested they start by experimenting with a variety of foods to find out what Cowper loved besides worms.

"Worms?" Florence asked on the first day of training. "How in the world did you figure that out?"

"I came into the barn to find the weasels laughing and tossing worms into the enclosure. Apparently, one of them nearly stepped on one, and when he went to throw it out of the barn, another weasel knocked into him, sending the worm into the enclosure, and Cowper gobbled it up. The weasels thought this was so funny that they dug up my tomatoes looking for worms in the garden."

Strong donned his welding mask, and Florence put on her mirrored sunglasses and covered them with a polarized and tinted face shield so Cowper would not see the mirrored surface. At the enclosure, they found the basilisk being fed night crawlers by Martin, one of the Nottingham weasels. "Here ya go, fella, eat up! That's a nice beastie! If ye let me wipe your eye, then you can hav' two wormies!"

Florence and Strong stared as Cowper blinked and ever so slightly nodded his head. Martin took a warm, wet cloth and dabbed at the crust around the creature's eyes. "There ya go, mate. Ain't that better? And"—he reached into an old coffee can— "here's the *yummy* wormies!"

Strong smiled. "Did I mention that worms are now our go-to dosing method for his antibiotics?"

At the training area, Florence and a couple of weasels went to one end of a PVC tube wide enough for Cowper to crawl through. Two additional weasels stood guard at the other end, and Martin guided the basilisk to the opening.

"Everybody ready?" Florence asked. The weasels nodded.

"Ready!" Strong said and rang a small bell. Florence inserted a long-handled spoon smeared with cream cheese and bacon into the tube and waved it at the basilisk. As Cowper moved toward it, Florence retracted the spoon and lured him up the tube until only his head and tail were outside the cylinder. When his head emerged, she let him lick the spoon, then fed him worms while the weasels lowered two portcullises: one to further stabilize the head and the other to, hopefully, keep the tail with its perilous spikes in check.

By the end of the day, Cowper was poking his head into the tube at the sound of the bell. "Should we try one more time to see how far he'll go up the tube?" Strong asked. "Maybe he'll even pop his head out without being lured."

"It does seem like he's awful close to doing that, but I'm worried that we might be pushing our luck," Florence said.

Cowper licked his lips then sniffed and nuzzled the tube.

"Okay, let's see what he does, but whatever the outcome, this is the last one for the day."

Everyone moved back into position, and Strong rang the bell. Cowper shot like a bottle rocket up the tube, emerging with his mouth opened wide.

"Holy cow, what was that?" Strong cried.

"Darn good training!" Florence said as she fed Cowper a jackpot of wormy delights. The weasels chirped and danced, and Martin high-fived Strong. Cowper slurped down the last night crawler and strained at the snug-fitting tube. The weasels raised the portcullises, and Martin escorted his charge back to the enclosure.

"I'm so glad you suggested we try one more time!" Florence gushed as they headed out of the barn. "Not only did it confirm that the training's working, but I got the impression that he *likes* it. What do you think?"

Florence had never asked for his opinion before. Strong took a deep breath. "I do think he likes it, and he's cooperative with all of it, but I can't help but think there's something odd about all this."

"You mean beyond a talking weasel feeding worms to a mythological killing machine we've taught to put his head in a tube?"

"Yes, beyond the obvious. This whole scenario doesn't make sense to me. Basilisks are supposed to fear and loathe weasels, but Cowper's obedient, almost obsequious. *Why?*"

"Well, maybe Jon is right, that positive reinforcement really does work—not just to teach something, but to change—attitude, emotion, whatever you want to call it." Florence stopped at the door to her car and turned to face Strong, who melted under her gaze. "I think you're right to be concerned, but I don't think Cowper seeks out things to kill. He just reacts to what he *perceives* as a threat. After all, if I understand this correctly, he lived for years at the back of your property, not bothering people at all. So, I'm gonna hold out hope that this training will tame him a bit and help him to trust that we're helping, not harming him."

Strong nodded. "I also hope we can tame him, but since we don't know much about him, I think we proceed with caution, and *never, ever* trust him."

Later that afternoon, Jonathan and Bingley arrived at Strong's farm. Madge had called him at Luckey Haskin's farm. "Strong insisted—*insisted* I tell you to stop by today. Said it had something to do with Gertrude."

Strong strode out of the barn with, as he called it, "the quandary" of border collies racing ahead and Gertrude waddling beside him. Jonathan noticed that neither she nor Storm were wearing their eye protection, and neither were they blinking at the bright afternoon light. He alighted from the truck as Bingley leaped from the passenger window and zoomed toward the pond with the collies. "Bring Storm back here when you can," he called after the furry cyclone.

"Hey, Doc," Strong said, "thanks for coming on short notice. I'd been thinking to call you for the past couple of days, and I *finally* remembered to call when I had my phone on me! Anyway, I wanted you to see how well Gertrude and Storm are doing. Storm still has some crusty stuff in the morning but is a lot less sensitive to light."

"Not a problem; this is a fine way to end the day. And that's great about Storm." He turned to Gertrude. "I see you aren't wearing your goggles! That's an improvement, eh?"

Gertrude nodded but hung her head.

Jonathan squatted down on his haunches and quietly asked, "How's the egg laying?"

"Vell, not so good. Not bad, but not good either." *Honk.*

Strong spoke up. "She's still not laying in color, but there are grays mixed in with the black and white now, so that's an improvement, don't you think?" He looked expectantly at the vet.

"I do! And the fact that you are less sensitive to light is also a good sign." He stroked Gertrude's neck, and she leaned into him, resting her head on his chest. He looked at Strong. "How are you doing on the meds? Do you need any refills for either of them? I'd like to keep everyone on them for another week."

"I think we're all set, but I will double-check before you GOOOO—" Strong's last word turned into a shriek as the quandary of wet dogs leaped between the two men, drenching them with pond water and sending Gertrude aloft in a huff.

Storm planted herself in front of Jonathan and, before he could stand, put her front paws on his shoulders and licked his face. "Enough!" He laughed as he fell backward into the grass. The dogs, of course, did not heed his words, but saw his rolling on the ground as an invitation to shower him with slobbery affection.

Strong laughed so hard he had to sit down, causing another riot of canine kisses, which ended only when an errant squirrel caught Bingley's attention and the quandary took flight once again. Strong sat up and looked at Jonathan lying in the grass, chuckling to himself. "Glad you have a sense of humor about all this! I don't know of many people who would find this so amusing."

Jonathan sat up and brushed himself off as best he could. He smiled at Strong. "Well, I'm not sure what else I could do. Get mad? At what? Their utter joy?" He stood and offered Strong a hand up. "I'm not sure that I would've always been so happy about something like this." He pulled the farmer to his feet and watched as his dog ran with complete abandon. "Then again, I've learned a lot lately about finding joy in the moment."

Strong followed his gaze and smiled at the dogs, some now collapsed in the shade of a giant oak tree, others rolling in the clover-scented grass. "They're great teachers, aren't they?"

"That they are." Jonathan scanned the bucolic landscape, his eyes finally resting on the barn housing the basilisk. *And Lord knows we need some levity right now.* He turned back to Strong. "How's the training going?"

"Great! Hey, let me get a couple of beers, and I'll tell you about our breakthrough today." Strong headed to the kitchen while the dogs zoomed by Jonathan, sending water, dust, and grass in every direction. He watched them plunge into the pond and drank in the scent of freshly mowed hay.

I don't know what's gonna happen with Cowper, but today, life is pretty good.

CHAPTER 22

Anita stood by the door of her work truck checking a text from her mother when she felt someone's eyes on her. She looked up to see Connolly Davis standing on the sidewalk in front of her truck.

"You headed in for lunch?" Connolly pointed to the deli. "Care to join me?"

"That'd be great." Anita stuffed her frantically buzzing phone into her purse.

"Do you need to get that?"

"Nah, it's just my mom complaining about one of my brothers—again."

Connolly snorted. "My mom does the same thing!" She held the door open for Anita. "So I always wonder what she's saying about me to my brother."

"Me too! And *every* time I ask one of them, they *always* say, 'I don't know, I wasn't listening.'"

"Exactly! How can they not hear even *one* word? Brothers!"

Anita laughed as she stepped up to order a tuna salad on rye with chips and an iced tea. Connolly added a chicken Caesar salad and iced tea.

"Put both orders on this." She handed Caroline her AmEx card.

"Thanks! You didn't need to do that."

"My pleasure." Connolly drew out the words as she signed the receipt and tucked a copy into her wallet. "Besides," she said, pointing to the last open booth, "I am hoping you can help me."

They sat down, and Connolly stirred sweetener into her tea before continuing. "I've come to find out that everyone knows you, and you," she looked right at Anita and smiled a half-smile, "due to your extensive civic involvement, know most everyone in return."

Caroline arrived with their meals, and Connolly flashed her a toothy smile. "Thanks! This looks great!"

"Enjoy," Caroline replied, glancing at Anita, who was uncharacteristically flushed and much too interested in her sandwich.

"We . . . I . . . will," Anita mumbled as Caroline turned and walked to the counter. When she was out of earshot, Anita looked up at Connolly. "My extensive civic involvement?"

Connolly took her time finishing her bite of chicken before she answered, "You are involved in a variety of things here in Carrollton, such as the Jaycees, the Papist Society, Rotary, right?"

"Yeah?"

"Soooo, as you know, I was told to investigate the impact of the oil money on this community. Monty introduced me to people who made the civic improvements possible, such as the renovation of the high school football stadium and training facility, the new playground, the library expansion . . . and all that is good."

"But?"

"*But* I also checked out police records for the last five years looking for unusual reports—like the 'flying monkeys' you mentioned—and you're right, there were some strange things sighted around here, always by visitors! In addition to the flying monkeys, gryphons, unicorns, and flying horses have been reported." She took a bite of chicken salad before continuing. "So, I looked at the reports to see which locals were contacted and their responses. *And* you were right there as well: nearly all the sightings were written off to drinking too much on nights with full moons. And, even more interesting, *none* of the people Monty introduced me to matched the locals contacted for the unusual sightings. So, I researched the land deeds for the residents listed on the police reports, and all of them are families that have been here for several generations, going back to the late 1700s, early 1800s. Names like Burgett, Haskins, Clegg, and *Lucash*—all the names you mentioned! When I said something to Monty about it, he dodged the question." Connolly paused to drink some of her iced tea. "So, this is where you come in. You know *a lot* of people, plus you're organizing the squash tournament for DeeDee's shindig. I was hoping you could introduce me to some of these families."

Anita recalled what Jonathan had said when she asked him about introductions. *It's none of my business.* She swallowed her mouthful and drank some iced tea before she responded. "Look, I'm not sure that I'm comfortable with this direct of an approach." Connolly's face darkened, but before she could respond, Anita continued, "*But* what I *can* do is sign you up for the squash tournament, which also gets you an invitation to the Millionaire's Ball. Between the two, there would be ample opportunity for you to meet people in a social setting. Then you can decide if there are any you want to follow up with."

Connolly looked past Anita and nodded as she watched the farmers and miners mingle in the line leading to the counter. She turned back to their conversation. "Okay, but playing as a single won't give me as much of an opportunity to meet people as playing doubles with *you,* would—"

"That would be great, except that I've never played squash."

"When is this thing?"

"In four weeks. Is that enough time—"

Connolly waved her off. "No problem! You can learn the basics, and it's probably better if we lose. Most of the time, winners are easier to get talking than losers."

"You know," Anita said as she waved a potato chip at the reporter, "the ball might be an interesting story itself. It's a fundraiser for the new clinic and might be another way to get people to talk."

"I never said I'd do a story on the ball."

"And I didn't say it had to be exclusively about the ball, but you *could* mention it as part of a larger story, no? After all, who doesn't want to brag about their civic work?"

"Good point." Connolly tilted her head to the side and squinted at Anita. "But I have to wonder, what's in it for you?"

Anita pressed her lips together. "The truth. I just want to get to the bottom of all this. The weird sightings, the beagles, the knowing glances . . ."

"Like between DeeDee and Jon?"

Anita's head jerked up from her iced tea. "You noticed that?"

"I'm a reporter. I notice everything." She shook her head. "Which you'd *think* would count for something when it came to assignments."

"I kinda gathered this wasn't your ideal story."

Connolly sighed. "No, it's not, it's actually my last chance.

The Zanesville story was just the first of several bad breaks, and Jack—he's my editor—told me that either I do this story, and do it right, or I'm gone."

"Bosses! What're ya gonna do?"

Connolly chuckled. "I don't know, play squash and then get the story of the century?"

CHAPTER 23

"Doughnut?" Xavier stood in the doorway holding a white bakery bag aloft.

"Always!" Jonathan stepped aside to let him enter. "Come on in. I just put on a fresh pot of coffee."

Jonathan poured Xavier a cup of black coffee and refilled his own mug. "When did you get back?" he asked as they moved outside.

Xavier sat down and looked around the shady deck and yard. "Last night, late, or I would have called. I hoped today might be as good a time as any to catch up?"

Jonathan nodded as he savored his Boston cream doughnut.

"So, how was it on your own?" Xavier asked.

"Well, in general, I think it went well and, for the most part, better than I expected, but I did want to talk with you about the eye problems that came up."

Xavier bit into his maple-glazed cruller. "Eye problems?"

Jonathan described the issues with Storm, Strong, and Gertrude, then added, "I was looking at Gertrude's egg up close, and I noticed an odd creature in the doorway of the barn. It looked like an iguana, and that seemed really odd to me, since Strong has never kept reptiles." Jonathan moved to the edge of his seat. "Moreover, it looked as if it had an eye infection! That got me to thinking that the cause of the problem might be in the barn, and perhaps this animal had something to do with it." He drained his coffee mug, then told Xavier about capturing and identifying the basilisk.

Xavier stopped eating and stared out at the lawn, his brow furrowed, his face darkening. "What did you decide to do?"

As Jonathan described their plan in detail, including the possibility of contact lenses, he failed to notice Xavier growing still and quiet. He was about to tell the older vet how they found the food that the basilisk liked and how the English weasels had trained the American weasels in the ways of basilisk management when Xavier said, "Do you have any idea what you've done?"

Xavier's pale face, taut shoulders, and deafeningly quiet tone stopped Jonathan cold. "What do you mean?"

Xavier took a deep breath. "Jon, I appreciate that you've tried to do the right thing, but there're serious consequences here. Let's start with the weasels. Did you quarantine them?"

Jonathan shook his head.

"Okay, so first, you've imported animals from another country without vetting them, literally, for diseases they may introduce, or protecting them from illnesses they may have no resistance to here. This could cause serious problems if they have a pathogen that spreads among the local weasels or other animals. Hopefully their only contact has been with a few Ohio weasels, is that correct?"

Jonathan nodded.

"Okay, well, let's put that issue aside for now, as there're other things to consider. Our weasels are now, for lack of a better term, trained prison guards, SWAT weasels if you will, skilled in control techniques and intimidation, which could be rather problematic. How'll they use these skills? Will they reserve them only for controlling the basilisk or will they use them against other animals?" Xavier took a sip of coffee.

Jonathan swallowed and shook his head. "I-I don't know."

"And then there's the basilisk. Who knows how long this creature has lived with us in peace? Now it's sick and displaced. I strongly suspect that this is the animal that lived in Strong's dell and killed the geese and the sheep, but there's no way to prove this. The question we need to be asking ourselves is, what do we owe it, even if it has the power to sicken or kill us or our livestock?"

Xavier paused, took a deep breath, and continued, "I'm keenly aware that this animal is dangerous and has the potential to be a deadly threat to the public, and that part of our oaths as veterinarians is to protect the public's health. But our oath also states that we will use our skills for the prevention and relief of animal suffering. So, wherein lies our compassion, if this animal is our enemy and it's also suffering? What's the quality of mercy we should have for it?" Xavier paused again.

Jonathan looked at his dog asleep in the sun, oblivious to the heavy burden settling down upon his person. He looked at Xavier and nodded for him to continue.

"Indeed, is it truly our enemy? If it was the animal in the dell, one could argue that it was just doing what nature intended for it to do: live its life according to its individual nature. Why did it suddenly take up residence in Strong's barn? If human activities caused its displacement, then an argument could be made that *we* created our enemy. Even legitimate and just activities can have unforeseen consequences, and Strong could not have known that the oil well, erected on what he thought was inconsequential land, would cause this problem. And, in fact, we cannot say for certain that it did.

"But, regardless, we have to acknowledge that with both the weasels and the basilisk, we have upset the natural order. Can it be repaired or restored? Or have we created a problem that is not only greater than we intended, but has broader-reaching effects beyond this immediate situation?" Xavier's frown deepened. "For example, if we do try something like contact lenses, which I doubt will work, have we interfered too much? Are there unintended consequences to disabling its powers?"

Jonathan's stomach twisted. "Probably, but that's why we intend to keep him in an enclosure, so we can monitor the situation for 'unintended consequences.'"

Xavier nodded. "That's good, but there're things to consider with that choice as well. You may recall that the day you were introduced to these animals, I mentioned that they do not thrive in captivity, and that they choose to live here, with us. What do our actions with the weasels and the basilisk say to the others who have chosen this place? Is it that we are protecting them from danger, keeping them safe from harm by incarceration of a deadly enemy? Or are we compromising their trust, safety, health, happiness? I'm not sure of the message we are giving them, but I do know that we must think about this situation seriously and try to find a solution that encompasses both mercy and prudence, as well as compassion and protection, or the consequences could be quite dire."

Jonathan put his head in his hands. He was grateful for Xavier's extensive use of "we," but he was keenly aware that he was the cause of the current situation and as such, would also be responsible for the resolution of it. *That is, if I can resolve it.* "Xavier, I am so sorry. I was trying to figure out what was going on with all the eye problems that weren't responding well to treatment. With the discovery of the basilisk, we found the source of the eye problems, and we *did* discuss the bigger issues like restoring the natural order, but maybe not fully enough—"

Xavier reached over the table and patted him on the shoulder. "I'm sorry I wasn't here to help you. Growing up here and spending my life in service to these animals means these questions are second nature to me. I guess I never thought about it *not* being second nature for you too. But why didn't you tell me about this earlier?"

Jonathan sat up straight and looked at Xavier. "At first, I didn't think it was necessary to tell you about eye infections. Then, you had the accident and were understandably very concerned about Janice and the RV, so I didn't want to add to your burdens. I had others to talk to—Strong, Tyrone, DeeDee—who could help with various aspects, and well, I thought we had it under control." His voice faded as he added, "But maybe not?"

Jonathan's phone rang. It was Madge. He put her on speaker phone. "Luckey Haskins just called. His yellow lab, Max, just came home with a nasty cut on his right side that will likely need stitches. He'll be at the clinic in five minutes."

"On my way." Jonathan hung up but didn't move, except to run his hands over his face and through his hair.

Xavier stood up, gathered the dishes, and walked toward the kitchen. "Let's go see a lab about some stitches, shall we?"

PART III

CHAPTER 24

"I won't be gone more than an hour! If you could finish up with the table and buffet flowers, ask the sound and light guy to double check the lighting for the mirror ball, and make *sure* the bartenders have the sparkling juices—I'm not sure they'll remember!" DeeDee grabbed her purse and keys and turned to leave, running smack into Jonathan, sending his tux sailing as he, Nathan, and Xavier entered the ballroom.

"I'm so sorry, Jonathan! Are you okay?"

"I'm fine. Not sure about my tux. I think you gave it a real fright! Where are you headed in such a hurry?"

"My mom won't let me come to the ball as Cinderella, so I am off to find a fairy godmother to transform me."

"Well, good luck with that. You might check in with Tyrone. If anyone would know of a fairy godmother, it would be him. But, on the off chance that all the godmothers are booked for the evening, he could do your hair. I know he's doing Janice's right now."

"Too true!" DeeDee laughed. "Tye does seem to know everyone, but he's mad at me right now because I told him he had to cut back on the mead or he was headed for some serious pancreatitis. If I asked for help now, there's no telling what the outcome might be!" With that, DeeDee Guzman whirled out the door.

Ninety minutes later, Janice Pratt, radiant in emerald green with a matching sling for her broken arm, entered the marina ballroom. DeeDee floated in behind her, resplendent in a midnight-blue backless gown trimmed with rhinestones. Her hair was piled in complicated swirls that hovered magically around her neck and shoulders, accented with three perfect gardenias, courtesy of Tyrone.

Jonathan and Nathan emerged from the restroom, bow ties in hand, salty words at the ready. "Madge, could you . . . uh, could you," Jonathan stammered as his eyes fell on the radiant DeeDee coming toward them.

Nathan, chuckling, finished the sentence for them. "Please tie these damn things for us? We are hopeless here."

"Apparently," Madge said as she watched the dumbstruck Jonathan attempt to regain his composure. "DeeDee, go get your father. He's over with Xavier." She turned back to the young vets. "If I have to do bow ties, I might as well do all of them at the same time."

Madge was working on Jonathan's when Anita entered in a black mermaid gown with a pearl choker hugging her slender neck. Her hair was swept up into a tight updo, much like Audrey Hepburn in *Breakfast at Tiffany's*. Connolly Davis arrived at the same time in an understated black gown and long pearl necklace.

They moved toward Jonathan and Madge, engulfing them in a thick atmosphere of perfume. Madge scowled, renewed her assault on his tie, and groused, "They look like Cinderella's stepsisters."

Jonathan snorted, coughed, and smiled at Anita.

"Jon! Don't tell me that you can't tie your own bow tie? I'm shocked!" Anita teased.

Connolly scanned the room. Her eyes landed on DeeDee. "If you'll excuse me, I'd like to catch Dr. Guzman before the evening gets underway." Her stiletto heels assaulted the dance floor as she pursued her quarry.

"There, *finally!*" Madge tightened the errant bow and brushed some invisible lint off of Jonathan's shoulder, nodded at Anita, glared in the direction of Connolly, and left to change her clothes.

"You look great," Jonathan said and gave Anita a kiss on the cheek. He knew better than to smear her ruby lipstick.

In short order, the hors d'oeuvres were circulating, big band music filled the air, and drinks were flowing. Xavier, along with Johnny T and The Imperials, kept the evening light and humorous. DeeDee glided effortlessly amongst the guests, thanking all the donors and reminding them of the many and varied items on the silent auction table. As the gong sounded for dinner, Xavier motioned for DeeDee to come to the stage to make her pitch.

"Thank you all for being here tonight. Despite our economic boom, we see the need for updated services on a daily basis as we strive to provide exceptional service to all who cross our threshold. I'm humbled and grateful for your support of the renovation and expansion of our clinic, including the addition of a substance abuse center, and I hope you all enjoy the evening."

DeeDee turned the microphone over to Johnny T and floated down to join Jonathan and the others at table number one. "Nice speech," Jonathan murmured as DeeDee slipped into the chair between him and Marcus. He leaned in for a fraction of a second, the fragrance of the gardenias in her hair intoxicating him, and added, "You look stunning."

She smiled.

Anita, seated on his other side, frowned—a fact that did not escape the attention of Connolly Davis, seated at the adjoining table.

Jonathan paid exclusive attention to Anita and Nathan as dinner was served. When the wait staff moved in with coffee and dessert, Xavier stepped toward the stage and beckoned to Jonathan as the band struck the first notes of "Sway."

Nathan cleared his throat, touched Anita's arm, and asked, "Did you know he could sing?"

Anita looked at Nathan's smiling brown eyes and shook her head. "Uh . . . nooo."

Nathan gently squeezed her forearm. "Then *you* are in for a treat," he said and nodded toward the stage.

The band was finishing the opening chords of their duet when Jonathan reached the apex of the stage, and Xavier handed him a mike with a wink and a nod, then crooned the opening lines of "Sway." Jonathan closed his eyes, leaned into the rhythm, and took the second stanza. The band swelled to meet the two singers as Johnny T's professional dancers swept middle-aged millionaire wives onto the dance floor. Spotlights hit the disco ball, electrifying the swirling dancers, then turned onto the duo as they brought the song to a sultry crescendo.

Jonathan and Xavier slapped each other on the back and bowed to the crowd, who jumped to their feet in a standing ovation neither had anticipated. Exhilarated, Jonathan left the stage, only to find DeeDee at the bottom of the stairs where she'd been talking with a potential donor. He smiled at the farmer, then took DeeDee's hand, guided her to the dance floor, and pulled her close as Xavier crooned: "*The summer wind came blowin' in from across the sea. It lingered there, to touch your hair, and walk with me . . .*"

The fragrance of the gardenias in the curls playing around her face and shoulders, the perfect fit of her waist in his hand, and the magic of soft lights and wistful music amplified the heady moment. Her ocean-blue eyes met his, and he bent low and kissed her softly behind her right ear, not knowing, much less caring, who saw. DeeDee moaned softly and melted into his embrace, but quickly recovered and pulled herself back. "Jon, no. Please . . ."

Nathan, on his feet with everyone else, saw the transformation on his friend's face. He flashed his brilliant smile at Anita. "Care to dance?" he asked, and before she had a chance to decline, swept her into his arms and onto the dance floor as far from their table as he could manage.

Marcus, having been at the bar getting drinks for the table when Jonathan stole DeeDee away, arrived back just as Lorenzo and Madge hit the now-crowded dance floor, leaving Janice alone at the table. Marcus set down the drinks and offered his hand. "Would you care to dance?"

Janice looked at her arm and up at him. "I would, but—"

"You will be fine! I'm an orthopedic surgeon, remember? Who better to guide you around the dance floor?" He smiled, took her good hand, and twirled her as they approached the swaying fray, careful to keep to the periphery to protect her wounded appendage.

Nathan spotted Marcus and Janice's entrance and maneuvered Anita in their general direction, hoping that he could switch partners with Marcus at the next dance, thereby giving Jonathan ample time with DeeDee. "Xavier certainly has a great voice. I think he could rival Sinatra," Nathan said in Anita's ear as he steered her away from the vet and the doctor and closer to the orthopedic surgeon.

"I agree! And you were right about Jon too. I had no idea he could sing like that!"

"He doesn't believe it himself. I am sure the only reason he agreed to do it was because of—" Nathan caught himself before he could say DeeDee's name, cleared his throat and continued, "Excuse me, because of the clinic. It's a worthwhile cause." One last turn and they were elbow to cast with Marcus and Janice.

Xavier wrapped up "Summer Wind," and the band slid right into "Beyond the Sea." Nathan looked at Janice and offered her a hand, while simultaneously handing Anita off to Marcus, who took the bait, picked up the pace, and spun Anita into the middle of the dance floor.

Jonathan lessened his grip on DeeDee's waist, spun her out and back into his arms. She looked up at him, smiling weakly and shaking her head. "Jon, I . . . I," she stuttered and then stared as Marcus dipped Anita low and pulled her up slowly into his arms.

Jonathan followed her gaze in time to see the heat pass between Marcus and Anita. "Holy cow! Who knew?" He looked at DeeDee's face. "Apparently not you," he said softly as tears slipped down her cheek. He scanned the room for an escape route and guided her off the dance floor toward the entrance to the stage and a nearby door that led to the service dock.

Jonathan caught Madge's eye as he steered DeeDee toward the exit. *She needs some air,* he mouthed to Madge. She nodded and rose to join them, instructing Lorenzo to corral Connolly onto the dance floor. "This is nothing *that* woman needs to know about!"

Jonathan guided DeeDee out the service entrance into the cool night air. He put his arm around her shoulder while he reached into his jacket pocket and handed her a linen handkerchief.

"Thank you," she snuffled into the handkerchief. "I'm *sorry,* I don't know what's going on with me! After all, it was just a dance."

"You really care about him, don't you?" He placed his tuxedo jacket around her bare shoulders and guided her to an upended crate.

Madge burst out the door and stood in front of her now-seated daughter. "DeeDee," she demanded, "look at me!"

DeeDee raised her tear-stained face toward the imposing Madge. "I don't know what happened, but I bet it had something to do with Marc."

DeeDee nodded.

"Whatever he did, or didn't do for that matter, isn't relevant at this moment. What *is* relevant is you getting a hold of yourself and getting back out there! I don't need to tell you that the success of this evening depends on you! So, here!" She shoved a makeup bag into her daughter's hands. "There's a mirror in there, so you don't need to go to the bathroom to tidy up."

DeeDee wiped her eyes then handed the handkerchief to Madge.

"Where did you get this?"

"From me," Jonathan said. "My father always had two handkerchiefs on him, one for himself, and one for whoever may need it—us kids mostly, I suppose. In any event, it always seemed so thoughtful that I decided to do it myself. Only, most of the time I forget."

Madge smiled and handed him the handkerchief. "That is very thoughtful and very gentlemanly."

Jonathan blushed and hoped that he was in enough of the shadow on the loading dock that they wouldn't notice.

DeeDee finished repairing her makeup, then handed Madge the bag and Jonathan his jacket. "Thank you, both of you, for taking care of me. I'm ready to go back. I shouldn't have let the dance affect me so, but Marc is—"

The door to the service dock flew open. "There you are!" Marcus exclaimed. "Xavier is about to sing 'Volare,' and since you've been humming it so much lately, I thought you'd want to dance to it." He took DeeDee's hand and pulled her close while nudging Jonathan to the side. "And, by the way," he said over his shoulder as he guided DeeDee back into the ballroom, "*your* girlfriend is looking for you."

CHAPTER 25

Nathan tugged at the bow tie with his left hand while he poured two Kentucky bourbons with his right. The bow finally gave way, and he chuckled as he undid the top button of his tuxedo shirt. "That was some evening—some weekend!"

Jonathan collapsed on the couch after starting a fire. He scratched Bingley's ear with his right hand as he loosened his own bow tie and top button with his left. "That it was."

Nathan gave Jonathan his drink and put the Four Roses Small Batch bourbon on the coffee table. As he sank into the sofa next to Bingley, he lifted his glass. "In the words of C.S. Lewis, 'There are far better things ahead than any we leave behind.'"

"Cheers!" Jonathan said. "And thanks for being here this weekend. Not sure I would have made it without you." He clinked his glass against Nathan's.

"I wouldn't have missed it for the world." He laughed. "Beating Dr. Pompous in squash was fun, but tonight was particularly, I don't know, entertaining. What exactly happened?"

"Heck if I know." Jonathan sipped his drink just as Bingley nuzzled his hand, nearly spilling the drink. "Okay, I got it, we aren't done yet. Just don't spill my bourbon." He moved his drink to his left hand and resumed the canine ear massage. Bingley groaned with delight.

"Well, let's start with the look on your face as you left the stage and corralled Dr. Guzman," Nathan said. "Luckily, I diverted Anita before *she* saw it. And maneuvered her to Marc to give you more time with the lovely DeeDee." He took a sip of his bourbon. "And you're welcome."

Jonathan sat up and started to rub Bingley's belly, who was now stretched out with all four paws pointed to the ceiling and his head hanging off the couch. "How can that possibly be comfortable with all the blood going to your head?"

Nathan looked at him and shook his head slightly.

Jonathan sighed and took a long swallow. "So, then DeeDee saw Marc dip Anita and started crying. I took her outside to compose herself, and her mom followed. Then, the next thing I know, Dr. 90210 is there to 'rescue' DeeDee, Anita is glaring at me, and you're dancing with Connolly! Have I missed anything?"

"Well, in case you didn't see it, sparks were flying everywhere! Strong danced all night with Florence, which"—he pointed his bourbon at Jonathan—"I am sure Madge will mention to you, as she mentioned it to *me* three times."

He poured another finger's worth of bourbon into his glass before continuing, "Marc and Anita *were* burning hot on the dance floor, so I think DeeDee had a right to be upset, and Connolly Davis came on to me! But I dodged that rather masterfully by escorting Janice to the dance floor." He untied his patent leather shoes and dropped them to the floor before putting his feet up on the coffee table.

"And you, sir, I have to say, handled the annoyed Anita rather well. I thought for sure that she was going to take you down, but I guess you have learned something from me, grasshopper."

Jonathan raised his glass to Nathan. "Thank you, sensei."

Nathan watched Jonathan rub Bingley's belly and scratch his ears affectionately, then gently queried, "Jon, I *saw* you and DeeDee, and this is more than friends. What's goin' on?"

Jonathan stopped stroking his dog and looked directly at Nathan. "Look, I'll admit that DeeDee is something special, but she made it clear when we were outside that Marc's the one for her, so I'm not going down that path." Bingley relaxed even more and started to slip off the couch.

"Just promise me you won't mope about DeeDee for two years like you did with Piper. Try to nip this one in the bud, okay?"

"I hear ya." Jonathan sighed. "Piper's 'Dear John' letter was a killer—I didn't know if I'd ever get over it." He tipped his drink toward Nathan. "But considering that DeeDee has never been a possibility, it should be relatively easy to consign this to the history books along with Piper. And besides, there's Anita. She's fun and pretty undemanding, and that makes her uncomplicated to date. So, I think I've got this."

Nathan nodded. "Well, if DeeDee isn't an option and Anita is just for fun, then it seems to me that you might want to consider a job opening at the Animal Care Center in Lexington. It's in internal medicine and the position has, in the past, also included a partnership with the University of Kentucky horse program. I thought it would be perfect for you. "

"Go on."

Nathan put down his drink and leaned forward, entwining his fingers and rubbing his left thumb with his right one. "I could be off, but I get the impression that things here, other than women, aren't what you thought they were going to be."

Jonathan squinted with one eye, bobbed his head back and forth a bit, then nodded for Nathan to continue.

"So, I thought you might like good hours, and good pay, in a city with a small-town feel." He stopped rubbing his thumbs and pointed both index fingers at Jonathan. "I talked with the director before I left and told him about you. He was really interested and authorized me to offer you a trip to Louisville to see the practice. If you like it and we 'like' you, it would save him the time, cost, and headache of advertising for the position. I have a description of the job in my stuff. Hang on." Nathan left to retrieve the information.

"Here ya go." He handed Jonathan the description, including the salary. He couldn't help but notice it was a hefty raise from what he was earning now. *But,* he cautioned himself, *remember that there is more to a job than salary.*

As Jonathan read through the job description, Nathan extolled the virtues of Louisville, the availability of advanced medical equipment, and the University of Kentucky. "Not to mention that you can get back to playing squash on a regular basis."

"Well, if that doesn't seal the deal, I don't know what will!" Jonathan retorted. "But seriously, I *will* think about this. The past year has been interesting, but I'd be a fool not to consider this possibility."

Bingley's momentum, coupled with gravity, overtook the friction keeping him on the couch, and he unceremoniously dropped to the floor. "Ummph! Ugh!" he grumbled and sat up.

Nathan stopped short. "Did he just say ugh?"

Jonathan and Bingley froze, and their eyes locked for an instant. Bingley shook off and headed over to his bed by the fireplace, circling three times before throwing himself onto it with an audible doggy-style sigh. "It did kinda sound like that," Jonathan admitted, "but I think it was just him hitting the floor."

"Wow. It really sounded like he *said* something, but maybe it's just the bourbon," Nathan said as he refilled their glasses.

"Bingley is the most, um, verbal dog I have ever met, so it doesn't surprise me that he sounded like he was talking, but I'm sure it was nothing unusual." *For him,* Jonathan added silently.

"Okay, but getting back to the job offer. Seriously, you've fulfilled your year-long contract, and if there isn't anything really compelling to keep you here, why not come to Louisville? At the very least, come for a visit so you'll be fully informed before you make a decision."

"You win. I'll look at the job, but no promises." He glanced at the peacefully snoring pup. "There are things that I really like about this practice that would be exceptionally hard to give up."

Later that night, after Nathan was in bed, Jonathan went to the back of his closet and pulled down a shoebox filled with assorted memorabilia. At the bottom lay a creased envelope, smoothed by the weight of time. He hesitated only a moment before pulling out the letter, expecting the familiar words to elicit a catch in his throat and a dreadful burning behind his eyes. When they didn't, he placed the letter back in its envelope, went down to the living room, and without reservation, threw it onto the embers of the fire.

CHAPTER 26

Madge was on the phone when Jonathan returned from lunch. She handed him his mail and the afternoon's files as he walked toward the back office. He was tossing assorted items into the trash, when something Madge said caught his attention. *Did she say engaged?* He stepped closer to the door of the office.

"Yes, Janice, that's what I said, engaged! . . . I know, I know. I was surprised too. They've been dating for what? Five years?"

Jonathan held his breath.

"DeeDee told me that it happened over the weekend," Madge added.

He sagged against the desk and stared at a catalog for ungulate wormers as if it held the answer to all life's questions. He heaved it into the trash, knocking over the waste basket.

"Everything okay in there?" Madge called to him.

"Yes. Everything is *just* fine. I'm leaving now." Jonathan grabbed the Lucash file and headed out the back door of the clinic.

"Okay, bye . . ." Madge stared after him, shook her head, and returned to the phone call. "I'm sorry, what was that?" Madge asked Janice. "No, no, they haven't set a date, but she's asked DeeDee to be her maid of honor, so there's that!" Madge laughed and added, "Well, I should go, these bills aren't going to send themselves out. Talk to you later."

Jonathan opened the door to his house and whistled for Bingley. Despite his deflated mood, he laughed as the sleek, black dog leaped into the cab of the truck and slathered his face with slobbery kisses. "Enough already!"

Bingley jumped into the backseat, and the now-somber vet maneuvered the wiggling flat-coat into his seat belt harness.

Bingley patted Jonathan's forearm with his front paw. "What?"

"I'll tell you as we drive to Cal's." He pulled onto County Road 613. "Well, it's been a very interesting day so far."

"Uh-huh," Bingley encouraged. "Did you break up with Anita?"

"Well, that's the first interesting thing." He checked both ways at the four-way stop and continued, "She broke up with me!"

"No!"

"Yes!" Jonathan snorted. "I was all set to let her down easy, when she told me that she thought our relationship would be better served as friends."

"And you said?"

"Well, nothing at first. My mouth was full of Reuben, and I literally couldn't talk."

"What have I told you about putting too much into your mouth at one time? You're going to choke to death one of these days!"

"*Really? Seriously?* A kibble-wolfing dog is going to tell me about eating too much, too fast?"

Bingley ignored the comment. "So when you finally swallowed, what did you say? Please do not tell me that you said,

'That's what I was going to say'!"

"No, I didn't say that, though truth be told, I thought it." Jonathan turned right onto the road to the Lucash farm. "But, having all that food in my mouth gave me a moment to think, and my reply was brilliant, if I do say so myself."

"Okay, so what *did* you say?"

"That I thought she was right and wise to end this while we could still be good friends. And I added that I thought she was terrific and deserved someone who could love her to the moon and back, and to be honest, that was what I wanted too."

Jonathan glanced in the rearview mirror to see Bingley nodding his furry black head.

"Good job, Boss! Now you can turn your attention to DeeDee!"

Jonathan's face clouded. "I don't think so."

"Why not?"

"I just heard Madge tell Janice that DeeDee got engaged this weekend."

"I don't believe it."

"You don't? Why not? *I know* what I heard."

"Because Duncan told me that DeeDee and Marc aren't getting along. Apparently, they had a fight over the phone, which I don't understand. How can you fight when you aren't in the same room to show your teeth to one another?"

Bingley looked out the window for a moment to contemplate the absurdity of human behavior, then continued, "DeeDee was mumbling something about it 'no longer working' as she folded laundry after the fight."

"When was this?"

"Time—you people are so concerned about time! I think it was just after we went to the stream, and you fell in and cut your paw, uh, hand."

Jonathan sighed and tried to think when that was. *Ten, twelve days ago?* "Huh. Interesting, but a lot can happen in a couple of weeks, so maybe they resolved whatever was going on."

He turned into the drive to the Lucash farm.

"I doubt it. Duncan was pretty sure things are not going well."

Jonathan turned off the engine to his truck and released Bingley from his harness. The dog leapt from the cab and took off with Jackson for a race about the barn.

As he gathered his medical supplies, Jonathan found his hope both rising and falling. *Could it be true? What about the engagement?*

"Hey, Jon. How's it going?" Calloway greeted his friend.

"Not too bad, how about you?"

"Not too bad either. It could be worse. It could be raining. And I could be out of beer!"

Jonathan laughed and thought, *He's right, you know. Even though things could be better, they could also be a lot worse.*

He smiled. "Well then, let's get started so we can get to that beer. Who's first?"

CHAPTER 27

"Fish tacos or chicken enchiladas?" DeeDee pondered aloud as she scanned the menu at El Pegaso.

"*Definitely* the chicken enchiladas," a woman's voice said behind her.

DeeDee whirled around to find Connolly Davis invading her personal space. She stepped back. Connolly moved in. With no more room to retreat, DeeDee raised the menu to chest height as she said hello and dropped her eyes to the menu once more.

Connolly leaned over the menu, pointing at the left-hand column. "Today's special is the chicken enchiladas, so they're a dollar off and come with a free twelve-ounce beverage." She smiled broadly.

DeeDee, always conscious of social distance with people she didn't know well, decided that the best defense would be a good offense, and moved toward Connolly. "Thanks for pointing that out," she said, then veered to the right, putting a large potted plant between them but sacrificing her spot in line. "It's definitely worth considering."

Connolly gave up her place in line and joined DeeDee behind the ficus. "I wanted to tell you how much I enjoyed the Millionaire's Ball, and that what you're doing is fantastic."

"Uh, thank you."

"I also wanted you to know that I'm including the ball as

part of my story on the sudden influx of money into this part of the state." She lowered her voice to add, "I was thinking it would be worthwhile to get the perspective of some of your donors, especially those who have been here for generations. Their long-term perspective could give me a better understanding of this area, and how money has affected it." Connolly smiled again.

"So?"

"So, I hoped that you might introduce me to some of them?"

DeeDee began to shred a leaf on the ficus. "I don't know . . ."

"Well, think of it this way," Connolly said as she flicked some dust off a nearby ficus leaf, "most people are eager to talk about what makes their hometown special." She lowered her voice again. "Doesn't *everyone* want their fifteen minutes of fame?"

DeeDee Guzman stood as tall as her five-foot three-inch fame would allow and turned to face the reporter. "Ms. Davis—"

"Connolly—please, call me Connolly."

"*Connolly*," she stammered, "I, um, look, I don't really feel comfortable with this conversation. You know, people live around here because they aren't publicity seekers, and it-it feels as if you are asking me to betray the trust of my donors." DeeDee's temperature rose as she saw surprise and amusement flash across the reporter's face. "Besides, I can't help but think there is something more behind your request—" Before she could say another word, the hostess tapped her shoulder.

"Dr. Guzman—"

DeeDee whirled away from the artfully composed face of the reporter and stared at the hostess.

"It's your turn to order."

"Oh, right. I'll have the fish tacos . . .to go."

CHAPTER 28

"So, you're okay with taking him for three days?" Jonathan asked. "I know he'd love spending time with Duncan."

"Absolutely!" DeeDee answered. "When Mom told me you were taking a few days off, my first thought was that if you weren't taking Bingley with you, Duncan would love to have him stay with us. Besides, it makes it a lot easier on me as I don't feel as guilty leaving him home when he has a buddy—so, you're *actually* doing me a favor!" She laughed.

"Well, when you put it like that, how can I refuse?"

"You can't! Now, since you leave on Thursday, why don't you drop him off Wednesday evening? That would make it easier on all of us, don't you think?"

"Yeah, I think you're probably right." He flicked a pen on the counter, sending it spinning like a whirling dervish. "Umm, can I buy you dinner on Wednesday as a thank you?"

"I think that can be arranged, but why not make it simple and get takeout from El Pegaso? I love their chicken enchiladas—hint, hint!" DeeDee laughed again.

"Done! See you Wednesday." Jonathan hung up and stared at the pen, now lazily circling the counter. "Why is it my heart pounds every time I talk to her?" he muttered.

"Because you *like* her," Bingley said as he trotted into the kitchen to get some water.

"Holy Mary!" Jonathan exclaimed. "How do you manage to sneak up on me *every* time?"

Bingley waved his tail as he drank deeply from his bowl. He raised his head and water poured off his face onto the kitchen floor. "It's a gift."

Jonathan scratched the base of his tail. "You'll be the death of me, dog."

Wednesday evening found Jonathan staring at his meager assortment of wine, trying to decide whether white or red would go better with chicken enchiladas. He tapped his right foot. "Hmm, maybe I should take both and let her decide?"

"Beer," Bingley said. "DeeDee likes beer with her Mexican food."

"How do you know?"

The dog sighed and stretched out on the sofa. "Everyone knows beer goes better with Mexican. The question should be: how do you *not* know this?" He wiggled back and forth, scratching an itch on his lower back.

"I don't know. Clearly, my education is lacking." He opened the refrigerator. "Luckily, I have a few Coronas, a couple of limes . . . I think we're good to go." He turned to see Bingley's gyrations. "That is, if you're finished grinding dirt into the sofa."

"I am. I was just waiting for you."

"Smells great!" DeeDee remarked as she leaned into the aroma wafting from the takeout bag. As Jonathan put the beer and the food on the counter, his arm brushed her hair as it skimmed the top of the bag. Butterflies sambaed in his stomach.

"Oh good, you brought beer too. Thanks! There's nothing better with an enchilada than a cold beer!"

Bingley nudged Jonathan's hand. "I told you so," he grunted.

"Why don't you go play with Duncan?" Jonathan grumbled. Then, looking at DeeDee, he said, "Well, I believe it is a universal truth that Mexican food is best served with beer, though I suppose you could make a strong argument for margaritas."

"You could, but you would be wrong!" DeeDee laughed as she got out plates, silverware, and napkins, and set them on the kitchen table.

"If you tell me where your opener is, I'll open a couple of these."

"Top drawer to the right of the sink," DeeDee said. "And there's a lime in the basket next to the blender if you want one," she added.

Jonathan wavered. *Do I just say thanks or do I produce my own? She needs to know I brought limes? Does it matter? If so, why would it matter?* He shook his head to clear it of the unheeded reverie. "Thanks."

He pulled the fruit from his jacket pocket, cut two wedges, and put them on the necks of the bottles and handed one to DeeDee. "Cheers!"

"Cheers," she replied, clinking her bottle to his. "Let's eat, I'm starving!"

DeeDee topped off Jonathan's coffee and handed him the container of half-and-half. "So, what's the word from the centaurs?"

"Well, so far, it's all good. At first, the pergolide suppressed Lucretius's appetite, which annoyed him." Jonathan offered DeeDee seconds from a box of cookies from the bakery. She chose a chocolate-dipped shortbread, and he took a double chocolate chunk brownie.

"That's no surprise."

"No, it's not, but, as it happened, the loss of appetite turned out to be a blessing in disguise." Jonathan leaned his elbows on the table. "Lucretius was always more concerned about Septimus than about himself. He was, *in no way*, convinced that diet and exercise would work, much less be enough for Septimus. But, when he discovered that eating better and losing weight made him feel and look better, you would have thought he invented the diet and exercise regimen. Now he, Septimus, and Flavia are all-in—and best of all—Septimus's A1C is routinely within normal range." Jonathan sat back in his chair and tucked into his brownie.

"Wow, that is—Duncan, what do you have?" DeeDee asked as the golden trotted over with a squishy purple ball in his mouth.

"That would be Blobby," Jonathan said. "It's the toy that Bing sleeps with every night—his emotional support toy. I know that Duncan is his best friend, but I'm a bit surprised that he is letting him hold it."

Bingley trotted over and leaned into his person. "It's okay, as long as I can have it at night."

"Of course you can! I'll make sure of it." DeeDee reached over and cupped the flat-coat's face in her hands. "And you are welcome to sleep on the bed with Duncan and me, if you'd like."

"Thank you." Bingley licked DeeDee's face before grabbing a nearby tug toy and inviting Duncan to play.

"You don't have to let him on your bed. He'll be fine on his," Jonathan said.

"Maybe, but I want him to be comfortable here, and since Marc is at a conference, there'll be no one around to scold me about it." She stood and started to clear the table. "Besides, I'm pretty sure that you'd do the same for Duncan."

Jonathan nodded. "Yeah, probably. Anita's just like Marc. She doesn't think dogs belong on couches, much less beds." Jonathan put the lid on the remaining enchiladas and put them in the refrigerator. "But I don't have to worry about that anymore." He turned to face DeeDee. "We broke up."

Was that a flash of relief that crossed her face? What does that mean?

"Oh, Jon, I'm sorry!"

"No, don't be. It was mutual. Anita's great, but we aren't suited for each other for the long run." *Unlike you and Marc.* "And I know Bing's relieved. She was never his favorite!"

DeeDee turned her attention to the dishes in the sink. "Well, break-ups are never fun—but if it's good for Bingley, that's all that really matters, isn't it?" She laughed.

"I suppose it is." Jonathan picked up a dishtowel and moved to DeeDee's side. "Do you want to wash or dry?"

CHAPTER 29

I wonder why I feel so good after only five hours of sleep? Jonathan pondered. The night before, after finishing the dishes and taking the dogs for a walk, he and DeeDee had talked late into the evening so that, by the time he got home, finished packing, and went to bed, there weren't many hours before his alarm would insist he rise.

He stretched as he walked to the window. Dew glistened on the wild roses edging the lawn, and he could hear distant cows lowing for their breakfasts. *It's a great morning for a run,* one part of him said. *It's also a great day for coffee on the porch before you leave,* answered the other side of his brain. "Coffee it is," he said aloud. *Besides, then I can get an earlier start. Maybe Nathan and I can get a game of squash in.*

As the coffee brewed, Jonathan showered and dressed. He had breakfast and his first cup of coffee on the deck, loaded the dishes in the dishwasher, filled his travel mug, and was out the door by 7:00 a.m. Though pleased by the efficiency of the canine-free morning, he nonetheless missed Bingley and was surprised by the number of times he reached out to pet him, look for him, or say something to him.

It's certainly a lot less complicated when he's not here, he thought as he hung the garment bag in the truck and tossed his duffle into the backseat. *But it's just not, I don't know . . . worth it.* He fastened his seat belt and pulled out of the driveway. *There's no doubt about it—simplicity is definitely overrated.*

Jonathan arrived at Nathan's office mid-afternoon and pretended to busy himself with a poster on Lyme disease prevention as Nathan wrapped up an endocrine consultation for a Great Pyrenees with Addison's disease. "I'm pleased with Kemen's response to the DOCP treatment, and I would recommend at this point that we recheck his electrolytes, as well as do a full blood panel in three months. If he remains stable, we can do those tests less frequently, say every six to twelve months, with a metabolic panel done every six months."

"Thank you, Dr. Jackson. We are so grateful to finally have our boy on the mend."

"You are most welcome. Now, a word of caution: any stressful event will mean he requires more cortisol, and that puts him at risk for a crisis. Symptoms to look for can be very subtle, such as shaking, loose stool, weakness, or decreased appetite. Please do not hesitate to contact us or bring him in if you see any signs that he might be struggling. We want to stay ahead of any crisis, because if he remains stable, you can expect a good quality of life for him."

Jonathan moved farther away from the door to Nathan's office when he heard chairs being pushed back and the *click-click-click* of Kemen's nails on the linoleum floor.

"Addison's, eh?"

Nathan looked up from his paperwork. "Jon!" He closed the file folder. "Yeah, truth be told, I am particularly pleased with this case. When Kemen started to lose weight and became listless, they didn't delay getting him seen. Their daughter had a standard poodle with Addison's, so they were at least familiar with it."

"Lucky for you!"

Nathan nodded. "Even more so for Kemen."

Jonathan nodded in turn. *If only all our cases could have such happy endings.* He punched Nathan lightly on the arm. "So, what's on the agenda for the rest of the day?"

"Glad you asked!" He pulled a sheet of paper from under the pile of files on his desk and glanced at the agenda for the next couple of days. "First, I'm to give you a tour of the facility, then you meet with the director of Human Resources at 3:30, the Medical Director and Clinical Director at 4:00, and, apparently, the Big Kahuna, our executive director, will meet with you first thing in the morning, and there are a whole lot of meet and greets, etc., tomorrow, but we can go over those later." Nathan grinned at Jonathan.

"Why are you smiling like that? What's going on?"

"Nothing. Well, almost nothing. Since you will likely be wrapping up around five, I have taken the liberty of arranging a squash match with some of the vets, followed by dinner at my place."

"You're cooking? Did you warn these people?"

"Ha-ha-ha. I am doing steaks on the grill, and I picked up some sides from Whole Foods, so don't worry. But for now, let me show you around. I think you'll be pleasantly surprised. Between us and the university, we have everything you could want as a vet."

Except for the most interesting clients in the world, Jonathan thought. "I bet you do!" he replied as another thought seeped into his consciousness: *And no DeeDee Guzman.*

The following Sunday, Jonathan and Nathan sprawled on the couch in Nathan's house to watch the final game in the Cincinnati Reds vs. Chicago Cubs series. Being the two worst teams in the league, they were evenly matched, and Jonathan was sure his beloved Cubs would take the series having won the first game and losing the second by only one run. Nathan was equally confident that the Reds would dominate. No matter the outcome, they were enjoying the chance to relax together over a friendly rivalry.

"YES!" Nathan jumped up, nearly spilling his beer. The Reds had just tied the score due to an unforced error on the part of Chicago's shortstop. But he was able to redeem himself, more or less, when the next batter hit a line drive right to him. It was the third out with two men left on base.

"You couldn't do that last time?" Jonathan scolded the TV and sighed. "Well, at least we stopped your rally."

"That you did, but we still have two innings left to score," Nathan said as "Take Me Out to the Ball Game" started the seventh-inning stretch. "Need another beer?"

"No, I'm okay," Jonathan replied as he strode out onto the patio and stretched. Nathan followed.

"So, what are you thinking about regarding the job? It seems to me that you enjoyed the visit and liked the people, or am I wrong?"

"No, you're not wrong. I really was impressed with the Animal Care Center and the university. I liked everyone I met. Well, with the possible exception of the HR person—Hillary, I think her name was. Is there some requirement that HR people be . . . I don't know, so self-important and serious?"

Nathan laughed. "I know exactly what you mean, but don't let that discourage you, especially since I'm pretty sure that the job is yours for the taking."

"It's very tempting, and I am leaning toward accepting."

"But?"

Jonathan took a deep breath and gazed out over the small but tidy lawn. *How do I explain this? Is there any other way besides letting him in on it?*

He turned back to his friend. "There's something I haven't told you about my practice, something that makes it very hard for me to step away."

"DeeDee?"

"No, I told you she was engaged, so that's not even a possibility, and you know Anita and I broke up, so it's not the human element." He paused and ran his hands through his hair several times before continuing. *What if I only told him one thing and somehow played down the mythological aspect.* "You know that I have always said we have a more *diverse* practice than you might imagine for a rural setting."

"Yeah . . ."

"And I've called you several times about this diverse practice."

Nathan grinned. "I assume you are referring to the Cushing's consult, the animal training referral, contact lenses—need I go on?"

"No, I mean, yes—I mean that you don't need to go on, but yes, those are the, uh, things, and they're not what you might think."

"Jon, what the hell are you trying to say?"

"Well, um . . ." Jonathan started to pace. *What do I say? Should I take Dad's tried-and-true legal advice and just "Answer the questions he asks*"? "We have . . ." He cleared his throat and tried again. "We have some patients that I never anticipated. They're *o-other* animals—some I never knew existed, and um, they have very special needs."

"Animals you never *knew* existed? What are you talking about? Jackalopes?"

"Not likely! Those are Western plain animals that rarely, if ever, migrate this far east."

"*Not likely?*" Nathan put down his beer and scratched the back of his head with both hands. "So, what *are* you likely to encounter?"

Well, for better or worse, I guess I'm committed now. Jonathan looked his friend right in the eye and said, "A basilisk."

"A what?"

"A basilisk."

"You mean an Australian frilled lizard?"

"No. A genuine basilisk . . . with an eye infection." He sat down, weak with relief from coming clean, but also terrified. *What have I done? Have I betrayed Xavier, Strong, Tyrone, everyone?*

Nathan paced the deck. "An eye infection?" He stopped and turned toward Jonathan and snapped his fingers. "Aha! Now I get why you're so interested in contact lenses for reptiles!"

Jonathan just nodded.

Nathan resumed pacing. Shaking his head, he asked, "How is this even possible? I thought this stuff didn't exist outside of myths . . . and legends . . . and . . . and *Harry Potter!*"

"Before coming to Carrollton, I would have agreed with you. But I swear, it's true."

Nathan stopped pacing, picked up his beer, stared at the label, and snorted. "Dragon's Milk, Bourbon Barrel Stout Ale!

Seems rather fitting for the occasion, but I think I need something stronger. How about you?"

Jonathan nodded as Nathan turned to go inside. *I do need to head back this evening, but I don't think that's going to happen any time soon, and a shot of whiskey might help.*

Nathan returned with some Jamesons and poured them each a shot and sat down across from Jonathan. He leaned in and lifted his glass. "To you, my good friend! Know that there are far better things ahead than any we leave behind."

"Hear, hear!" Jonathan replied, and they downed their shots.

Nathan made them each a Jameson and ginger ale. Then, settling back in his chair, he shook his head and said, "I'm not sure I'm ready for this, but . . . tell me everything you know about this guy."

CHAPTER 30

Jonathan was about an hour into his roughly five-and-a-half-hour drive to Carrollton when he stopped to use the restroom and get himself another cup of coffee. Though he hadn't left as late as he feared, he hadn't hit the road as early as he would have preferred either, so he called DeeDee and asked if she could keep Bingley another night.

"Absolutely! He's been the perfect house guest, and I think Duncan believes he has moved in for the duration."

"Thanks, DeeDee. I appreciate it, and I'm glad he's been a good boy. I hope I can reciprocate the hospitality some time."

"I will keep that in mind, though I am not sure Duncan will be as well behaved as your Mr. Bingley!" She laughed.

"I'm quite sure he will be a perfect gentleman should the occasion arise." Jonathan swallowed the lump collecting in his throat. "But, I should probably hang up now, as I am driving, and the traffic around Cincinnati is remarkably bad for a Sunday night. I'll see you in the morning."

"Sounds good. Drive safe."

Jonathan dropped his phone onto the seat next to him, wishing he had an excuse to call her again, but, as it was, the heavy traffic quickly forced thoughts of DeeDee Guzman aside.

When the traffic thinned, the decisions that refused to be ignored, resurfaced. Coffee, he hoped, would coalesce his scattered thoughts. Well, that and Mozart. When he was in high school, his father suggested that Mozart might help him concentrate when he studied. He scoffed, of course, then tried it one night when his parents were out for the evening. The next day he scored the highest mark on the biology midterm, besting even Yale-bound Parker T. Styvescent III. From that point, any time serious thought was required, Mozart was on deck.

As the Jupiter symphony swelled in the background, Jonathan thought about the two jobs. *It's really hard to compare them. They're so different, and not just like apples and oranges different. It's more like, I don't know, apples and parking spaces! I'm not sure how to weigh them against one another.*

The next exit was twenty minutes away. Mozart would have to suffice for the moment. *So maybe I don't try to compare them side by side, but instead ask myself what do I want more? Stability, salary, fixed hours, and clients who are just one species and not a combination . . . or lower pay, odd hours, difficult treatment plans, and animals who can kill you by just looking at you?*

He laughed. *When I put it that way, it hardly seems there's a choice. Who wouldn't take the road less deadly?* He passed a trucker with a load of pigs, then eased into the right lane. *Still, something draws me back. What? Duty? To whom? Xavier, the creatures, the people?*

Jonathan hummed along to part of the *Allegro Vivace* to distract himself, but something niggled at the back of his mind. *Okay. I do owe something to Xavier, no doubt about that. He took a chance on me, and I can't leave without cleaning up this basilisk mess and helping him find a replacement.*

He rubbed the back of his neck. *Ugh, and now I have to tell him Nathan knows about the basilisk. He won't be pleased. But, c'mon—we wouldn't have a solution to this without his help. Besides, who's Nathan gonna tell?*

The niggling persisted.

What the heck is catching me up here? Is it DeeDee? It can't be—well, at the very least, it shouldn't be. Though I would just as soon avoid seeing her as Mrs. Doctor 90210. But, no, that's not it . . . it's something more.

Thoughts of Bluebell nudging him with her horn for a treat, Lucretius stamping his foot and raising enormous clouds of dust, Delta and her new foal, Melina, Gremsboc's volume, and Tyrone's melt-in-your-mouth scones surfaced, unbidden but not necessarily unwanted. *And Gertrude. I've gotten so good at making dandelion tea. Who knew that would be a valuable vet skill?* He felt a dull ache in his chest when he thought of not seeing any of them again.

He took a deep breath, and the tightness eased. *Okay, these animals and the people who watch over them are my friends, and of course I will miss them when I leave, but that could be said about any job! I mean, it was hard to leave Spain. I had good friends there, but I was fine.*

A small voice whispered, *Fine is not the same as good.*

I know that! Jonathan argued with the voice. *Sometimes fine is all we get; sometimes good is not an option! And who said that this Carrollton job was good anyway, that this whole situation is good? Seems to me, all it has done is cause me a ton of grief.*

The voice persisted. *But the other side of grief is what . . . joy?* It was then that he knew what was holding him back. *What has given me more joy in the past year than anything else?*

Bingley. He sighed.

Is that enough reason to stay? He can't go with me. I can't risk exposing him, but . . . is that really, truly, reason enough to stay?

Jonathan bit his lower lip and concentrated on merging onto 70E from 71N, but the thought of leaving Bingley behind scratched at his consciousness. *Hold on. Didn't DeeDee just give me the way out, if I want it? I bet she'd take him, and then he* would *be with Duncan for the duration.*

He shook his head and turned off the highway to use the bathroom and get another coffee. *I don't know what I'm going to do,* Jonathan lied to himself, *but at least I know what the obstacles are.*

DeeDee set the now-silent phone on the counter, kinda wishing she had an excuse to call Jonathan back. She turned to the two expectant faces earnestly gazing up at her. "Seems Jon left later than he expected and won't be home till after midnight—so Bingley, you are our guest for one more night."

Worry flashed across the black dog's face as he reached for Blobby. DeeDee squatted down and scratched his ears, then wrapped her arms around him as he put his head on her shoulder and softly squeaked the toy in her ear. Duncan, not wanting to miss out, waved his tail and leaned into her on the other side, causing the trio to cascade onto the floor.

"Enough already!" DeeDee giggled as she put her arms over her face in a vain attempt to quell the canine ablutions. She somehow managed to sit up and lean against the refrigerator. Duncan and Bingley quieted themselves and, each claiming a side of her, laid their heads on her lap.

"I guess I'm not going anywhere—at least for the time being." She sank her hands into their soft manes and stroked the sighing beasts. It hit her, not for the first time, how right it felt to have two dogs, not any two dogs, but these two dogs in particular. "We're lucky, you know, that Marc isn't here. He's fine with one dog, but I don't think he'd tolerate two, much less two who pin you to the ground."

Bingley sighed again and let go of Blobby. It rolled between his front legs. He wrapped his left paw around it and pulled it close to his chest. It reminded DeeDee of a toddler she'd seen this week who'd clung to her well-loved bunny while sitting frozen in place. DeeDee offered to listen to the toy's heart first, and the three-year-old hesitated only momentarily before holding up BunBun for his examination. The rest of the visit, much to the mother's relief, continued without a hitch. Marcus's only comment was, "That's great. Maybe I should get stuffed rabbits for all my linebackers."

Duncan stretched and draped his front leg over DeeDee's lap and onto Bingley's shoulder. "Oh, Duncan! You do love Bingley, don't you?" She dabbed at her stinging eyes with the cuff of her hoodie. "I'm sure Jon would appreciate you taking such good care of his buddy—I know I do." She stroked the canines' soft ears, and smiled as she remembered Jonathan's unrehearsed affection as he massaged Bingley's ear the day of the thunderstorm. "How *does* he get the right spot every time, huh, guys?"

"It's a gift," Bingley grunted. The phone sprang to life just as Bingley snuggled in closer and put his leg across Duncan's. DeeDee, now officially held captive by two retrievers, felt like Tantalus as she grasped for the phone. Just before it went to voice-mail, she broke free of the dogs and grabbed it.

JULIE FUDGE SMITH

"Hello! We've been trying to reach you concerning your vehicle's extended warranty. You should have received a notice in the mail about your car's extended warranty eligibility. Since we've not—"

"Oh, for crying out loud!" DeeDee snapped. She turned to encounter two bewildered and somewhat distressed retrievers.

"What was that all about?" Bingley reproached. "We were comfortable back there."

"I'm sorry. I thought it might be Jon."

CHAPTER 31

Tyrone luffed the barber's cape onto Xavier as the vet popped the last of his blueberry muffin into his mouth. "That was really good," he said, spewing crumbs down the front of the cape. "May I have another, please?"

"Certainly—when I finish with this mop you call hair! When was the last time you got a haircut, Xavier? 2010?"

"Not quite, but it's been a while. Since retiring, I haven't paid much attention to haircuts. Janice finally said that she'd attack it while I was sleeping if I didn't get over to see you, and you know that Janice is a woman of her word!"

Tyrone nodded. "That she is! Now, what are we doing here?"

Xavier gave a vague description of what he wanted and sighed. "Do whatever you think will make Janice happy."

As Tyrone launched his assault, Xavier eyed the muffins and tried to calculate if he could reach them from his current position. He couldn't, at least not without the risk of being stabbed in the jugular by Tyrone's flying shears, so he turned his attention elsewhere. "Jon tells me that you are working on an article about marginal hybrids?"

"I was! I just finished it and sent it off to the editor for *The Bestiary Society Annual Review.* I was quite pleased with it, if I do say so myself, and I hope Lawrence likes it as well." Tyrone moved to the front of Xavier to see if his sides were even. They were. He nodded to himself and started on Xavier's bangs.

"Ptooey." Xavier spat out the small hairs from his bangs. "Is Lawrence the editor?"

"Yes, Lawrence Pendergast-Jones, to be precise." Tyrone stepped back to view his work, shook his head, and launched a new attack on Xavier's bangs.

"He's tough, demands solid research and citations, but," Tyrone snipped some stray hairs from over Xavier's left ear, and moved to tidy up the back, "his periodical is *the* best in the business and very prestigious to get into. There you go!" Tyrone handed Xavier a mirror.

The vet nodded his approval. "Much better than when I came in, but I think it could use a bit more off the sides. What do you think?"

The faun studied Xavier from the front. "I agree." He picked up his shears and began snipping. "Do you know what marginal hybrids are? I ask because most *people* do not."

"I do! I have a bestiary that was my grandfather's, and I remember asking him about the creatures in the borders. He called them marginal hybrids."

Tyrone nodded. "I'm not terribly surprised. According to my mother, Rupert was a clever and witty man, but I don't think she knew he had a bestiary." He stopped to survey his work, then continued, "I think she would have told me about it since I love comparing animals across different bestiaries."

"So, what do your different bestiaries say about basilisks? Mine has nary a mention."

Tyrone stopped snipping. "There isn't a lot in any of the bestiaries, so you must grab bits and pieces where you can. There is, however, good information about basilisks in *The Feejee Mermaid*. Have you read that?"

"No, I don't think so."

"Let me get it." Tyrone put down the shears and left the kitchen for the library. Xavier seized the moment and grabbed another muffin. He had the paper off and a large bite stuffed in his mouth when Tyrone entered the kitchen with the book.

"Aha! So, all this talk about the basilisk was just a ruse to get another muffin?" Tyrone picked up the wrappers from both of Xavier's muffins and popped them into his mouth. "What can I say, it's my favorite part!"

"Your secret is safe with me, Tyrone," Xavier said. "But really, I'd like to know more about this creature. We've never had one before—at least that I know of."

"Here, the relevant chapter starts on page 161." He handed Xavier the book. "It's out of print now, but not too hard to find a used one online. And there are several bestiaries online with wonderful illustrations. The texts are generally in Latin, so let me know if you need any translated."

Xavier thumbed through the chapter, alighting at the picture that had captivated Jon and Strong. "Do I have this right?" He pointed at the illustration. "This basilisk was tamed?" He scratched his nose and sniffed from the fine hairs dusting his face, then before Tyrone could answer, he added, "You know, apparently Strong and Florence are making great headway with training Cowper."

Tyrone took a deep breath, set down his shears, and handed Xavier the mirror once again. Xavier nodded his approval. Tyrone stood behind him, and as he removed the barber's cape, he tapped his hoof and grasped Xavier by the shoulder. Looking in the mirror, he caught Xavier's eye. "I *do* understand and *deeply* appreciate the effort being put into trying to save and re-establish the natural order of things. I do."

"But?"

Tyrone exhaled and squeezed the vet's shoulders. "Xavier, if I may be so bold . . ." He shook his head as if to clear any resistance. "I've been thinking that the most prudent course of action may be to euthanize Cowper. I shudder to think of what may happen should he escape and kill someone. Police investigations, reporters snooping around—what if they find Delta, or Bluebell, or me? We'd lose *everything*."

Xavier turned and looked at Tyrone. "*Thank you* for telling me this, Tyrone." He swallowed before adding, "But we have committed a lot of time and energy to this plan, and though I share your concerns, and will relay them to Jon, I am inclined to go ahead with the ocular inserts, wait a month to see if they work, and make sure the enclosure is *truly* secure. We can always choose to euthanize, but I—we—want to be certain there are no other viable options."

Tyrone took another deep breath and nodded. "I understand, but *please* remember, this animal is cleverer than you may think and not as passive as it may appear. The passivity may be due to its illness, so I am warning you, *do not take it for granted, do not underestimate it, and never, ever trust it.*"

CHAPTER 32

On the Friday after Xavier's haircut, Nathan arrived with the polarized lenses for Cowper, several practice lenses, and an amiable iguana named Billy Bob, who was used by the vet school for demonstrations of reptile care—including ocular inserts. Nathan was currently "babysitting" Billy Bob while his owner, Victoria, a research vet at the university and Nathan's current love interest, was on vacation.

Jonathan was glad to see his friend but nervous about him meeting the "Cowper Crew," as they called themselves. DeeDee was the only one who trusted his judgment about disclosing the situation to Nathan. Florence had stared at him, and Strong shook his head when he told them.

"You're absolutely sure we can trust him?" Strong asked.

"Yes. I have no doubt, *whatsoever*, that he can be trusted."

The farmer shook his head again, but it was Florence who spoke up. "I don't envy you having to explain this to Xavier, and I wouldn't want to be on the receiving end of whatever he has to say."

As it turned out, Xavier didn't say anything when Jonathan told him that Nathan knew about Cowper. But his stony silence spoke volumes, and Jonathan knew his work was cut out for him when it came to proving Nathan was worth the risk.

Although they'd all met Nathan at the ball, dinner that Friday evening was for the express purpose of the crew getting to know, like, and hopefully, trust him. The Kentucky bourbon, courtesy of Nathan, flowed freely, and the outsider did his best to answer questions, and not ask too many.

"I can only imagine how uncomfortable this must be for you," Nathan said as he mixed another drink for Xavier. "Is there anything you'd like to ask me?"

Xavier took a draw of the expertly mixed cocktail. "Why should I trust that you won't tell anyone about this?"

"You probably shouldn't. I wouldn't in your situation." Nathan motioned for them to sit at the table for two by the window. "Except for one thing."

"And that is?"

"Jonathan. Do you trust him? Has he ever acted in a way, other than telling me about the basilisk, that would make you think he has acted outside the best interests of this practice or this community?"

Xavier furrowed his brow as he sipped his drink.

"Look, in his first year, Jonathan asked me a few endocrine questions but didn't reveal anything. Even at the Millionaire's Ball, he said nothing. If he wanted to spill the beans, don't you think he would have said something sooner, before things got messy?"

Xavier raised his eyebrows and nodded.

"So, if you trust him, and he trusts me, I am asking you to give me a chance. I'm here to help, and I promise that I'm not going to say anything to anyone about this."

Xavier sat back in the chair and looked Nathan in the eye. "I do trust Jon, and we do need your help. So I guess I have to take a chance that you are a man of your word." He offered Nathan his hand.

Jonathan watched as the men smiled and shook hands. As he massaged the back of his neck, DeeDee passed by him headed to the dinner table with the salad. She turned and beamed. "I told you it would work out."

Xavier, Jonathan, Nathan, DeeDee, Strong, and Florence gathered the next morning at the clinic to plan and practice their strategy for inserting the contact lenses into the eyes of the basilisk.

"I experimented with polarized panels on Cowper's enclosure," Strong said as he handed a face mask to each participant. "The polarization not only seemed to protect anyone looking at the beast, but also prevented mirrored sunglasses from killing *him*. So, I made these to use when training him, and I thought we ought to wear them during the procedure."

"I think you'll find that they are surprisingly comfortable and give something like 270 degrees visibility and protection," Florence said as she demonstrated how to put it on like a welder's mask. "And they fit over glasses, so we'll have double protection."

"These are fabulous, Strong!" Nathan declared as he adjusted his head band. "I think there might be a huge market for these babies!"

"Because there are so many people doing ocular surgery on killer reptiles?" Jonathan quipped. "Not that they aren't fabulous, because they are," he said as he winked at Strong. "I'm just not sure what the market would be for 270-degree polarized face masks."

"What about spitting snakes?" DeeDee asked. "They might be useful when dealing with dangerous reptiles—though I'm not sure why they would need to be polarized for that."

"Or llamas," Nathan added. "They spit, don't they?"

"Only when provoked, and not as much at people as they do at other llamas," Xavier said. "A female will do it to tell a male she is not interested in his advances."

"You know, that's not a half bad idea! I wonder if that would work on the males of our species?" DeeDee laughed and exchanged glances with Florence.

"Yes, it would," Nathan said.

"You know this from . . . experience?" Jonathan asked.

"No comment," Nathan replied, his neck and ears growing red. "Okay, so now that everyone has their gear in place, let me show you how this is done."

Strong and Jonathan wrapped Billy Bob tightly in a towel and held him in place as Nathan showed them how to insert the lens into the iguana's eye, as well as how to remove it. "Not that we have any intention of removing this thing, but it is useful to know, just in case."

Jonathan struggled with the procedure, but eventually got the hang of it. Xavier was adept, but it was DeeDee who mastered it effortlessly.

"Fabulous job, DeeDee!" Nathan effused. "You have incredibly fine motor skills. I'm surprised you aren't a surgeon."

DeeDee, unaccustomed to flattery, flushed, but retained her composure as she removed the lens and dropped it in the stainless steel bowl filled with optical saline solution. "Thank you, Nathan. I did enjoy my surgical rotation, but I missed the personal interaction that comes with family practice." She straightened up and stretched her back. "And I knew that I'd be coming back to Carrollton, where the need for family medicine is high. Still, it's *fun* to stretch my skills!"

Nathan laughed. "That's exactly what I said when Victoria showed me how to do this!" He high-fived DeeDee.

Xavier nodded to Jonathan and Strong to put Billy Bob back into his crate. "So, I think we are all in agreement that, to get this done quickly and efficiently, DeeDee is our best chance. Although I have to say this makes me uncomfortable."

DeeDee squeezed Xavier's upper arm. "Thank you for your concern, Xavier, but I do think I am the right choice. Besides, if you continue to protest, I might have to spit on you!"

Everyone laughed but sobered up when Nathan asked, "What about sedating him for this procedure? Would that make it easier or safer?"

Jonathan sighed. "I'm reluctant to do that since the last time we sedated Cowper, it took several days to wear off, even though I used *less* sedative the second time than the first. And, he had his eyes tightly shut the entire time, so I am not sure we could even get the contacts in."

"Also," Florence said as she glanced at Strong, "we've been working with Cowper regularly, and he is trained to go into the tube and be still."

"Not to mention the weasels," Strong added.

"Weasels?" DeeDee and Nathan said in unison.

Jonathan was reminded of how little Nathan knew about this practice and wondered just how much to divulge. "Yes, weasels are the natural enemy of the basilisk and the only ones unaffected by his—um—powers. So, we have some trained weasels who guard Cowper 24/7."

"Trained weasels?" Nathan asked. "Where, pray tell, does one find weasels trained to guard a basilisk?"

"Nottingham."

"England?"

"Yes, of course!" Jonathan replied. "Is there any other?"

"I have no idea, but even if there were, why would you go there for weasels when, I presume, the best guard weasels come from the original Nottingham . . . forest?" Nathan sat down.

"Exactly!" Jonathan laughed and squeezed Nathan's shoulder.

Jonathan grew somber. "Look, *I know* this is a lot to take in, and it absolutely boggles the mind. But I also know that I have to trust the people in this room. They've lived here all their lives and know best how to approach the situation at hand. And, best of all, they'll have your back, no matter what."

Nathan stood up and inhaled deeply. "You're right, this is a lot to take in," he said as he surveyed the room. "But I'm grateful to be here, and I'll do what I can."

"Thanks, Nathan. That's all we ask," Xavier said.

CHAPTER 33

Jonathan stood in the doorway of the old barn, contemplating the heat waves warping his view of Strong securing livestock in the other barn. *Hmmm. The air has been still all day. I wonder how little a breeze would be needed to sweep away the heat waves?*

"Jon?" Xavier called, startling him from his reverie.

Jonathan turned and entered the old barn. Large fans mounted at either end of the hay loft kept the building cool, and sent the sweet smell of timothy hay floating down to him. He took a deep breath and sighed as he watched barn swallows swoop in and out of the barn with food for their chicks. *Probably the second brood for most of them. Whoa! I thought for sure that one was going to hit the wall!* He shook his head and tossed his keys onto a hay bale alongside his ball cap. *Just a fraction of an inch difference, or moving a second too late, and . . .*

"Can you tighten this up for me?" Xavier asked Jonathan as he arrived at the older vet's side. "I can't seem to get it cinched." The Cowper Crew was now assembling at Strong's barn after honing their plans over lunch.

Jonathan looked at the polarized face mask that Xavier was attempting to adjust and cinched it a bit tighter. "I think that's all the farther it'll go."

Xavier frowned and shook his head. "Okay, it feels a bit loose, but it seems to be staying in place, so I guess I'm good to go. DeeDee? How about you?"

DeeDee shook her head vigorously to the left and right and gave a tepid thumbs-up. "Mine feels fine."

Jonathan and Nathan secured their masks and set the lenses on the instrument tray along with other medical supplies in a secured area. Everything was ready, including posting Strong outside as a lookout in case someone should come onto the property unexpectedly, but Xavier did not give the go-ahead. Instead, he paused and looked at each of them in turn, then took a deep breath. "Look, I know this is unorthodox and dangerous, but I also know that each of us is dedicated to the preservation of life whenever possible. Let's work toward a restitution of the natural order, to the best of our abilities, and to the health and comfort of the animals and the people in our care. May God guide our hands. St. Blaise and St. Francis of Assisi, pray for us."

Xavier rubbed his hands together and nodded. "Let's do this." They donned their eye protection, and Jonathan signaled to Florence to bring in the basilisk.

"Come on now, Cowper," Florence cajoled as she led the creature, surrounded by three weasels, to the pipe. Strong rang the bell, and Cowper's head, up to his shoulders, popped out the far side, leaving only his tail hanging out the entrance. The portcullises were lower, and one weasel stationed himself at Cowper's head, while the other two were relegated to tail duty.

"Now, let's roll him gently onto his right side so we can do the left eye insert," Xavier instructed.

Nathan and Jonathan carefully maneuvered the creature onto his side. Xavier nodded to DeeDee. She took a deep breath and reached for the first lens. Xavier reached over and held the basilisk's eyelids open. DeeDee skillfully inserted the lens, stepped back, and exhaled. She took another deep breath. It rattled out slowly. "Whew! One down . . ." She attempted a smile.

Nathan and Jonathan exchanged glances while Xavier looked directly at her. "Are you okay?"

"Yeah, I guess I'm just a bit—"

But before she could finish her sentence, several things happened at once. When everyone, including Florence and the weasels, looked at the stammering DeeDee, the basilisk rolled and flicked its tail toward Xavier. The hooked barb caught the vet's face mask and flung it across the room, dislodging his sunglasses in the process. Before Xavier could retrieve his glasses, Cowper looked him straight in the eye with his right eye. Xavier gasped and sank to the floor. DeeDee and Jonathan rushed to his side. He wasn't breathing. DeeDee checked for a pulse. Finding none, she and Jonathan started CPR. As Jonathan began compressions, DeeDee called 9-1-1.

Meanwhile, the weasels jumped onto the basilisk, subduing it on its left side. Nathan, not realizing the full extent of what had happened, stayed focused on the task at hand and looked for something to cover the basilisk's head. Florence was ahead of him, however, and threw a towel over Cowper's head. They both knew this was a temporary fix.

Nathan looked at Florence and tilted his head toward the instrument tray with the lens for the right eye. Florence nodded and turned on the weasels. "You hold him *tight*, you hear me?"

The weasels doubled down on the creature.

". . . and thirty," Jonathan said.

DeeDee gave two breaths, and Jonathan started compressions again.

His counting did not register with Nathan, who was concentrating on finishing what they'd begun. He picked up the lens. "Okay, so here's what we do. You lift the towel and hold his head still, and I'll insert the lens. Then we get this guy outta here before the paramedics arrive."

Sirens could just be heard in the distance.

"Got it."

"Ready?"

"Yes."

"Go!" he said, and Florence ripped off the towel.

Nathan moved quickly to insert the lens. The basilisk hissed and jerked its head, but Nathan, albeit clumsily, edged the contact into place. Cowper quieted as the weasels loomed over him. Nathan slumped onto a bale of straw, resting his head in his hands as he tried to steady his breathing.

Florence ordered the weasels to back the creature out of the tube and, together, they moved Cowper into his enclosure. She warned Martin, the senior weasel from Nottingham, "Under *NO* circumstances can you allow this beast to get out, nor can any of you make *any* noise until otherwise instructed. *Have I made myself clear?*"

"Yes, mum—crystal." Martin turned and chirped at his small battalion of basilisk guards. Silence fell upon the enclosure as the wailing sirens grew louder.

Florence walked swiftly out the side door of the barn.

"Strong!"

He turned, and one look told him something was terribly, terribly wrong. He rushed over to her. "Florence, what is it? Are you okay?"

"I'm fine." Her voice trembled as she added, "But Cowper got Xavier, and he collapsed. They're doing CPR." She swallowed, took a deep breath, and continued. "I got it back in the enclosure and told the weasels they have to be silent. The squad is on its way. Can you bring them in when they get here?"

"Yes, of course! Is there anything else I can do for them, for you?"

She threw her arms around Strong's neck and whispered in his ear, "Pray."

"I already am," he whispered back. Florence let go and headed toward the barn.

"Has anyone called Janice?" he called after her, but she didn't respond. The sirens were closing in. Strong closed his eyes as he pressed the heels of his palms into his forehead. "*Shit,* what do I do? Do I call her? Do I go ask?"

He felt something, *someone* nudge his leg. He opened his eyes to see Gertrude gazing up at him. A single tear slid down her cheek. "Call her. It vill cause no harm to care."

"Thank you, Gertrude." Strong pulled out his phone. Not having her cell number, he dialed their home phone, uncertain as to whether or not he wanted her to answer.

Florence reentered the barn and headed toward DeeDee and Jonathan. Nathan intercepted her. "Thank you." He squeezed her upper arm. "I, we couldn't have done this without you." She glanced at Nathan and gave a half smile.

". . . and thirty," Jonathan said yet again.

DeeDee gave another two breaths.

Florence hugged herself while tears coursed down her cheeks as she prayed for deliverance.

Only then did Nathan grasp the full extent of what was happening.

Jonathan, sweating profusely, was visibly tiring after twenty minutes of CPR. So, after DeeDee gave another two breaths, Nathan stepped in and took over the compressions.

Jonathan resisted, but DeeDee pulled him away. "Let him help, Jon." She squeezed his hand and knelt next to the inert older vet. "Please come back, Xavier, please . . ."

She gave him another two breaths, and Nathan started the next round of compressions while Jonathan paced and begged God to spare his friend.

The ambulance screamed into the farmyard. Strong threw open the barn door, and the paramedics rushed in with a defibrillator.

DeeDee rose to greet them.

"How long have you been doing CPR?" a paramedic asked.

"Um . . . um . . ." Jonathan stuttered.

DeeDee shook her head.

Nathan kept compressing Xavier's chest, too preoccupied to answer.

"Twenty-three minutes, more or less," Florence replied. "Dr. St. Roche and Dr. Guzman started the compressions as soon as Dr. Pratt collapsed, so they wouldn't have checked the time."

The paramedics exchanged looks. "Any return of spontaneous circulation or breathing?"

"No," DeeDee said, then sighed. "Florence is right. We

started CPR within a minute or so of Xavier collapsing, but despite that, there has been no ROSC."

As DeeDee talked, the paramedics prepped Xavier for defibrillation. "CLEAR!"

KA-THUMP.

Nothing.

"Again," said a paramedic.

KA-THUMP.

Nothing.

"Again," DeeDee ordered.

KA-THUMP. Nothing.

"AGAIN!" DeeDee demanded.

The paramedics paused and looked at DeeDee. "Dr. Guzman," one of them whispered.

DeeDee's shoulders slumped as she shook her head almost imperceivably. The paramedics receded to the background, and she knelt down next to her friend. She stroked his forehead, smoothing his, for once, neatly cut bangs into place. Tears brimmed, but she kept them at bay.

Looking at her watch, she said in a clear voice, "Time of death, 4:32 p.m."

Xavier Doolittle Pratt was gone.

PART IV

CHAPTER 34

The only sounds in the barn were Florence's soft weeping and the hushed, efficient movements of the paramedics preparing the body for transport to the hospital morgue.

Jonathan stared at Xavier, daring his friend to defy death. *Get up! You've just fainted or been knocked unconscious.* But the bruises from the compressions belied this alternate reality. DeeDee was still kneeling next to him, unable, *or was it unwilling*, to leave Xavier's side, thereby making it harder for the EMTs to do their job.

Jonathan stepped over to DeeDee, guided her to her feet, and folded her into his arms. His throat tightened as she pressed her face to his chest and gave herself over to grief. Stroking her hair, he tried to think of words that would comfort her and, if truth be told, himself. He knew of no such words, so he simply held her as she wept.

Nathan sat on a nearby straw bale, numb and exhausted. He looked over at Strong, who was holding Florence, and asked, "Do you know if anyone called Xavier's wife?"

"I did. I left a voicemail for her to call me as soon as she got the message, but I haven't heard anything from her." He shifted

Florence a bit to his left and retrieved his phone from his hip pocket. He frowned. "Still haven't heard from her."

"How about if I call her? You and Jon have your hands full."

"No!" DeeDee and Jonathan said at the same time. The paramedics stopped what they were doing and looked at them. Nathan, Strong, and Florence stared as well.

DeeDee stood up straight, wiped her eyes, and said, "What I mean is, I'm the physician who called it, so I should be the one to tell Janice that Xavier died."

The paramedics nodded as they moved Xavier to a collapsible gurney and covered him with a sheet. "Since there was a doctor at the scene to sign the death certificate, we don't need anyone to accompany the body, but we do need you to finalize the paperwork," one of them said as he handed DeeDee a clipboard.

Jonathan caught her by the arm as she started to follow them out and, gently lifting her face to his, he said, "*We* will tell Janice what happened."

"Okay," she acquiesced. "Just let me give them the paperwork."

He let go of her arm and turned to face the others. "I'm so sorry for everything that's happened. None of you deserved to go through this."

"Nor did you, Jon," Nathan said, gripping Jonathan by both shoulders. "Nor did you."

Jonathan put his hands over Nathan's and leaned into the support of his friend, head bowed. He took a few deep breaths and stood up straight. "Thanks, Nathan—I'm grateful you're here."

They heard the gravel crunch under the tires of the ambulance as DeeDee walked back into the barn. She looked at Jonathan. "I think we should find Janice and take her to the hospital. I don't want her going there alone."

"Good, that's good," Jonathan said. "Um, let me get my keys." He patted his pants pockets, then looked around the barn. "Or should we take your car? That way Nathan has—"

"Don't you worry about me. You just focus on what you and DeeDee need to do," Nathan interrupted. He nodded toward Strong. "We'll take care of everything else."

The sound of a car coming to an abrupt halt in the drive startled them into silence. A car door slammed, and Janice Pratt appeared, white-faced, in the door of the barn. "What happened? Why was there an ambulance leaving here?" She stepped into the barn, looked at their tear-stained, grief-stricken faces, and whispered, "Where is Xavier?"

That broke the spell, and they all started talking.

"STOP!" she ordered. "I can't understand what happened when you all talk at once!" She pointed at DeeDee and Jonathan. "But I did gather that something happened with the basilisk, you two did CPR, and he's in that ambulance, correct?"

They all nodded.

DeeDee opened her mouth to speak, but Janice held up her hand. "Save it! You can tell me on the way to the hospital." She pointed at Jonathan. "You drive! I need to focus on what happened." She moved toward the door. "Let's go! My car! Now!"

DeeDee pulled her keys from her left front pocket, tossed them to Strong, and dashed out to get her purse and cell phone from the front seat of her car.

Nathan grabbed Jonathan's arm and said in a low voice as they headed outside, "Let DeeDee tell the story, and don't interrupt unless Janice asks you something. It will be easier for her to hear it from one person, beginning to end."

Jonathan nodded.

"And one more thing, I know you. Don't take the blame for what happened. If asked, just tell what happened and let her digest that, which is plenty for now. Don't burden her with your supposed guilt."

Jonathan half-smiled and nodded again. "Thanks, Nathan. I don't know when I'll be back."

"Don't worry about a thing. We'll see you when we see you."

They sat in silence as Jonathan sped toward the hospital. His throat constricted, and his eyes burned, but he swallowed the urge to cry.

"Janice, how did you know to come to Strong's?" DeeDee's voice quivered.

"Strong called and left a voicemail. The sound of his voice scared me." She took a tissue from the console, wiped her eyes, and took a deep breath. "So, I just got in my car and drove over."

Jonathan stopped for the left turn into the hospital. Sirens screamed behind them, and an ambulance careened toward the emergency entrance. Janice blanched, and DeeDee feared she would faint, but Janice took some deep breaths and her color slowly returned.

"Janice, why don't you stay here in the car, and I'll go find out where Xavier is. Then, I'll come get you."

"No." She reached over the seat and took DeeDee's hand

as Jonathan parked the car. "I'll go crazy waiting. We'll face this together. That's what I think Xavier would want. I know it's what I want."

"Did Xavier say anything before he collapsed?" Janice asked as she and Jonathan waited while DeeDee gathered the necessary paperwork.

"No. He went down too quickly."

He watched Janice's face fall and guided her to a nearby bench as he added, "But before we started, he reminded us about the importance of preserving life and the natural order, and using our abilities as best we can. And—being Xavier—he asked for the intervention of St. Blaise and St. Francis."

"The old fool! I told him that one day he would die with his boots on. I am so angry, and yet so proud of him." Tears streamed down her face, falling unchecked onto her linen pants. Jonathan, choking on his own grief, handed her a handkerchief, then went to the vending machine across the hall to get some water for all of them.

DeeDee appeared with forms for Janice to sign, but setting them aside, she slipped her arm around the older woman's thin shoulders. Janice leaned into the comfort as DeeDee's tears co-mingled with hers.

Jonathan set the water bottles down and knelt in front of the two women. He handed his second handkerchief to DeeDee, who smiled at the familiar gesture. Before Jonathan could speak, DeeDee pulled Janice closer and whispered, "This is all my fault! I distracted Xavier, and that allowed the basilisk to rip his eye protection off. I am *so, so* sorry."

"DeeDee, please," Jonathan said. "It's not your fault—it's mine. I mishandled it from the beginning, and—"

"No, no, no!" Janice interrupted. She reached for a bottle of water and took a long drink. "If it's anyone's fault, it's that creature's!" She closed her eyes tight to stem the onslaught of tears. "You know, it's probably good that he died doing what he loved, but . . . but he didn't die with *who* he loved."

DeeDee looked at Jonathan, but before either could respond, a portly man in a navy suit walked up to them. "Mrs. Pratt?"

Janice opened her eyes and looked up. Tears cascaded down her face.

"I'm Orville Wellinger Jr., Orville Wellinger's son." He turned and shook hands with Jonathan. "From Wellinger and Son's Funeral Home."

Orville pulled an unopened packet of tissues from his suit-coat pocket and offered them to Janice. "I am so very sorry for your loss. My father knew Dr. Pratt from Rotary and always said how wonderful he was with cats. It's my sincere hope that I can now help you navigate this difficult time."

He nodded to the paperwork next to DeeDee. "Is there anyone else you would like me to call?" he asked as he helped Janice to her feet, and offering her his arm, led them to Xavier.

CHAPTER 35

As they watched Janice's Ford Explorer speed south, Gertrude waddled over and wedged herself between Strong and Florence. Strong stroked her head and put a finger to his lips to warn her not to speak in front of Nathan.

"He doesn't know about you," the farmer mouthed to the goose.

She nodded, honking softly. Silver tears traced her iridescent cheeks.

Nathan turned at the sound. "Hey, Strong, that's some goose you got there," he said.

Strong smiled down at Gertrude. "Yes, she is pretty special."

The way he said "special" made Nathan pause. He sounded exactly like Jonathan when he described the "other" animals in his practice. He took another look at Gertrude. This *really* was no ordinary goose.

"Strong," Nathan said and cleared his throat, "when you say *special*, exactly what do you mean?"

Strong looked at Florence, who looked at Gertrude, who looked at Nathan, and said, "My name is Gertrude Van Gans, und I'm happy to meet you, even under dees conditions." She bowed her head at Nathan but did not leave the security of Florence and Strong.

Nathan stared at the trio, unable to speak.

"Nathan," Florence said, "you should sit down. You look rather pale." She guided him to a bench under a nearby oak and sat down next to him. "I do understand that this is a lot to take in, but considering what you already know and what happened today, this isn't such a big deal, is it?"

He stared at her. "A talking goose, not a big deal? What, exactly, would you call a big deal?"

Florence held his gaze. "If she laid golden eggs, now *that* would be a big deal!"

"Does she?"

"Does she what?"

"Lay golden eggs?"

"No! Of course not." Florence laughed. "That would be ridiculous!"

While Florence tended to Nathan, Strong escorted Gertrude to the new barn. "Gertrude, I fear we may have overwhelmed Jon's friend back there, so why don't you rest in the barn while we tend to him? As soon as I can, I will bring you some tea. Okay?"

Gertrude nodded and climbed onto her nest, tucking her head under a wing. Strong hurried back to Florence and Nathan just in time to hear Florence's declaration that Gertrude did not lay golden eggs.

"Ridiculous!" echoed Strong.

Nathan closed his eyes and put his head in his hands for a long moment. When he raised his head, Strong and Florence were looking at him, concern knitting their brows. He smiled. It'd been a long time since anyone, besides Jonathan, had befriended him like this. He took Florence's hand and kissed the top of it. "Thank you." Looking up at Strong, he added, "Jon's right about you, you know. You're a good guy, a good friend. He's lucky to know both of you."

Before either could reply, Nathan stood up. "Think we should check on Cowper?"

"I'm not sure that I want to check on him as much as kill him," Strong said as they walked to the barn.

"I'm right there with you," Nathan replied, "but I don't think we can actually *do* that." He held the barn door open for Florence and Strong. "At least, not until we talk with Jon."

"I agree," Florence said as they reached the exam table and put their protective eyewear on. "I also think Janice should have a say about it."

Cowper stood in the far corner of the enclosure, facing them, but completely, eerily still.

"Can we get him closer so I can see his eyes?" Nathan asked.

"Sure," Florence said and moved toward the phalanx of weasels huddled near the door to the enclosure. She whispered to the head weasel, "Martin, can you move him closer to us please? And make it look like I'm giving you signals about what to do, okay?"

The head weasel nodded, and softly chirped at three other weasels snacking on boiled eggs. As Florence whistled "commands," the four lanky individuals cajoled Cowper to a spot right in front of the polarized panels. The basilisk's eyes were watery, and a bit crusty in the corner of his right eye, which was also pinker than the left. The lenses, however, were clearly visible.

"I'm ninety-eight percent sure the lenses are in correctly, what do you think?" Nathan asked the farmer.

"I agree," Strong said, "but I am worried that his right eye seems to be infected again."

"Yeah, damn it! I was afraid I might have scratched his cornea." Nathan sighed. "We should probably start him on some antibiotics. Will he take oral antibiotics?"

"Yes, I'll see to it," Florence replied. She didn't think it necessary to elaborate about Martin and his earthworm treats.

"The left eye seems normal," Strong said, "so I was wondering if we should test the lenses—see if they actually stop him from killing something."

Nathan looked at Strong. "Are you volunteering?"

"No! I was thinking of using a mouse. We, uh, I have been using crickets, worms, and mice to test Cowper's recovery." He turned and looked at Nathan. "We wanted to see the effect on different species."

Nathan thought about this for a moment and nodded. "And?"

"Well, as his sight improved, so did his killing power, on all three species." Strong took a bandana from his back pocket and wiped his brow before adding, "But, interestingly, if he looks at any of them through the polarized panels, they don't die, so I am hoping the lenses work the same way."

"Huh, no wonder Jon wanted them polarized." Nathan rubbed the stubble on his chin. "Anyway, I'm game to try, how about you, Florence?"

She nodded and wrinkled her brow. "Why don't you see if there are any antibiotics in Jon's truck, that way we can get him started right away. And Strong and I will get the mice."

Nathan nodded, grabbed Jonathan's keys, and headed to the truck.

"Martin!" Florence waved the weasel over. "We need a couple of mice to test Cowper's eyes. Can you get me two and put them in a live trap?"

Martin nodded and hustled off to procure the volunteers.

Strong stayed at the enclosure while Florence went to intercept Nathan and prevent any unnecessary interactions with the weasels. But just as he returned with the antibiotics, the weasel crew zoomed past, chirping and squealing. "Careful, boys! Watch where you're going," Florence admonished.

It did not escape Nathan's notice that the large mahogany-colored weasel named Martin shot Florence a look and seemed to understand everything she said. He shook his head. "Nope, don't want to know, don't need to know," he muttered as they reached the enclosure.

"Know what?" Strong asked.

"Nothing," Nathan said and took a deep breath. "So, how do you think we should do this? I'd like to try to test both eyes, even if one is infected."

"Well," Strong said as he warmed to the topic, "what if we release a mouse on the right side of Cowper near his back leg, then he will most likely see it with his right eye first. If that works, we can repeat it on the left with the second mouse."

"Sounds like a plan to me. Who's going to release the mouse?"

"I think I can get Martin to do it. He's the best trained," Florence interjected.

"I bet he is," Nathan said.

Florence led the weasel to the entrance at the back of the enclosure, out of sight and earshot of the men.

"Don't want to know, don't need to know how," he mumbled again as they gathered at the polarized panels.

Martin climbed into the enclosure with the trap containing the two mice while the other weasels kept Cowper from looking at Martin and his vermin sacrifice. Once he was behind Cowper, Martin placed a mouse by the basilisk's hind leg. As if on cue, the mouse ran forward, attracting Cowper's attention. The beast looked at him with his right eye, as the mouse ran toward the wall of the enclosure where the humans were watching. It veered left and crossed in front of Cowper, who then followed it with his left eye. The mouse raced to a back corner of the enclosure and scurried along the baseboard with Cowper in hot pursuit.

The weasels jumped up and down, squealing and chirping. One of the weasels knocked into the trap in Martin's hand, sending the second mouse somersaulting through the air and landing with a splash in Cowper's water bowl. The basilisk turned and charged the newest contestant, who leaped out of the bowl and fled for its life. Reaching the wall, mouse number two, like his compatriot, raced along the baseboard, desperately seeking an escape hatch. Cowper, with the weasels close behind, eventually cornered both mice. He stared at them, and though they didn't move, neither did they die.

Strong, Nathan, and Florence hugged one another, grateful that *something* had gone right that day, while the weasels squealed amongst themselves. No one, animal or human, noticed Cowper open his mouth and exhale on the mice. The rodents swooned and swayed and stumbled over one another as if intoxicated, before passing out, but they did not die.

Cowper backed away from the comatose mice and let the weasels move in for the final kill. He turned and looked in the direction of the ecstatic humans. Something about him sent chills down Nathan's spine. Then he saw it. The basilisk was smiling.

Nathan shook off the chill and turned, with Strong and Florence, to the sobering task of cleaning up from the procedure. "I'll pack the medical supplies," Florence suggested, "and you two can clean up the disposables. It shouldn't take long."

And she was right. In fifteen minutes the barn was back to its normal chaos.

"Well, I think that's it." Nathan looked around for any errant item. "Florence, do you want me to take the medical supplies to the clinic?"

"They're already in my car. I will bring them to work on Monday, but thanks for offering. Oh, and Nathan?"

"Yes?"

"If you need anything before Jon gets home, don't hesitate to call either one of us. Being alone can be tough."

"Thanks, Florence. I'll keep that in mind." He leaned over and kissed her cheek. He shook Strong's hand, then climbed into Jonathan's truck and punched the "Home" button on the GPS. "Funny thing," he muttered to himself as he headed down the driveway, "I kinda feel like I *am* going home."

Bingley heard the truck rumble down the long gravel drive. He stretched and trotted to the back door to wait for his person to cross the threshold.

"*Finally*," he muttered as the car door shut and footsteps crunched in the gravel.

Wiggling and tapping his front paws, left, right, left, right, left, right, he positioned himself for maximum effectiveness. When the lock turned and the door swung open, he launched himself at Jonathan, asking, "What took you so long? What happened with the contact—" Only, it wasn't Jonathan, it was Nathan! He backed away and sat down, his tail twitching back and forth.

"What did you say?"

"Bark."

"No, you didn't."

"Woof?"

Nathan stepped into the house and closed the door. He leaned against it and rubbed his eyes with the heels of his hands while shaking his head. He slid down the door until he was sitting on the floor, head resting against the door, legs stretched out in front of him, eyes closed. Bingley wiggled in between Nathan's legs, one front paw gently patting his friend's thigh. Nathan slumped, and the dog leaned in, rested his head on Nathan's shoulder, and wuffled in his ear.

The comforting warmth of the dog brought Nathan to the brink. He gave himself over to the rising sorrow, wrapped his arms around Bingley, and wept. The musky smell of pine needles and clover from the back of the dog's neck soothed his raw nerves. He had no idea how long it was before he opened his eyes and smiled at the earnest black face.

"Thank you, Bingley. I really needed that." He massaged the dog's ear with his left hand and smiled as Bingley leaned into it and moaned with delight, eyes narrowed to sleepy slits.

Nathan switched hands, and Bingley melted to the right and began slipping into a prone position. Nathan took advantage of the dog being off his guard and murmured, "What did you say when I came in the door?"

"What took you so long and what happened with the—" Bingley bolted upright and closed his mouth.

"So you *can* talk!"

Bingley nodded but avoided eye contact and licked his lips several times.

Nathan mussed the hair on Bingley's head and got to his feet. "I know I should be more shocked, but this has been one helluva day, and right now, I could use a drink."

He walked to Jonathan's liquor cabinet, pulled out a bottle of Jameson and a can of ginger ale, and mixed himself a drink. He made Bingley's dinner, and as he set it down, his pocket buzzed with a text message from Jonathan: *On our way back to Janice's. Should be home within the hour. Will catch up then.*

Nathan replied: *I'll see you when you get here.*

He forwarded the exchange to Strong and Florence and headed out to the deck to watch the twilight acrobatics of the local bat population. As he collapsed into a deck chair, Bingley draped over his feet, he noticed the glittering of fireflies from the pachysandra to the treetops. His mother's voice drifted in from a dusty memory. *You're right, little one,* she'd said as she knelt down beside him. *The ones in the bushes are fireflies.* She pulled him close and lowered her voice so only he could hear. *But the ones in the treetops, my love, are fairies.*

Nathan leaned his head back, sank deeper into the cushions, and sighed. "Maybe she was right, and reality really is the stuff of myths and legends."

CHAPTER 36

At 10:01 Wednesday morning, Father Douglas rang the funeral bell and walked into the sanctuary of Our Lady of Peace to offer Mass for the soul of Xavier Pratt. "Please rise."

He turned to face the casket. "The grace and peace of God our Father, who raised Jesus from the dead, be always with you."

"And also with you," the packed church responded in unison.

He sprinkled the casket with holy water as the organist played the opening to "Be Thou My Vision." Father Douglas turned, and the procession began. The casket, pushed by Orville Wellinger Jr., came next, with Janice and Jonathan following Xavier down the aisle.

Jonathan found it nearly impossible to concentrate on the Mass. He stood, he prayed, he sang, and he even gave a handkerchief to Janice, but his mind was stuck on that day, that moment when Xavier was taken. He didn't know what to do with the complex emotions that sometimes paralyzed him but other times made him so antsy he thought his skin would fly off. All too soon, he heard Father Douglas inviting him to "say a few words."

Janice reached over, squeezed his hand, and pressed a folded piece of paper to his palm. He rose, walked to the lectern, and withdrew the eulogy he and Nathan had composed from his pocket. He smoothed it into place and cleared his throat.

"Janice asked me to thank you all for being here. She is very grateful for your love and support." He cleared his throat again. "Xavier Pratt was an important and well-loved member of our community who left us way too soon." He paused then looked down at the carefully crafted words. As grateful as he was for Nathan's help, these were not the things he needed to say. He turned the paper over and looked out at those gathered to mourn Xavier.

"He was my boss, my mentor, my friend. He had the remarkable ability to make a firm and honest connection with everyone he met. I . . . I think that Xavier made these connections because he not only believed in the dignity and sanctity of life, in all its many forms, but he put that belief into action every day, with every person, and every animal.

"Many of you have known him far longer than I have, and I'm sure you could tell many wonderful stories that would bring him to light. But I was with him on the day he died, and I want to share with you what he said just moments before he collapsed, because I think his own words tell his story better than any that I could muster." He closed his eyes and forced his mind past the trauma to the hope. "'I know that each of us is dedicated to the preservation of life whenever possible—so, let us work toward a restitution of the natural order, to the best of our abilities, and for the health and comfort of the animals and people that we serve. May God guide our hands.'"

Jonathan knew he didn't get it exactly right but hoped it was close enough. He opened his eyes and took a deep breath. "I'm so sorry that I couldn't save the life of Xavier Pratt. I'll carry that burden for the rest of my life." He swallowed the lump rising in his throat. "Even so, I'm grateful to have known such an honest and faith-filled man for what little time was given to me." He clenched the paper from Janice. "And may the memories you have of this remarkable man bring you comfort, solace, and ultimately, joy."

Jonathan pocketed his speech and returned to his seat, calmer than he'd been in days and no longer dreading the rest of the day. *I said what I needed to say.*

His thoughts were interrupted by Janice reaching over and squeezing his hand. She smiled, then turned her attention to the priest. The organist struck the notes of the closing hymn, "Let All Things Now Living," a favorite of Xavier's.

Jonathan reached for the hymnal, and the small piece of paper from Janice fell from where it had stuck to his damp palm. He picked it up and opened it up to see Xavier's handwriting: *The creatures of this world do not belong to us. We choose to be of service; they choose whether or not to accept it.*

Two days after Xavier's funeral, Jonathan was standing in a shady corner of the deck filling a plastic wading pool for Bingley when he heard the slam of a car door and Nathan's voice. "Well, hey there, Janice, this's a pleasant surprise!"

Is it? Jonathan mused.

He left the hose in the pool and went to turn off the water, arriving back on the deck at the same time Janice, Nathan, and Bingley walked out of the house. Bingley plunged into the cold water, repeatedly immersing himself, then rising like a phantom from the deep. Water streamed from his mouth, head, and body as he exited the pool, being sure to stand next to Nathan before shaking off.

"Hey!" Nathan yelped. "This's how you thank me for taking you for a run?" He laughed and added as he opened the screen door, "Guess that's a hint I need to shower!"

Nathan left, and Jonathan turned to Janice. "Coffee?" She nodded, and he returned with two steaming mugs. They sat in the shade of the birch trees while Bingley snoozed in a sunny part of the deck.

"Jon, the day of the funeral, I didn't get a chance to tell you how moving your reflection was. I loved hearing Xavier's last words again, and you were right, they did show who he was."

"But?"

Janice smiled. "Yes, there is a but." She took a sip of coffee. "*But,* I am not sure you *really* heard what he was saying."

"And what would that be?" He tried not to sound irritated.

Janice ignored his tone. "Xavier believed that genuine happiness required cultivating a life of virtue, humbly grounded in service to others." She leaned toward Jonathan. "He didn't always believe that way." She paused and looked at the yard for a moment. "Or, maybe it's more accurate to say, he had to learn it the hard way."

She blew on the hot liquid before taking a small sip. "Xavier's father, Doolittle, impressed on him the importance of respecting the dignity of these incredible animals, and Xavier really thought he did."

"But?"

Janice smiled again. "*But* . . . he was just out of vet school and filled with the wonder of modern medicine, so when Lucretius's gout flared, Xavier was quick to prescribe prednisone, convinced it'd be *the best thing* for him. Lucretius wasn't so sure since Colchicine had worked well, and he was reluctant to try anything new. But Xavier pushed back, insisting that this was a far better treatment, and Lucretius should trust him.

"Unfortunately, Xavier somehow missed the fact that the centaur had a fungal infection brewing in one of his hooves."

Jonathan winced. "So let me guess, the prednisone made the fungal infection worse."

"Worse? It nearly killed him! Xavier pulled him off the prednisone immediately and, thank goodness, he recovered. But it was touch and go, and Lucretius ended up with a permanent limp."

"I noticed that when I was there for his PPID but decided that I wouldn't ask about it. I'd already irritated him."

"Good call! He's sensitive about others noticing the limp." Janice paused to watch the chipmunks dart along the garden wall. "You know that piece of paper that I gave you at the funeral?"

Jonathan nodded.

"Well, Xavier wrote that shortly after the incident with Lucretius and kept it in his wallet as a reminder that not only were he and his father here to be of service, but that *he especially*, had to be willing to let the animal being treated refuse that service." Janice pulled a packet of tissues from her purse and dabbed at her eyes. "The problem was that Xavier focused *exclusively* on his duty to these animals."

Jonathan furrowed his brow as he shook his head.

"What I am trying to say is that, in protecting the dignity of these animals and being of service to them, Xavier tended to overlook the part of the veterinary oath about *protect the public health*."

Jonathan's forehead softened ever so slightly. "I don't know, Janice. I think his philosophy worked pretty well. And I don't think he forgot his obligation to the public. We talked about that *very thing* when we discussed what to do with Cowper. If anything, he was *exactly* right. If *we* don't fully commit to protecting them, who will? How many times did he say that we are morally obligated to defend and preserve them, and their right to live and live well?"

Janice took a long sip of the now lukewarm coffee before answering. "You're right, Jon. Rupert, Doolittle, Xavier, and now you, do have a commitment to these creatures to protect and care for them. But, like any good intention, it can be taken too far. Virtue, if I remember my Aristotle correctly, is found in the middle, and Xavier—for the most part—did not reside in the middle ground between service and unnecessary sacrifice." She drew a long breath. "Balance."

Jonathan tilted his head and squinted at her.

"Maybe it was because we couldn't have children, or maybe it's because we worked together and didn't have enough other interests but, whatever the reason, Xavier lacked balance, perspective, and as a result, these animals animated everything in his life." She sat up straighter and focused on Jonathan's hands, white-knuckled on his coffee mug. "He didn't die because of anything you or DeeDee did or did not do, but because he was doing what he loved and believed in, *regardless* of the consequences."

Jonathan stared at his coffee and shook his head, his eyes now brimming. Janice lifted the mug from his trembling hands and placed it on the table. She wrapped his hands in hers and looked into his troubled eyes.

"Jon," she whispered, "I want you to understand two things. First, I don't hold you responsible for Xavier's death. It was his choice to do what he did and to accept the risks. And second, I want you to learn from his life, his mistakes. Find balance in how you work and live with these animals *and* this community. And find love outside of your work. I'd bet *anything* that if you do, not only will you care for these animals with compassion and dignity, but you will serve a greater good, and *truly* honor the memory of Xavier."

As Janice spoke, Nathan stood silently by the door to the porch. He was about to ask if anyone would like eggs Benedict, but the intense and intimate scene made him pause. When Janice glanced his way, he lifted his mug to her and mouthed, *Thank you*.

Jonathan closed his eyes and slowly lowered his head onto their entwined hands. Janice slipped a hand out and stroked the back of his head. Bingley, awoken by a pesky fly, padded over to rest his chin on Jonathan's shoulder and wuffle softly in his ear.

For the first time in a very, very long time, Jonathan Francis St. Roche wept.

CHAPTER 37

"You are one lucky woman, Anita," the baker said as he carefully wrapped the warm cookie. "This is the last one! The assistant manager at First National just came in and bought the rest for a staff meeting."

"Thank you, Austin. I'll be sure to enjoy it to the fullest," Anita said and headed out the door. Since her breakup with Jonathan, she'd taken to eating her lunch on the road most days, telling herself, and anyone who'd listen, "It's really a lot more economical to pack your lunch. You wouldn't believe how much I'm saving by not eating out every day!"

Which is why Anita was now sitting on the passenger seat of the animal control van with the door open, enjoying the breezes and contemplating the quiet beauty of rural Ohio from the crest of Rottingdam Road. "Sandwich first, *then* coffee and cookie," she said out loud as she unwrapped the everything bagel stuffed with tuna salad.

Three bites into her lunch, her phone unexpectedly buzzed and burst into song. "YIKES!" Anita shrieked, dropping the remainder of her sandwich in the dirt. "Darn it! I thought there wasn't any cell service here. Damn fracking!" she mumbled as she reached for the nearly hysterical appliance.

"Hi, Connolly, what's up?" Anita asked while futilely brushing off her bagel. Giving up, she threw the remains into her lunch bag.

Connolly cleared her throat. "Hey, I've contacted the people I met at the tournament and the ball, but I'm being stonewalled. I've tried to get interviews—asking about fracking, local philanthropy, the ball—anything I can think of, but none of the 'old' families will talk to me, much less invite me to their farms. The newer families who'll talk to me, show off their new barns and livestock and ramble on *forever* about what the fracking money has done for the community, but when I hint at unusual happenings, they all stare at me as if my hair is on fire. Then, *every one of them* tells me about McKinley and the wild boar, saying, 'There hasn't been a wild boar sighted in the area since then. Isn't that unusual?'"

As Connolly vented, Anita looked out at the rolling green hills and cornflower-blue sky. She caught the sound of an Amish barn being raised, but it was the yellow swallowtail butterfly hopscotching along the Queen Anne's lace that brought home the graceful beauty of this place and the people who lived here.

She wiped at her eyes with her sleeve. "Soooo, what exactly do you want me to do?"

"Could you maybe call some of them? Perhaps they'd be willing to let me visit if you introduced me or went with me?" Connolly sounded desperate. Maybe there's someone on the outs? Someone with a bone to pick with one of the other families that's been here a long time? Maybe we could get an in that way?"

Anita's heart beat in rhythm to the hammering. "I don't know, Connolly."

"Anita," the reporter interrupted, "*you're* the one who brought this to my attention, and if *you* really want to find *the truth*, as you claim, then you're gonna have to help me. I don't want to destroy anyone. I'm just trying to find the in that'll lead us to an explanation. That's what journalists *do*. We look for answers, and we don't stop until we find them."

"Okay, okay." Anita sighed. "I, um, do know of someone who's upset with Luckey Haskins. I was getting coffee at the deli a while back, and I overheard Tony Gregory say something to Elmer Stubb like, 'Haskins has more to lose than he realizes. He doesn't know what *I know* about him.' I didn't think much about it at the time, but it occurs to me now that Tony might have some useful information. Let me make some inquiries, but I'm betting he'll want to talk."

"That's exactly what I meant!" Connolly said. "I can be ready anytime, so call me when you have something."

Anita hung up, poured herself some coffee, and took out the butter brickle pecan cookie. The sound of hymns sung in time to the rhythmic hammering rose on a column of warm air. She dunked the cookie into the steaming liquid and said to the dancing swallowtails, "I wonder what stories you could tell?"

Later that afternoon, Anita turned into the parking lot of the Microtel to find Connolly dressed in nondescript jeans and a sleeveless blue button-down shirt and typing angrily on her phone.

"I see you finally took my advice to dress down."

Ignoring the comment, Connolly climbed into the truck and put her phone on the center console next to Anita's. "So, what's the story?"

Anita headed east out of the parking lot toward Rottingdam Road. She planned to stop at her lunch spot before they deposited the truck at the Animal Control Office and headed to the Gregory farm. This stop took them a few miles out of the way, but Anita hoped to give Connolly a more expansive perspective of the county. "Tony Gregory is the third or fourth generation to farm this land, and I heard that he was recently on the verge of bankruptcy." Anita slowed down and pointed toward the valley stretching out to the right. "Just as a point of reference, that ridge on the other side of the valley is Hipster's Ridge."

Anita pulled into her lunch spot and rolled down the windows. The still air was punctuated by a distant cicada chorus and the sound of the barn raising. "In order to raise cash, Tony leased some land to Luckey, who sublet it to an oil company."

Anita looked at the bewildered Connolly and added, "My cousin Frank filled me in. He's been Tony's best friend since high school. They played basketball together and even introduced me to my high school boyfriend, Jim Peterson, but I digress.

"Tony claims Luckey doesn't have the mineral rights and sues. But the oil money starts coming in, none of it goes to Tony, and Luckey uses it to improve his farm. That hammering you hear? That's Luckey's new barn being raised." Anita swallowed hard. "Tony's a good guy, but he's being pushed to his limit, and that's why he agreed to talk. I think he's looking for leverage against Haskins, if not full-blown revenge."

A loud rustling in the weeds alongside the road caught Connolly's attention, interrupting her contemplation of local mineral rights. "What the hell is that thing?" she asked as an animal sauntered across the road.

"I don't know. It looks like some sort of lizard or iguana, but what would an iguana be doing here?" Anita asked. "And what's it holding? A beagle?"

"I think you're right! Drive over there!"

Anita put the truck into gear and inched toward the animal that was now in the weeds about two feet from the shoulder of the road. It seemed oblivious to them, so she crept the truck closer and closer until they were less than ten feet away.

"I'm going to get a catch net from the back. You stay here until I signal that it's safe for you to get out," she whispered. Anita slid out of her door and closed it without catching the lock. She walked to the back of the truck and opened the rear door.

Connolly, meanwhile, grabbed her phone from the console and got out, not bothering to close her door. She snuck toward the animal, her phone at the ready. As she approached, she noticed that the scaly tail of the animal was poking out of the weeds, and it had two spikes on the end, one curved and one straight. She bent closer and snapped a picture. The animal spun around, dropped the inert beagle, and stared right at Connolly. The reporter's eyes stung and started to water, but she still managed to snap a burst of photos as the animal lunged at her, growled, and blew its foul breath into her face.

Anita rounded the corner of the truck just in time to hear the reporter scream and see her stumble backward, slip in the gravel alongside the road, and crack her head on the corner of the open door. Connolly hit the ground and didn't move.

"Connolly!" Anita screamed. She rushed to her side, dropped the catch net, and checked to make sure the reporter was breathing. She was, but it was shallow and labored. Her head wasn't bleeding, but a bump was rapidly appearing, and she was non-responsive to sound or touch. Anita grabbed the phone out of Connolly's hand and dialed 9-1-1, thankful this time that the oil boom had brought better cell service to the county.

"9-1-1, what is your emergency?"

"I have someone who's hit her head and is unconscious. We need an ambulance, as her breathing is shallow and she's nonresponsive. We're on Rottingdam Road, about a half mile or so, I think, north of the intersection with New Rumley Road." Anita looked up to see if there was a mailbox nearby with a number on it. There wasn't, but she did notice that the animal was still in the weeds.

"How long has she been unconscious?"

"Just a few minutes at most. I saw her slip on the gravel and go down. She hit her head on the car door and passed out."

"I've dispatched an ambulance, and they should be there shortly. Keep her warm and don't move her, in the event she has injured her neck."

"Got it! Thank you." Anita hung up and dashed to the back of the truck. She grabbed the first-aid kit and knelt down to put a crushable ice pack on Connolly's head and cover her with one of the blankets from the kit. A growling from behind her reminded her that the animal was still close.

"That's weird. Why has it stuck around?" she mumbled as she turned on her knees and saw the animal just a few feet away, standing over its prey and looking away from her toward the valley. She noted the scaly body, the folds of skin along its side, and the hooks on the end of its tail. "What are you?" she whispered as she grabbed the catch net and crept toward the creature. She slowly raised the net into position and brought it crashing to the ground, missing the animal by a breath. It turned and erupted into a piercing scream that could wake the dead but did nothing to arouse Connolly.

Anita dropped the net and scrambled back toward the truck, heart racing and eyes watering. She pushed her sunglasses onto the top of her head, wiped her eyes with her shirttail, and looked for the animal in the tall grasses lining the road. She couldn't see it, but she could hear its screams mingling with the approaching sirens, which soon overwhelmed the animal's lamentations.

She leaned against the truck and took several deep gulps of air. When her heart rate slowed, she stood up, checked on Connolly, and picked up the phone that the reporter had dropped. "Huh, I never noticed that we had the same phone," she said as the ambulance and the sheriff pulled alongside the truck.

While the EMTs tended to Connolly, the sheriff took a statement from Anita.

"Yes, Morgan, I did have a civilian in my truck. But, as I told you, I picked her up on my way back to the office, as it made the most sense logistically. I asked my supervisor if I could since she is a reporter and was interested in a story on us," Anita fibbed.

"And you stopped here, because . . .?"

"Connolly wanted to learn more about Carroll County, so I drove this way because there are some of the best vistas here, and I thought she could get some good pictures. We stopped, and when she got out, she slipped on the gravel, lost her balance, and hit her head on the truck door."

The semi-conscious Connolly groaned as they lifted her onto the stretcher. "Hang on a second, let me give them her things," Anita said, looking at Connolly's phone in her hand. She dashed to the cab of the truck to grab the reporter's satchel, and something about the phone on the middle console caught her eye. Though it was face up, Anita could see the case was pink, not orange like hers, like the one in her hand *right now*. She stuffed her phone into her pocket, grabbed the reporter's phone and satchel, and turned to find the sheriff standing right there.

"Jesus, Mary, and Joseph! You scared the heck out of me, Morgan!"

"Sorry about that!" The sheriff smiled. "I'll take her things to the hospital and try to contact her next of kin."

"She works for *Ohio Monthly*, so if you can't find an address book or get into her phone, try calling her office."

"This isn't my first rodeo, Anita, but thanks." He signaled to the ambulance that he had Connolly's personal effects, and they screamed off in the direction of the new trauma unit.

Anita sank into the passenger seat of the truck, pulled the phone out of her pocket, and opened the camera. The last photo that Connolly took was of the animal staring at her with its mouth wide open, eyes blazing. "Holy cow . . . is that thing spitting at her? What kind of lizard spits?"

She lowered the phone to her side and looked out at the now-peaceful countryside. The sun danced along the edge of the tree line as the sound of the barn raising wound down. "Damn," she said with a sigh and dialed Jonathan. If anyone would know what this thing was, it was probably her ex-boyfriend.

CHAPTER 38

"Umph." Jonathan grunted as he repositioned Bluebell's leg to better trim her hoof. "Okay, girl, I know this isn't your favorite thing, but it's got to be done if you want to feel more comfortable."

The unicorn whinnied and gently poked the vet with her horn.

"Strong! Seriously, I need you to keep her from poking me. It will only make this take longer."

"Bluebell," Strong cooed, "stop poking the vet with your horn." He pulled a peppermint from his pocket. Bluebell sniffed at it, gave him a look, but ate it anyway. Jonathan's head snapped up at the smell of the sugary treat.

"Really, Strong? Candy? *This* is how Bluebell got into this fix in the first place!"

"Those were toffees, and this is *one* peppermint. Besides, it's keeping her calm so you can finish charging me an indecent amount of money for your manual labor!"

Jonathan squinted at Strong. "Yes, but it's still *sugar*, and that's the reason for the laminitis. If she needs something to keep her occupied, give her some lavender to chew. That's a treat with *no sugar*."

Jonathan's phone rang. Seeing that it was Anita, he let it go, but a minute later, it rang. Again and again.

"I thought you two broke up," Strong said as the phone refused to cease and desist.

"We did," Jonathan grunted as he released Bluebell's leg, "but apparently there is something important or she wouldn't have called right back." He grabbed the phone and answered it just before it went to voicemail.

"Hey, Jon, um, it's been a weird afternoon, and I think . . . well, um, you, um," Anita stammered.

"Anita, what happened, are you all right?" Jonathan headed to the open barn door to get a better signal.

Strong hit Jonathan on the arm as he walked away. "What?"

Anita took a deep breath. "Okay, here's what happened. Connolly and I were on Rottingdam Road, and we stopped to look at some weird animal by the side of the road. I told her to wait until I could get a catch net from the back, but she got out anyway, and before I could get to her side of the truck, she screamed, fell back and hit her head on the door, knocking herself out."

"Is she okay?"

"I think so. She's on the way to the hospital, so I don't know for sure, but I think she'll be okay." Anita cleared her throat and continued before Jonathan could reply, "The reason I'm calling you is because she picked up my phone by mistake and snapped a couple of pictures of this thing before she fell."

Jonathan broke out into a cold sweat as the color drained from his face.

"*What?*" Strong mouthed again.

He held up a hand to Strong and shook his head. "I'm a bit confused here," he said to Anita. "Did you see the animal too? And where *exactly* were you?"

"On Rottingdam Road, just north of New Rumley Road. I did get a glimpse of it as it disappeared into the brush heading toward Dog Hollow. It looked kinda like an iguana, but it had folds of skin along its side and a double-spiked tail. Do you want me to send you the pictures she took?"

Jonathan sank down onto a bale of straw and turned to Strong, who was exiting the stall where he had ensconced Bluebell. "Cowper, he's escaped!" he mouthed.

"Holy shit!" Strong cursed, as he tossed timothy hay into Bluebell's stall.

"Yes, yes, *do* send the photos." He exhaled the breath he didn't realize he'd been holding. "Where are you now?"

"Still on Rottingdam Road, but I'm supposed to be dropping off my truck."

Jonathan's phone pinged. He put Anita on speaker and opened the text. His heart crashed against his chest. "Can that wait? I'm at Strong's farm, can you come here?"

"Yeah. Let me call my boss and say that I got delayed for some reason. I'll be there in fifteen minutes?"

"Good. And Anita, don't show the photos to anyone, okay?"

"Again? We have to capture this thing again?" Strong whined as he filled the unicorn's water bucket and secured the two halves of the stall door.

"Apparently, but I don't know how we're going to do it!" Jonathan paced the corridor, rubbed his palms together, interlaced his fingers, and stretched his arms above his head. "Plan Giancarlo was never supposed to be implemented."

Strong joined the perambulation. "Okay, let's start with what we know. It's escaped, and was last seen where?"

"Rottingdam Road north of New Rumley Road and headed toward Dog Hollow, according to Anita."

Strong stopped pacing. "That's about a mile or so from its enclosure, and if it's headed toward Dog Hollow, then it's headed in the direction of the enclosure." He snapped his fingers. "Could it be heading *home*?"

"I wouldn't count on it, but it's worth noting." Jonathan stopped walking and looked at Strong. "If the thing escaped, why didn't we hear anything before this?"

Strong pulled his phone from his back pocket. "Let me call Tyrone."

The noise of a truck on gravel drifted into the barn, and Jonathan went out to meet Anita. "So, you've had a rough afternoon."

"You could say that." She waved her phone at Jonathan. "And I didn't know what to think about this—"

"I, um, do know what this, uh, is, and—"

Strong trotted toward them, shaking his head. Anita watched Jonathan blanch. She looked at Strong and then back at her ex. "What?" Her voice was trembling now. "I could've shown these photos to the sheriff, but I chose to show you, *trust* you!" Anita growled. "So *please*, stop playing games with me and tell me what's going on!"

Jonathan and Strong exchanged a glance, which did not escape Anita's notice.

"You're right. You are owed an explanation," Strong said.

Anita's shoulders loosened slightly.

"And we will give you one, but why don't we sit down?" He steered her toward the screened-in porch.

She settled onto a sunny-yellow loveseat. Jonathan took the chair next to her, while Strong headed to the kitchen and returned with three beers, some peanuts, and a bag of Doritos on a tray. *The Feejee Mermaid*, tucked under his left arm, fell onto Jonathan's foot as he set the tray on the coffee table.

"When'd you get this?" Jonathan asked as he picked it up.

"I found a copy on eBay a few months back. It's really interesting, and well, you *know*, relevant."

Anita took a swallow of beer, munched on some peanuts, and said, "I'm *so* glad you two have found common literary ground, but I'm not here for book club."

"No, you aren't," Jonathan said, "but Strong is right. This is relevant." He turned to the chapter on the Warsaw basilisk, bookmarked by a folded sheet of paper, and handed both to Anita. "I'm not sure how to begin, but this might be as good a place as any. Take a look at the picture on the left as well as the one on the paper."

Anita set her beer on the table and looked closely at the illustrations. Her eyes shot up to meet theirs. "You're telling me that animal, that *thing*, is a basilisk?" she croaked.

"Yes." Strong nodded. "We found it living in my old barn."

"In your barn? It was living *in your barn*? Why was it living in your barn?"

Exactly how many times could *she say "in your barn"?* Jonathan wondered. He chimed in, "Yes. Apparently, the fracking on Strong's land drove him—it—out of its habitat and into Strong's barn." He hesitated, then added, "With an eye infection."

Anita sat shaking her head, unable to respond with anything other than, "IN your barn. In YOUR barn. In your BARN?"

Apparently, she can say it an infinite number of times, Jonathan mused. "But that's only the beginning," Jonathan said. They told Anita about researching basilisks and their plans for it, but left Tyrone, Gremsboc, and the weasels out of the narrative. One fantastical animal seemed sufficient for the moment.

"So, Xavier and I decided that polarized contact lenses were the best option to prevent him from harming anyone." Jonathan swallowed hard. "But before we could get both of them in, the basilisk knocked off Xavier's eye protection and looked him right in the eye. He was killed instantly." He dropped his hands to his lap, his right thumb massaging circles into his left palm.

Anita gasped and threw her hands over her mouth, her forehead deeply furrowed. "Oh Jon, I am so sorry! I thought it was a massive heart attack."

"It was, sort of. Technically, he collapsed due to cardiac arrest," Jonathan replied, sidestepping the fact that DeeDee declared the cause of death. *She doesn't need to know that DeeDee was involved, especially since I'm pretty sure she knows I'm in love with DeeDee.* He stopped massaging his hands and looked out the window. He saw none of the bucolic scene, as his thoughts veered in a new, not unpleasant direction. *Am I? In love?*

Anita dropped some Doritos in her lap. She didn't notice Jonathan's faraway look as she tried to flick the chip dust off her khakis. Strong did, however, and picked up the story. "So then, we released him into the enclosure, thinking he couldn't escape because—"

"Speaking of escaping, didn't you just talk to our, um, enclosure manager?" Jonathan interrupted.

Anita stopped sweeping her pants. "You have an 'enclosure manager'?"

"Apparently," Strong mumbled and cleared his throat. "Yes I did. He said that this was news to him, and he would call back as soon as he had an update."

"So where is this enclosure?" Anita asked.

"Not too far from where you saw it on Rottingdam Road—about a mile or so east, as the crow, or in this case the basilisk, flies," Strong said.

Jonathan glared at Strong. "Ha-ha. Except he *can't* fly, remember? We clipped his wings."

Anita did some quick calculations. "Do you think it might be headed back to the enclosure?"

"That's exactly what I said!" Strong poked himself in the chest with both index fingers.

"Even if he is, how are we supposed to find and capture him?" Jonathan asked as he began pacing. "There's no way he'll go anywhere near a live trap again." Jonathan snapped his fingers. "On the other hand, is this his first escape or does he come and go, sneaking out when no one's watching?" He stopped circling the porch. "So the question is: where will he go that he thinks we won't look for him?"

Anita nodded. "You mean, will he hide in plain sight in the enclosure? Or will he try to hide for real?"

"Exactly!" Jonathan replied.

Everyone stopped as the Toreador song from *Carmen* burst from Strong's pocket. He pulled out the operatic phone. "Hey, Tyrone, what'd you find out? Really? You're sure it's not a new opening?" Strong laughed.

It was Jonathan's turn to mouth, "*What?*"

Strong waved him off. "Yeah, I think that's right, don't touch or fix the hole yet, as he may be headed back—" Strong stopped mid-sentence, pulled a bandana from his pocket, and wiped his now-sweaty forehead. "Thanks, Tye, that's a good reminder."

Anita and Jonathan looked at one another, then back to Strong's ashen face.

"Seems this guy dug a hole under the straw in his nesting box, and added a tunnel that opens outside the fence in some weeds. No one noticed the hole until they actually looked for it." Strong chuckled. "But the best part is that a few feet from the hole is a gas line flag that says, 'Call Before You Dig.'"

"He marked it with a flag?" Anita asked.

"Well, they don't know which came first, the hole or the flag, but that's irrelevant. The relevant part is that the dirt around the opening is tightly packed down, *meaning* that this hole has probably been used for a while."

"Which means he comes and goes!" Jonathan exclaimed. "So you were right, and he could be headed back there now."

"Yeah, which is probably a good thing—but hang on a sec!" Strong dashed into the house, returning with a thick file folder.

"Tye reminded me of something that Pliny the Elder wrote." He pulled a sheet from the folder: "'It destroys all shrubs, not only by its contact, *but those it has breathed upon;* it burns up all the grass too, and breaks the stones, so tremendous is its noxious influence.'"

"Holy cow," muttered Anita as she got to her feet. "That must have been what caused Connolly to collapse! It breathed on her."

"But it didn't kill her," Jonathan interjected. "So its breath isn't strong enough to kill, just incapacitate, at least for now." He slumped onto the loveseat and put his head into his hands. He rubbed his temples. "We're going to have to euthanize, aren't we?"

Anita squatted down in front of Jonathan. "Look," she said, "I know you'd like to fix this somehow, but really, *there is no other option.*" She paused to clear her throat. "Think about this: What if Bingley had come across *him* rather than the weasel trap, or worse, what if a child encountered him?"

He blanched, remembering Janice's words: *any good intention can be taken too far.* He looked at Anita and nodded. "Thank you. You're right."

"So, let's think about what we need to do," Anita said as she stood up.

"We?" Jonathan looked at her. "I'm not sure that's a good idea. We needed your help to find its location, but—"

"Yes, *we,*" Anita interrupted. She looked at each of them in turn. "Look, I capture dangerous animals for a living, so it seems to me that I am *exactly* who you want to have along."

"She's right, you know," Strong mumbled. "And with three of us tracking him, we increase our odds of finding him," Strong continued, warming to the idea of a hunt, even if it was for an elusive killing machine. He checked the time. "He's been on the move for about an hour, so he's conceivably getting close to the enclosure. I say we start there, moving out toward him. That'll give us the element of surprise, because I bet he thinks that if anyone is tracking him, it will be from behind. And, hopefully, we can get him before he encounters anyone else."

"And before he figures out that he shouldn't return to his enclosure," Anita said. She pointed at Strong. "You said something to the enclosure manager about 'a good reminder'? What was that all about?"

Strong dabbed at his forehead again. "Yeah, Tye reminded me that this guy never makes the same mistake twice, so if we don't get him this time, we might never capture him."

"Then we have no time to lose." Anita swallowed the last of her beer. "Let's go. We'll take my truck. It has everything we might need."

"Except for luck," said Jonathan.

CHAPTER 39

"Pull in there." Strong pointed to the left. Anita turned into a small clearing where a tall hedgerow obscured the truck from the road.

Jonathan loaded his tranquilizer gun and shouldered a backpack containing euthanasia supplies. Anita found N95 masks for everyone and equipped Strong and herself with tranquilizer guns. She secured her work belt, which contained a handgun she prayed would not be necessary.

"Okay, I suggest that we split up and spread out at 30-degree angles, heading west toward Dog Hollow. The wind is blowing toward the east, and that'll help keep our scent downwind," Strong said and waved his arm in the general direction of west. "I suspect he'll use trails and crop rows rather than bushwhack his way back home. Corn rows would be the easiest to traverse. They're tall enough to hide him and, if they sway, it'll look like the wind blowing."

"We'll need to signal to one another," Anita said.

"Can you guys whistle?" Strong asked.

"Yes," they replied in unison.

"Good. Let's keep this as simple as possible." Strong let loose with one long whistle for: *I've shot it; come and help,* followed by three short notes for: *I need help.* They repeated after Strong.

"Perfect! Now, Anita, you take the left path, I'll go down the middle, and—"

"Hold it a sec," Jonathan interrupted. He pointed to the gun in Anita's belt. "I just want to emphasize that we are out to *tranquilize* him, then *humanely euthanize* him. I fear that if we were to shoot him outright that we would only wound him, and he would hunker down somewhere, truly suffering. But *moreover*, we might never find him, and the problem would remain."

Strong looked the vet in the eye. "Jon, we are all on the same page, but it isn't wrong for Anita to have a gun to defend herself if needed."

Jonathan sighed. "Okay, fair enough."

Strong and Anita plunged into the woods.

"All I wanted was a simple, uncomplicated, rural practice," he muttered as he readjusted his backpack and went in search of a mythological killing machine.

Jonathan walked as quickly and quietly as a non-hunter could, scanning the ground and the horizon, keenly aware of every twist of a branch, flicker of light, and snap of a twig.

Huh, I'm both enjoying and dreading this. At the sound of rustling, he dropped to his haunches, gun at the ready, but it was just a chipmunk scurrying along a fallen tree. He took a deep breath and stood up.

Funny, I feel kinda the same way about this job. Despite what Janice says, I really feel as if I failed Xavier, and I've messed up this whole basilisk thing, so it's probably better that I leave. He catapulted into the air, heart racing. *Was that a whistle?* He whirled around and saw the trunks of two white pines rubbing together in a high-pitched imitation of Strong. He took a deep breath, wiped his forehead on his sleeve, and went on.

But—is there a but? Haven't I already decided to leave? I mean, what is there to stay for? DeeDee is engaged and probably moving to Pittsburgh. He stopped and looked around. *Hmm, maybe that's actually a plus! If she's not around, it will be easier to forget her—do I want to forget her?* He shook his head to clear the image of DeeDee on the night of the ball and forced himself to take note of the perfectly formed oyster mushrooms on a nearby tree.

If I were to list the pros and cons, I'd have to say that I've made some good friends, and I really enjoy the diversity of the practice. He smiled and chuckled softly. *Plus, I have the best dog ever!* He looked to his left. *Why is that corn row moving? There isn't any breeze.*

Jonathan inched toward the field, keeping low. Whatever was in the field was moving in his general direction. *Should I whistle? Probably not until I'm sure it's Cowper.*

Six or seven crows landed just in front of the movement, which stopped suddenly at their appearance. Jonathan hunkered down and crept toward the murder of crows. *Maybe I could be a hunter if it weren't so hard on my knees.* He watched as one of the crows sitting on a sturdy bunch of stalks started to preen under its wing, confident that there was safety in numbers.

He caught a whiff of something noxious and brought his gun into position just as the basilisk sprang, shrieking toward the unsuspecting crow. Jonathan fired and hit the beast in the soft spot just below his iridescent wing, sending him to the ground on top of the dead crow. The rest of the murder took flight right at

Jonathan, sending him backward several feet from the incapacitated basilisk.

He loaded a second dart and pointed it at the woozy animal, who was lying there as though he'd decided a nap was just the ticket on this lovely afternoon. Its eyes were shiny, its gaze was soft, and it snuggled into the crow as if it were a downy pillow. Jonathan kept the gun pointed at it as he started to whistle like a crazed cartoon dwarf.

At the shriek of the basilisk, Strong and Anita ran toward the sound. "Jon," Anita panted as she came into sight, "are you okay?"

He put a finger to his lips and pointed at the recumbent creature who was watching a yellow swallowtail butterfly flit about. Cowper batted at it.

"Is he playing with it?" Strong asked.

"Sure looks like it," Jonathan replied. "Who knew?"

"Not me," Anita said. "But then, I didn't even know it existed until this afternoon."

"Makes me want to try to save it, maybe work on taming it some more," Strong whispered.

"I know what you mean," Jonathan said. "Seeing it so playful makes me wonder if we *could* contain the danger it poses—"

"You can't be serious," Anita interrupted. "This thing nearly—"

WHOOSH! Cowper exhaled. As the butterfly froze mid-flutter, the basilisk jumped up and swallowed the insect with a loud and satisfying smack of his lips. He turned to the three of them and smiled, his gaze sending an icy chill down their spines. Jonathan knew it was over. There was no redemption for this animal, no more second chances. He pulled the trigger and hit Cowper in the chest with another tranquilizer dart. The basilisk fell back onto the crow and closed his eyes, his breathing shaky and shallow.

Jonathan pulled the euthanasia kit from his backpack and made sure his mask and sunglasses were secure, as did Anita and Strong. They held him as Jonathan located a vein in one of its rear legs, inserted the needle, and depressed the plunger. Cowper's eyes flashed open. He looked directly at Jonathan, but there was no emotion, just cold blackness, and he was gone.

CHAPTER 40

It wasn't until Jonathan confirmed that there was no pulse or heartbeat that Anita and Strong lessened their grip on the basilisk. Jonathan sat back on his haunches and only then realized that tears were streaming down his face. Anita reached into her pocket, pulled out a tissue, and handed it to him.

Jonathan took the proffered tissue. "Thanks, Anita, I, um…"

"Hey, I've witnessed enough euthanasias to know that even when it's completely justified, it takes a toll. Ending a life always does." She sighed wearily and cleared her throat. "I guess this is as good a time as any to tell you that this is the last month for me as an animal control officer. I've taken a job with a wildlife rescue and sanctuary."

"Really? Where?" Strong asked.

"Upstate New York."

"Good for you, Anita," Jonathan said as he pulled a rubber-backed sheet from his backpack to wrap the basilisk in. "You've seen the hard, dark side of things, so I know you'll handle the difficult parts well." He took some rope from his backpack, and Strong helped him to secure the beast in the sheet. "And I hope—no, I believe you'll really appreciate doing something more positive, something that makes life better."

"Thanks, Jon."

He nodded and squeezed her arm. "Now, let's get this guy outta here."

Anita opened a kennel on the side of the truck. "Put him in here. It'll keep him secure and out of sight, lest we meet anyone on our way back to Strong's."

"*Umph,*" Jonathan grunted as he and Strong lifted the bundle into the kennel. "Hopefully it'll keep the smell contained too!"

Purple martins careened after mosquitos, and the smell of cut hay floated in the open windows as they pulled into Strong's farm. "Thanks, Anita, for everything," Jonathan said as he lifted the beast from the kennel and secured it in the back of his truck. He pulled her into a hug. "We couldn't have done this without you," he said into her hair.

Anita exhaled her weariness as she pulled away from Jonathan. "Well, gentlemen, it's been a most interesting afternoon." She picked at the dirt under her nails. "Um, don't worry about Connolly and what she might have seen. I'll make sure *nothing* comes from today. Since she used my phone by mistake, she doesn't have any pictures, and I'll delete the ones on my phone, so there's no evidence." She hazarded a glance at Strong. "Besides, she told me that no one will talk with her about anything, so I don't think she could get a story if she tried. Plus, who knows what she'll remember if—or when—she recovers." She pointed toward Jonathan's truck. "I'd ask what you're going to do with *it*, but I'm not sure I really want to know."

"I'm not sure we know either," Jonathan replied, "but we'll figure out something and be sure not to tell you."

"And I will be sure not to tell anyone about any of it—not

that anyone would believe me if I did," Anita said, as she climbed into the truck, waved goodbye, and drove out of his life.

Jonathan turned to Strong. "What *are* we going to do with this thing?"

Strong grinned. "As a matter of fact, I was thinking about that on the way back, and I think I've got the perfect solution. The centaurs!"

"The centaurs?"

"YES! We have them build a Roman pyre, and we cremate him!"

Jonathan rubbed his chin. "Do they even know about basilisks?"

"You remember I mentioned Pliny the Elder?"

"Yeah."

"Well, Tyrone was the one who told me about Pliny, *but* the Centaurs are the ones who introduced Tye to Pliny, so I'm pretty sure they have at least a passing knowledge of his works."

"But why would they do this for us?"

Strong shook his head and squinted at Jonathan. "You seriously don't know?"

"No."

Strong took a deep breath and smiled at his friend. "Because you're a vital part of this community. Tye told me that Lucretius is very fond of you. He wasn't happy that you told him that he has an incurable disease, but he was very touched by how hard you worked to make it better for him."

"Huh. I thought he saw me as a fool and a bother."

"No, not at all. And Jon, I can't think of anyone who does—well, except for Marcus, but who cares what that pompous windbag thinks."

Jonathan smiled back and murmured, "Thanks, Strong, that means a lot." *It sure complicates the decision to leave, though.* He shook his head and said, "Okay, so how do we get this party started?"

Twilight was descending as Jonathan St. Roche, Armstrong Clegg, and Calloway Lucash headed to the centaurs. "So glad you're with us, Cal. Neither Strong nor I can whistle a tune, much less 'Volare'!" Jonathan said as he pulled up to the trailhead to Tangled Hollow.

"I wouldn't have missed this for anything!" Calloway laughed as he shouldered a bag containing a bottle of Lorenzo's mead as well as two bottles of his favorite red wine. They were grateful that the supermoon illuminated the path, as the rank smell of Cowper encouraged them to move as quickly as possible down the seldom-used trail. When they turned the last bend before the entrance, Calloway whistled loudly.

Hoofbeats sounded as the centaurs, vested with boughs of ivy and pine and enveloped in dust, stormed into view with Tyrone and Gremsboc close behind.

"Welcome, dear friends, welcome!" Lucretius roared over the stamping hoofs. He pointed to the sheet slung between Jonathan and Strong. "Septimus! Octavius! Relieve them of that vile burden!"

The two young centaurs wrinkled their noses as they took the basilisk from Jonathan and Strong and galloped back to camp.

"This is for you, Lucretius," Calloway said. "A thank you from us, for doing this."

Lucretius pulled the mead from the proffered bag and shot a look at Jonathan. "Is this the same ambrosia you brought before?"

"It is."

"All the better then, to toast our heroic slayers of deadly beasts and dragons!" Lucretius bowed slightly and trotted off to see to the festivities.

Aglow from earlier toasts, the faun and the flying monkey led the men toward a table laden with horns of wine. "When I told them what you had done, Lucretius was dumbfounded. He refused to believe it at first!" the Faun gushed and picked up a large vessel of mead. The men followed suit.

"BUT WHEN TYE HERE SHOWED 'EM THE PICTURE STRONG SENT, WELL 'E JUST ERUPTED, 'E DID!" Gremsboc boomed.

"Indeed, he did—praising you, thanking Zeus, giving orders, singing, drinking." Tye took a sip of mead. "I can't remember the last time I saw him so happy!"

Everyone moved toward the large pile of wood holding the unwrapped body of the basilisk. Lucretius, along with two centaurs carrying torches, stepped into the ring between the log seats and the funeral pyre. He stamped his hoofs and called out, "Quiet! Quiet!" The laughter and talking died away.

"Dear friends." He nodded at Tyrone, Gremsboc, and the three men, then threw his arms wide. "Fellow centaurs, we are gathered here to send into eternity the earthly remains of the creature known as the basilisk.

"We hold that life is a gift from the Gods and therefore should not be taken in vain. *However*," he bellowed, "no matter how worthwhile life may be in the abstract, what you do with that life truly matters. So, when you're a dangerous and deadly enemy of all worthy creatures, justice can and should dictate a fitting end to that life."

"Huzzah! Huzzah! Huzzah!" the centaurs cheered and stamped and drank deeply from their horns of mead.

"HEAR, HEAR!" Gremsboc bellowed. He, Calloway, Jonathan, Strong, and Tyrone raised their glasses to the crowd, and found them filled to the rim after every swallow.

"And today, the life of the basilisk came to a just and fitting end at the hands of our noble and heroic slayers of deadly beasts and dragons," Lucretius roared.

More cheering and more stamping emanated from the crowd. Jonathan, Calloway, and Strong were brought in front of the centaur chief. "And so, I ask you to raise your horns in salute to our champions." He raised his own horn. "To the Good Spirit! To Zeus! To health! And to those we choose to call friend!"

"Hear, hear!" burst forth from all sides, along with much back slapping and refilling of horns for man and beast alike.

Lucretius signaled to the torch bearers to come closer. He took one torch and handed it to Jonathan, then offered the second one to Strong. The farmer shook his head. "No, sir. I think you should have that one, Lucretius."

Calloway put his hands behind his back and stepped into the shadow by the logs before Lucretius could offer it to him.

"Very well," Lucretius said and nodded at Jonathan.

Centaur and man stepped to opposite ends of the pyre and raised their torches high. Lucretius looked at Jonathan and nodded once again. They dropped their torches onto the pyre where the dry wood cracked and sputtered. As the beasts and the men moved away from the intensifying heat to eat and drink through the night, magnificent blue-and-yellow flames spiraled into lapping tongues that swallowed everything they touched without regard for wood or flesh.

CHAPTER 41

"Jack, you're not listening to me!" Connolly Davis sat on the edge of her chair in front of her editor's desk.

"Connolly," he soothed, "yes, I am. You want me to run a story about an odd-looking iguana that breathed on you and made you faint. How exactly is that news, much less a feature story?"

"Jack, I *know* this sounds bizarre, but I swear it's an important story! I think it's a whole new species, or maybe an ancient one that was thought to be extinct but has been hiding in Nowheresville, Ohio. You know, like ghost sharks that seemed to appear out of nowhere!"

Jack pulled a pen knife from his pocket and started cleaning his nails, not looking at her.

Connolly leaned in toward her boss's desk. "This could be our *Loch Ness monster*," she enunciated. She exhaled on the words, "*but real.* There isn't an oil story—at least not an interesting one. Sure, there're more Jet Skis on Tappan Lake, but the new millionaires mostly used their wealth to build clinics, trauma units, and sports facilities." She slumped in her chair.

Jack leaned back in his chair and pressed his fingertips together in front of his mouth. His face was serious as he spoke.

"Connolly, you hit your head *hard* when you fell, then they discovered you had angina—those are two good reasons for you to pass out."

Connolly opened her mouth to protest, but Jack held up a hand. "Try to understand this from my point of view. First, you saw an odd-looking reptile whose breath, you claim, knocked you out. Second, you're calling it a new species? Third, it might even be 'our Loch Ness monster'? And, fourth, you have no photos, physical evidence, witnesses, or collaborating testimony."

Jack softened his tone. "Connolly, think about it, in all likelihood, it was probably someone's escaped iguana, and I *cannot* run a feature story in *Ohio Monthly* about an escaped pet, *no* matter how odd it looked or how bad its breath was."

He cleared his throat and leaned toward her. "Look, whatever happened, it was obviously traumatic for you, so I suggest that you take some time off to recover from this and—"

Connolly was on her feet and headed toward the door. "F-f-f-ine! I'll take some time off." She turned and fumed at her editor, "But I *know* what I saw!" Then she stormed out without waiting for a reply.

CHAPTER 42

The Wednesday after the cremation, Jonathan stood at the reception desk of the clinic. With the clinic closed to patients on Wednesdays, Madge and Jonathan used those mornings to catch up on paperwork. "Could you follow up on the blood test for Cooper Wilkins, please? We should've had his Lyme results by now." He flipped through the files on the desk until he found the right one. "And have you called Natalie Perkins about Buttercup's hyperthyroidism? I should be the one to call to discuss treatment options, but I can't tell from the notes if someone already did."

There was a loud knock on the back door. Bingley leapt from his bed behind Madge, barking as if the clinic were on fire and he was Lassie needing to evacuate everyone. Tyrone's face pressed against the glass.

"Good lord, dog, you're going to be the death of me!" Madge scolded as she rose to unlock the door.

"You look a bit gray, Tyrone," Madge commented. "Very similar to Dr. St. Roche earlier in the week."

Tyrone flushed.

"Never mind her. She's just jealous she missed such a great party." Jonathan winked at Madge. "Let's get your allergy shot, Tye." They walked into exam room one and shut the door.

Tyrone giggled. "It *was* a good party! I just wish I remembered more of it. If I have to feel this bad for this long, I'd like to know what happened!"

"Suffice it to say you sang *and* danced . . . a lot, as did Gremsboc." Jonathan drew the medicine into a syringe and tapped out the bubbles. "Who knew he could dance a jig like that? It was quite impressive. Now, hold still." Jonathan delivered the shot into the faun's left tricep, then pointed to the dry, scaly skin on the inside of Tyrone's elbow. "Your eczema seems worse."

"It is, and the aloe vera isn't working like it used to."

"Well, let's try some topical corticosteroid cream and then recheck in a few weeks." *If I'm even here. Maybe I should suggest he see DeeDee?*

Jonathan got the meds and joined Tyrone at the reception desk, where Strong was now standing with Gertrude and Janice. "Um, y'all know we're actually closed Wednesdays, right?" He handed the meds to Tyrone. "But still, I'm glad that you're here, as there's something I want to tell you."

He folded his hands into a steeple and pressed his index fingers to his mouth as he looked around the room. *How do I even start to tell them I'm leaving?*

"I, um, I've been doing a lot of thinking the past few weeks, months really." Bingley walked over to him and leaned against his leg, warm and silent. Jonathan's hands reached for the silky ears. Bingley leaned harder.

"And . . . and . . . I have decided . . . um." The words refused to come.

"HONK-CHOO!" Gertrude sneezed, not once, not twice, but three times.

"Are you all right?" Jonathan knelt next to the iridescent goose and gently stroked her head. "Do you need some tea?"

"Jah. I fine, itz just the nettles are in bloom, and they makes me schneeze. But I didn't come here for that. I vant to give you dis." She looked up at Strong, who held out a small box. "Itz for you."

Jon stood up, set the box on the counter, and lifted the lid. In a nest of tissue paper lay a beautiful, full-color egg depicting the familiar scene of Strong's farm: the tidy yellow house, the two barns, the crowd of chickens, ducks, and geese, and five of Strong's border collies. *I could have sworn he has six.*

"Why, Gertrude, this is magnificent!"

Strong reached over and turned the egg one hundred eighty degrees. There, in perfect, minute, action-packed detail were Storm and Bingley running to the pond as Jonathan and Gertrude watched.

Jonathan handed the egg to Tyrone and knelt by Gertrude again. "Is this your first colored egg since the incident?"

Gertrude nodded. "I vanted you to have the first vun as you ver so good to me."

His eyes brimmed, and he whispered, "Thank you, Gertrude. It's the nicest thing anyone has ever given to me." He took a handkerchief from his pocket, wiped a tear from her cheek, and dabbed at his own. He straightened up, and Tyrone passed him the egg.

"Jon," the faun said, "I don't know if you know this, but I've been cataloging all of Gertrude's eggs, and I know for a fact, there've only been three other people featured on any of Gertrude's eggs—and then, *only* after she'd known them for many years: Rupert, Doolittle, and Xavier Pratt. You are certainly in good company."

"I don't know what to say," Jon said, his voice almost inaudible.

"I do!" Janice spoke up. "Well, maybe I should say that I *have* something to say, not that I know what to say." She smiled and looked at the goose. "Gertrude, this is beautiful. I know how much Xavier treasured the ones you gave to him, and I'm sure Jon will treasure this just as much.

"But that's not what I came here to tell Jon." She directed her gaze at the vet. "You remember that I had a meeting with an insurance agent a while back?"

"Yeah, that's why you couldn't stay for eg—brunch with Nathan and me," he said, remembering at the last moment to avoid saying eggs in deference to Gertrude.

"Well, it turns out that Xavier had a million-dollar policy on himself that I didn't know about!" She beamed. "I got to thinking about what I told you about finding balance, and it hit me that one reason we didn't find it was because there was no other vet in the practice. Xavier had assisted his father, and Doolittle had helped his, but we did it on our own for years. It wasn't until you arrived that we finally took a vacation!"

Madge was nodding vigorously at this and opened her mouth to speak, but Janice preempted her, "So, I've decided to use part of the insurance money to fund another vet for the practice. I just left the lawyer's office, and the paperwork should be ready for us to sign next week."

Janice stepped over to Jonathan, who was shaking his head, eyes wide. She put her hand on his arm. "Jon, please let me do this for you—for all of us." She waved at the circle of friends with her other hand.

"But Xavier intended this money for you, to take care of you," he protested. *Besides, I'm leaving . . .*

"Please don't worry about me. Xavier and I planned for retirement, and I'm just fine." She let go of his arm. "Besides, I'm not giving you *all* the money!" She chuckled. "Just enough to hire a second vet and fund the position for about five years. After that, you and Dr. Whomever are on your own."

"I don't know what to say. This is a lot to take in . . . and . . ."

"Yes. The word you are looking for is *yes*," Madge interrupted. Everyone laughed and began talking at once.

Jonathan looked at the joyful, smiling faces and felt the pressure of Bingley leaning into him. As he caressed his dog's ear, it hit him that for one of the few times in his life he *was* exactly where he wanted to be. He thought of DeeDee and her engagement to Marcus and, though it grieved him, a small voice reminded him that every choice brings loss, and that no matter where he was, grief and pain would be there too. *Because they're part and parcel of life and can't be avoided. Maybe that's what Janice wants me to see, that in caring for* both *creatures and community there's an obligation to serve them honestly, and sometimes that means making decisions that are awful, no matter how you look at it. So, if I can't escape the sorrow, where do I find the joy?*

Bingley pawed at his leg and looked up at him with that earnest expression he loved. He squatted down. "What's up, Bing?"

The dog scooted closer, put his head on Jon's shoulder and sighed, and Jonathan St. Roche had his answer. *It's here. Joy is found right here.*

CHAPTER 43

Jonathan woke to a chill in the air that hinted at the approach of fall. Though there would be several more weeks of fair weather, color was creeping into the black tupelo tree next to the barn, and the silver birches were looking threadbare. Bingley snuggled close, and Jon was tempted to stay in bed, but he forced himself upright. Bingley groaned as he stretched and rolled onto his back to wiggle an itch away.

"Time to get up, Bing. We've got plenty to do today."

"Does Nathan come today?"

Jonathan laughed as he rubbed Bingley's belly and kissed him on the nose. "No, you silly goose! I told you he'll be here in two weeks! You really don't understand time, do you?"

He jumped off the bed and shook. "I understand it's time for breakfast."

"That it is, and coffee. It's definitely time for coffee."

He prepared Bingley's breakfast, then started his to-do list as he waited for the coffee to finish brewing. "So, what's first on the agenda for today?"

"Going for a run," Bingley said between mouthfuls of kibble.

"Not when you've just eaten. We'll go this afternoon." He wrote *Go for run* near the bottom of the page.

"You should be proud of me, though! We don't have patients this morning. I told Madge to have Florence help with the paperwork and ordering supplies, so we have the whole day to get stuff done."

"You took off an entire Wednesday?" Bingley walked over to the door to the yard.

"Yup." Jon followed and opened the sliding door. "I decided Janice was right about finding balance, so I'm taking today off."

"Radical move, Jon." Bing trotted into the yard.

"It is, actually," Jonathan said, even though the dog was out of earshot. He returned to his task via coffee and composed a list that reflected the flurry of activity since he decided to stay:

1. 11 a.m.: attorney—review partnership agreement, fax it to Nathan.
2. Get paint and supplies for guest bedroom and apartment.
3. See Harley about adding office space to clinic.
4. Call Strong: name and number of sign maker.
5. Call sign maker.
6. Call Nathan: new logo, moving plans—need me to come down?
7. Go for run.

Jonathan let Bingley in, then paused in the doorway to breathe in the morning air. He closed his eyes and let the sun warm his face as he caught the far-off lowing of cattle.

"Ahem," Bingley interrupted Jon's reverie. "I thought you said we had a lot to do today."

"Indeed, we do!" He turned to see the dog stretched out

on the sofa. "So why don't you get started on your morning nap while I shower?"

Jon exited the offices of Danbury and Smith, Attorneys at Law, and stopped to throw his jacket through the open window of his truck. He checked his list and the time. *Eleven thirty. Do I have time to grab some takeout from Caroline's?*

"Jonathan!"

His head snapped up at the sound of DeeDee Guzman's voice. "DeeDee, hi. How are you?"

As she walked toward him, her hair, released from its customary ponytail, played around her shoulders in the breeze. "I'm good! Hey, my mom told me that Nathan is joining your practice? Congratulations! I think that's fabulous. He's a great guy."

"Yeah, he is, to both!" Jonathan took a tentative step in her direction. "I understand congratulations are in order for you as well." He swallowed. "Tell Marc that I think he's a lucky man."

DeeDee narrowed her eyes and tilted her head as she approached the car. "Sorry, I'm a bit confused here."

"Your engagement to Marc."

"I'm not engaged." She smiled ever so slightly as she added, "In fact, we broke up."

Jonathan's palms moistened. "But, I heard your mom tell Janice that you were engaged." He paused to review the conversation in his head. "At least, I *assumed* it was you."

DeeDee giggled. "Suzanne, my nurse practitioner, is engaged! That must have been what you heard."

"Well, congratulations to her, then!" Jonathan beamed.

Bingley, having tagged along in the hope it would hasten his run, recognized DeeDee's voice and sat up. Seeing no one besides his two favorite people, he leaned out the window. "Kiss her!" he barked.

DeeDee jumped and stumbled into Jonathan. For a moment their bodies pressed into one another. Their eyes met as he steadied her. "You okay?" he asked.

The now-blushing DeeDee nodded and took a step back.

"What was that?" Jonathan turned to address his dog.

"You're deaf now?" Bingley asked.

"No, um, you startled me, that's all," Jonathan said as he wiped his palms on his jeans.

DeeDee giggled. "Me too. I didn't expect that."

The dog sighed. "Why don't you just kiss her and quit talking her to death?"

DeeDee blushed again and looked down.

Jonathan looked sheepishly at the ground. Then, all at once and without reservation, he reached out and pulled DeeDee into his arms. Tucking her windblown hair behind her ear with his right hand, he lifted her radiant face to his, caressed her cheek, and kissed her.

And this time, she kissed him back.

THE BEAST KEEPERS BESTIARY

There are a number of mythological animals in this book, so here's a short glossary of terms that may help you to keep them straight, as well as some resources.

THE BEASTS:

Jackalope: cross between a pygmy deer and a killer rabbit. Found in the Western parts of the United States. According to legend, jackalopes can imitate the human voice, their milk has medicinal uses, and they're rare because they are unable to breed except during electrical storms with hail.

Gryphon (griffin): body of a lion, head and wings of an eagle. Legends of Mesopotamian and Egyptian gryphons date to 3300 BC. One legend says that Alexander the Great (356-323 BC) harnessed eight gryphons to a basket which he flew to heaven. In medieval times, Christians saw the combination of beast and bird as a symbol of Christ's dual natures of human and divine.

Flying monkey: winged monkeys who first appeared in L. Frank Baum's book *The Wonderful Wizard of Oz*, published in 1900. They are playful, intelligent, and speak English.

Pegasus: the flying horse of ancient Greek mythology, usually portrayed as a magnificent white stallion. The most often told story about his birth is that he sprang from the neck of Medusa when Perseus beheaded her. Pegasus was also the horse that Bellerophon was riding when he slayed the Chimera.

Unicorn: hoofed animal with a single horn. In Western lore it is depicted most often as a horse, sometimes a goat. (*Note:* Unicorns are also found in Middle Eastern and Eastern folklore and may have the body of an antelope, the mane of a lion, or the tail of an ox.) They are often imbued with noble qualities, such as courage, virtue, and strength.

Phoenix: a long-lived bird that immolates and rises again from the ashes. (Found in legends from Asia, the Middle East, and Europe. The Greek historian Herodotus, c. 484-425 BCE, mentioned one in his histories.) A phoenix can live as long as 500 years. In the Middle Ages, the legend was that, at the end of its life, the bird built a pyre of twigs, faced the sun, fanned the fire with its wings, and was consumed by the flames. From the ashes, a new phoenix is born. (Herodotus says a small worm crawls from the ashes, and the sun's rays turn it into another phoenix). Medieval Christians saw this rising from the ashes as a symbol of the Resurrection.

Thunderbird: an enormous multicolored bird from Native American folklore. Its wingspan can be as wide as two canoes from wingtip to wingtip. Ahusaka is Winnebago for "wings." The Winnebago tribe were originally from Wisconsin and had a legend about the thunderbird.

Centaur: body of a horse, torso of a human. From ancient Greece, they were considered to be uncivilized and easily intoxicated. A few centaurs have been notable for their nobility, such as Pholus, who entertained Hercules. The noblest was Chiron, respected for his knowledge and his skill in medicine. He was a tutor to Achilles (Trojan War), Jason (Captain of the Argonauts), and Asclepius (famous Ancient Greek physician).

White hart: an all-white, mature stag, magical in nature. Legend says that the white hart was sought by the Arthurian knights. (Hart is an archaic word for stag.) Apparently, at the wedding feast of Arthur and Guinevere, a magical white hart rode into the hall and circled the round table.

Faun (satyr): both have the torso of a man with the horns, pointed ears, legs, and tail of a goat. The Greeks referred to Pan (a faun) as the spirit of wild nature and protector of woodlands. Satyrs, on the other hand, were depicted as rural fertile spirits, their torsos were covered with hair, and they were companions to the god of wine. Both played pan pipes.

Vishap: a type of Armenian dragon closely associated with water. But they may rule or live in the sky, bringing thunderstorms, whirlwinds, and eclipses. Mount Ararat was the main home of the Vishap.

Basilisk: The basilisk is described in various ways, from a snake-like animal with a crown-shaped crest to an animal with two to many legs, wings, no wings, etc. The common elements are that it can kill any living thing by looking at it, and/or breathing on it, and according to some sources, with its voice. I based my basilisk on the basilisk found in the bestiary of Anne Walshe, the only known children's bestiary.

Basilisks can be confused with the following:

Cockatrice: a basilisk-like creature with the head, neck, and legs of a cockerel, with dragon-like wings.

Wyvern: a winged, two-legged dragon with a barbed tail.

Dragon: In the European tradition, a winged, fire-breathing creature with four legs.

Marginal hybrids: beasts found in the margins of medieval manuscripts that have the features of two or more types of animals.

Aesop's Fable: The Dog and His Master (Bingley claims to be a descendant of this dog):

A certain man was setting out on a journey when, seeing his dog standing at the door, he cried out to him, "What are you gaping about? Get ready to come with me." The dog, wagging his tail, said, "I am all right, Master; it is you who have to pack up."

SOURCES

BOOKS

Aesop, The Complete Fables, translated by Olivi and Robert Temple. Penguin Books, 1998.

Beasts, Factual & Fantastic, edited by Elizabeth Morrison, The J. Paul Getty Museum, 2007. (*Book of Beasts: The Bestiary in the Medieval World,* a large, hardcover book was published by the J. Paul Getty Museum in 2019, on the occasion of the exhibition by the same name.)

Bestiary, MS Bodley 764, translated and introduced by Richard Barber, The Boydell Press, 1993. (The Folio Society did a beautiful version of this in 1992.)

The Canterbury Tales, by Geoffrey Chaucer, translated by Burton Raffel, Random House, 2008. (The Parsons Tale mentions a basilisk).

The Fantasia of Leonardo Da Vinci, His riddles, jests, fables, and bestiary, by Ross King. Levenger Press, 2010.

The Feejee Mermaid and Other Essays in Natural and Unnatural History, by Jan Bondeson, Cornell University Press, 1999.

The Mythical Creatures Bible, by Brenda Rosen, Sterling Publishing, 2009.

Mythic Creatures, And the Impossibly Real Animals Who Inspired Them, adapted from an exhibition curated by Laurel Kendall & Mark A. Norell, with Richard Ellis. American Museum of Natural History, Sterling Publishing, 2016.

The Naming of the Beasts, Natural History in the Medieval Bestiary, by Wilma George & Brunsdon Yapp. Gerald Duckworth & Co., 1991.

ONLINE

The Natural History, by Pliny the Elder. On basilisks: http://www.perseus.tufts.edu/hopper/text?doc=Perseus:text:1999.02.0137:-book=8:chapter=33&highlight=basilisk

ONLINE BESTIARIES

The Bestiary of Anne Walshe: https://williammorristile.com/medieval/bestiary_of_anne_walshe.html

The Medieval Bestiary: https://bestiary.ca/beasts/beastalphashort.html

British Library Bestiary: https://www.bl.uk/manuscripts/Viewer.aspx?ref=add_ms_11283_fs001r

University of Wisconsin Library–*The Book of Beasts:* https://search.library.wisc.edu/digital/APVFA6XOOSG2448C

Selections from the Bestiary of Leonardo Da Vinci: https://www.jstor.org/stable/537007?refreqid=excelsior%3A51e5cae5b-b744984ae546c6be35cc2d2&seq=2#metadata_info_tab_contents

ACKNOWLEDGMENTS

I *always* read the acknowledgment section of a book because I am sure that someday there will be an author who has written and edited the book solely on his or her own. I remember thinking many years ago (which, by the way, started my acknowledgment-reading-obsession): *How is it that there are always so many people to thank and the ubiquitous, and seemingly breathless, expression of fear that the author has somehow forgotten a vital contributor, not to mention the desperate plea for forgiveness and/or pardon for this lapse of memory or judgement? Isn't this the work of the author alone?*

Clearly, I had never written a book. Since I have now done so, I *reallio trulio* (thanks to philosophy professor Dr. Steven Snyder for that phrase) understand that a book is never written in a vacuum. (Or conversely, if it is, you probably don't want to read it.) And I am now ready to humbly admit the following: 1) there is an incredible number of people who influence, contribute, cajole, criticize, and support you through this process; 2) I will undoubtedly forget some of the contributors; and 3) for that omission, I am genuinely sorry.

As I worked through this book, I found that I needed the help and advice of people in different categories: Technical advice and writing advice/process advice. So here goes:

I. Not being a veterinarian (and I don't play one on TV), I found that my many vet contacts were extraordinarily helpful and generous with their time, talent, and knowledge.

In no particular order:
Dr. Wendy McElroy (horses)
Dr. Chad Herrick (and his FABULOUS staff at
Northtowne Animal Clinic, general information)
Dr. Erin Malone (cancer)
Dr. Leanne Lily (treatment for exotics)
Dr. Jim Carlson, whose response to my questions
about acupuncture in "other" animals sparked the
idea for the book.
Dr. Natalie Theus (skin conditions)
Other technical help came from Dave Kishler on
how EMTs respond.

II. Many of my dog-training friends have helped me over the years to be a better person, a better trainer, and given me the insights needed to write from a positive reinforcement perspective. Colleen Pelar, Robin Bennett, and Tina Spring, thank you for bringing light to my darkness. To all the others I have known and worked with: Thank you.

III. While the content of this book is mine, it would not be the work that it is without my writing partners and editors. Laura Sommers and I have been meeting to write, twice a week, for something like a millennium, and without her steadfast support, humor, insights, and questions, I would not have a story, period. Brian Nutwell, my other writing partner, has also been crucial in helping me find my path at various times. The book would not be here without him either.

Brad Pauquette (formerly of Columbus Publishing Lab and now of The Company, a writing school) offered a four-week novel-writing class (where I met Brian) that I decided to take because I was floundering. *It changed everything.* It set me back on the road to writing a novel by giving me the process that I needed. Moreover, his guidance as initial editor was invaluable. I am more grateful to these three than words can express.

Emily Hitchcock, Heather Shaw, and Melissa Gray of Boyle & Dalton were there at precisely the right moment. Heather's skillful developmental editing was brilliant and helped me to craft a real book, while Melissa Gray's copyediting corrected all my grammatical foibles. Thank you so very much.

There are others who have helped in subtler ways, my daughters, Ellie Hicks and Emma King, have asked critical questions at key points ("Exactly why are they trying to save the basilisk?"), and editorial help ("None of your characters are using contractions. Why is that?") that helped to keep me on course. Thank you. You are the best thing I ever did.

My husband, Brad, has been a stalwart supporter of this project and has helped me in a thousand different ways, from giving me legal quandaries to ponder, to songs for the characters. He has helped me to develop the backstory on many of the characters, suggested names (Florence Burgett is his), given me history lessons, and never doubted that I could do this. Without him, the time and space for this book would never have happened. I love you lots and lots.

As a dog trainer for nearly 20 years, I have worked with countless owners and pets, and I am profoundly grateful that so many people have allowed me to share both the joy and the sorrow that comes with loving an animal. You have inspired me to be the best that I can be and to admit when I have failed. Hopefully, this has also made me a better writer, and my love for your animals comes through these pages. Thank you.

Over the course of 40+ years of marriage, we have had twelve dogs and four horses share our lives. I am so grateful that I married someone who loves dogs and has been willing to ride the roller coaster of emotion that comes with opening up your heart and home to these fur balls. Every animal who passed through our life has gifted us in some way, and I have loved all of them. But, as any dog lover will tell you, if you are lucky, there will be a dog that is your champion, your all-star best friend who not only loves you unconditionally but lights up your world like a lighthouse on a stormy night, pointing you toward a safe harbor and a warm place to rest your heart. For me, this was my flat-coated retriever, Mr. Bingley. Hopefully, his presence in this book will bring you a bit of the joy that radiated from him every day of his too-short life.

And lastly, I should mention that this is a work of fiction, a story from my imagination, and not intended to bear any likeness to real people (real dogs have already been addressed). I have, however, intertwined some real Ohio history into the story. If this is confusing, I am sorry, but please feel free to fact-check me! I am also deeply and profoundly sorry if I missed anyone who contributed to this book. As Mr. Darcy would say, "The fault is mine and so must the remedy be."

ABOUT THE AUTHOR

J ulie lives in Galena, Ohio, with her husband, flat-coated retriever, and Clumber spaniel. She recently retired from training dogs professionally to write, travel, and spend time with her nine grandchildren. She also has a podcast called Your Family Dog. This is her first novel.

www.ingramcontent.com/pod-product-compliance
Lightning Source LLC
Chambersburg PA
CBHW020941260626
47169CB00006B/1762